GW00457155

THE MAT ....

Book 1: Valentine's Day

by

Claire Elaine Newman

To Iris & John

All my love
from
Claire!
xxx

Claire Elaine Newman

Copyright © 2018 Claire Elaine Newman

All rights reserved.

ISBN: 9781980847342

Dedication

For my parents
and Bridie

CONTENTS

ACKNOWLEDGMENTS i

Chapter One 1

Chapter Two...23

Chapter Three 44

Chapter Four 78

Chapter Five 99

Chapter Six 114

Chapter Seven 134

Chapter Eight... 173

Chapter Nine 194

Chapter Ten... 225

Chapter Eleven 245

ABOUT THE AUTHOR 271

ACKNOWLEDGMENTS

Many thanks go to the Pasadena Area Screenwriting Group, who provided feedback on this story when it was still just a TV pilot script, and to my wonderful friends Joy and Louisa, who read through the entire manuscript and provided me with comments.

Special thanks, however, must go to my parents for their continued support of my dreams - whatever those may be! - and especially to my mother, who was the first person to ever read "The Matchmaker." I love you both very much.

Chapter One.

In my thirteen years on the job, I had seen the City of Angels at its most depraved; at its lowest. I'd raided meth labs and hooker motels. I'd been at crime scenes that had made me want to lose every meal I'd ever eaten. But what had been done here? It was worse. Everywhere I looked, there was red.

It was plastered all over the convenience store: the shelves, the walls, the floors.

Red.

And *pink*.

I fought the urge to turn around and march out the door. Instead, I grabbed a basket and stomped down the nearest aisle in disgust.

February 14th. *Valentine's Day*. What a con job. Just an excuse to raise prices by sticking candy and perfume in a cheap heart-shaped box, or stamping a big "I Love You" on the front of some cheap-ass soft toy that'd be in the trash by March. Or falling apart at the seams. Probably both.

As I passed a display of sappy Valentine's cards my eyes snagged on a particularly gruesome one perched on the top. Because, first, the thing was huge - way too big to fit on a mantelpiece or dresser. Nope - that sucker would stand proudly on a coffee table, or not at all. Then there was the glitter. *Right.* Because nothing says "I love you" like tiny, shiny bits of foil that explode out the envelope and disappear into your carpet and sofa. And what was with the giant teddy bear? What did that even mean? Was it like, "Honey, I can't figure out how to tell you this, but I'm a Furrie. Tell you what: you rent the costumes, I'll meet you in the parking lot at sundown, and you can go all Yogi on my ass"?

I forced myself to walk past the display without stuffing the offending card down the back of it. Moving down the aisle toward the rear of the store, I loaded up my basket with power bars, even though just looking at those slabs of cardboard made my stomach clench, then grabbed a six-pack of energy drinks from a cooler cabinet. Catching sight of my reflection in the glass, I couldn't help wincing a little. It wasn't like I had high standards - I was sartorially-challenged at the best of times. But even for me, I looked bad.

My blue eyes were bloodshot, with dark bags under them. My light brown hair was now bordering on shaggy, since I'd been too busy (and too lazy) to get it cut for weeks. It also stuck out from my head like a bad wig, thanks to my having slept on and off in the back seat of my car for the last two nights. For the same reason, my white cotton shirt was covered in wrinkles, and even in the fuzzy reflection I could see the residual stain on the front where I'd spilled ketchup down it and my jeans last night, as I scarfed down a fast food burger in between stakeouts. I needed to start wearing darker colors.

Sometimes it freaked me out how different I looked from when I'd been in homicide. Not like I'd shown up in designer duds, but at least I'd always stuck gel in my hair when I didn't have time for a shower, and pulled on a fresh shirt and clean pants or jeans before heading out. Hell, I'd even ironed my shirts on a weekly basis and gotten a suit dry-cleaned once in a while. These days, I seemed to be going for 'perpetually rumpled.'

Maybe that was why Kaylee had started calling me 'Columbo' to my face?

What the hell. If people didn't like it, they didn't have to look at me -

"Fuckin' stick it in the bag!!"

The voice sounded agitated, like someone trying to keep quiet who'd gotten just pissed enough - or scared enough - that he couldn't keep it down.

"Sir... sir, please...!"

The second voice was definitely scared. And from the faint Indian accent, it sounded like it belonged to the store clerk I'd noticed when I came in the door.

Crap. I felt my heart put on a quick burst of speed. Lowering my basket silently to the ground, I glanced up at the nearest corner, where there should be a... Great. Just an empty space instead of a fish bowl mirror. On the plus side, at least I didn't have to worry about the robber spotting *me* in it.

"Come on, Kumar - hurry up!"

I crept slowly down the aisle furthest from the store counter, keeping my head down and carefully edging around yet more Valentine's Day crap sticking out from the shelves. So far I'd only heard one threatening voice, but that didn't mean jack. For all I knew, the entire front area and parking lot was filled with more assholes, carrying two machine guns apiece. Okay, so they'd have to be the quietest, most disciplined fighting force in LA history... but as a patrol cop I'd learned the hard way not to assume anything.

I reached the end of the aisle and tilted my head cautiously around it, ready to pull smoothly back if there was even a chance someone might notice me. Planning to pull back anyway, once I'd gotten a snapshot of the scene, some idea how the bad guys were armed. Very, very slowly, I moved my head a fraction of an inch around the edge of a shelf -

- and found myself staring into the face of a small child. *Jesus!* I yanked my head back around the corner, heart pounding. Way to make my adrenaline spike.

So... the bad news was I'd just been startled by a freaking *Cupid* ornament. The good news was that - even in the fraction of a second I'd had before my autonomic nervous system had ordered retreat (from an inanimate flying baby, which was just plain embarrassing) - I had managed to sweep the scene in front of me. The bad guy was definitely armed, and although he might not actually want the store clerk dead, it was downright scary how easy it was for a gun to go off in your hand.

My own hand headed to my belt at that thought, reaching for -

- the empty space at my hip.

Double crap. I'd applied for a concealed weapon permit the same time I applied to become a PI, and I'd had one for the past six months now. Even though they'd jerked me around at first for a few weeks. Okay, a few months, and it wasn't exactly a mystery why.

But by the time I'd been able to carry, I'd decided maybe it wasn't the best idea after all. Sure, if I was planning on going somewhere dicey, I'd wear a gun. But chasing down lost dogs and runaways? Taking photos of middle-aged businessmen picking up hookers? The odds of needing a gun for protection on those kinds of jobs was pretty low. No, I didn't like making assumptions... but I was also acutely aware that Things Had Changed since I'd left the job. These days, I couldn't take someone down and expect the detectives to give me the benefit of the doubt, like they would with an officer-involved shooting call. And even if I was cleared on the homicide, it was a given *somebody* would sue.

On the other hand, litigation was looking pretty good at this moment, compared to being a stain on the floor tiles -

"That's it... that's all of it!" The clerk sounded terrified.

Screw being sensible or cautious.

Shifting forward onto the balls of my feet, I braced my hands to take a longer look through the ornaments... and realized the entire display unit I hid behind was top-to-bottom Cupids. Everything from balloons to chocolate ones to... garden ornaments? Yeah, because nothing says 'I love you' like a creepy garden gnome. Not that any place deserved to be robbed, but seriously, way to go overboard with the romance bullshit. It was just typical of my recent luck that I'd ended up trapped in a store full of the stuff.

Okay, now I was just stalling.

Leaning further forward, I peered out. Behind the counter, the store clerk held his hands over his head, looking as terrified as he'd sounded, while the robber waved the shotgun around erratically as he inspected the money he'd just grabbed. By the way he skittered around on his feet, he was obviously on something: probably crack or meth. Which meant it was a coin toss whether he'd accept his good fortune at getting anything at all and boogie happily on out of there, or decide the clerk was trying to cheat him out of the millions a small, independent convenience store *obviously* took before noon.

"I swear, that's all - see, you can check the register!"

The robber nodded vigorously - presumably to himself - and clutched the bag to his chest, turning toward the door.

I willed the guy to leave. Right now.

Because right now, there was no sign of other customers to get in his face, and nothing in the tiny parking lot except my own beat-up old Toyota (it was great for stakeouts in bad neighborhoods) and one of those green VW bugs that all the cool kids started driving around in a few years back. It had to belong to the perp. Didn't seem like a great match to the badly-groomed unstable guy waving a gun around, but maybe it came from a previous life before some drug dealers got their claws in him.

As I watched, though, he stopped and turned to face the clerk again.

"No-no-no...." But my under-my-breath entreaty to the gods of bad situations had no effect. The perp stepped back, away from the door, and waggled the shotgun at the clerk's head. Or rather... at something *above* his head.

"And the bear!"

The clerk's face showed his confused dismay. "Y-you want the *bear*?"

"*Yeah!!*"

Not the smartest move, second-guessing an armed gunman, but I had to admit I was pretty damn surprised too. Under the heading of 'demands made during hold-ups' I was pretty sure that stuffed toys didn't come up too often. Although... I had to admit, that was one eye-catchingly huge polar bear. The thing hung, King Kong-like, high over the counter, its white fur gleaming in the store's bright lights. It had a bright red bow around its neck and the obligatory "I Love You" stamped on its chest. Not to mention it dwarfed both men.

Still, the guy had to be high as a kite being flown off the top of the CN Tower... in a hurricane. Even if they could get it down somehow, he'd never get it out the front door, let alone stuff it into that tiny car of his. They probably had to stuff the thing in place, just to get it up there. But I guessed logical thinking was too much to expect at this point.

As the perp took a furious step closer, the clerk visibly flinched then made his biggest mistake of the night... after showing up for work, that is. "B-b-but... why do you want it?"

Definitely the wrong thing to say.

Dropping the bag of money, the perp brought up both hands to aim the shotgun at the clerk's head. "It's for my girlfriend! You wanna make something of it?!"

Watching it all go down, all I could think was: *Where the*

fuck are the good guys? I was willing to bet that a store like this, in this area, would have been robbed before. No question, a panic button was located somewhere back there. But if the clerk had stepped on it as soon as this all started, the nearest patrol should've already been here. I flicked my gaze from the counter to the parking lot visible through the front window... and froze at the sight of a heavily pregnant woman helping a young child out the back of the green bug.

Shit. The bug didn't belong to the perp at all, but to a couple more innocent victims who were about to walk into all of this.

Three, if you counted the unborn kid.

I felt cold dread fill my stomach, shoving bile into my throat. I could almost see the aftermath: the flashing lights of the paramedics and police vehicles; the tape securing the crime scene; the sobbing husband and father pleading to see it, then losing his stomach contents if someone was dumb enough to let him through.

Sad thing was, I barely had to use my imagination. I'd seen this scenario play out in real life too many times before.

"Get it down!"

"B-but I can't! I-it's attached to the wall!"

"*Get it down!!*" The perp stepped closer, the shotgun barrel shifting erratically in his trembling hands as it pointed into the shaking clerk's face.

I shot another glance outside. In the parking lot, the woman took the child's hand in hers and headed for the door.

And that was it. I couldn't wait for the cavalry; or for the shotgun to fire; or for a five-year-old and her mother to walk unwittingly into a potential bloodbath.

I stepped out from my hiding place, grabbed something from the nearest shelf, and was at the perp's back in three long strides. Alerted - by a noise, or a reflection, or maybe just the slight involuntary widening of the clerk's eyes - the perp started to turn around -

THWACK!

- then experienced instant blackout as I slammed a bright pink Cupid garden statue into the back of his head.

I bent down to feel the pulse in the man's neck where he lay sprawled on the ground. Slow but steady. He'd have a real thumper of a headache when he woke up. I figured a gun butt or a baseball bat would've hurt worse. Although... taken out by a flying baby garden ornament? The guy's prison time would be a *nightmare* if that got out.

Plus the fact that he'd screwed up an easy getaway by getting hung up on a *bear*?

For his *girlfriend*?

Because it was *Valentine's Day*?

I shook my head as I carefully shifted the shotgun away with my foot. "Schmuck."

"Oh, my God - thank you! You saved my life!!" The store clerk had clearly emerged from his state of temporary shock.

And just in time, too. Even as I started to wonder what had happened to the incoming woman and little girl, the door was yanked open abruptly. Two uniformed cops charged through, weapons aimed squarely at my chest as they yelled at me.

"Get away from the gun!"

"Put it down! Put it *down*!!"

Put *what* down?

"Drop the Cupid on the ground!"

Right. I slowly lowered the Cupid gnome I'd hung onto in case the perp didn't stay down, careful to keep both hands in view at all times. "Guys, I'm the good Samaritan here -"

"Stay down! Get down on your knees!"

The store clerk spoke up, coming out from behind the counter. "No - no, you don't understand, sirs, he -"

"Not now!" The more senior of the two cops - aka

Dumbass #1 - glared at the clerk, then turned his full attention back to me. "Down on the ground!"

I tried one more time. "Look, my name's Lyle Thatcher. I'm an ex-cop -"

"On the ground! *Now*!!"

I hadn't been expecting a commendation from the Mayor or the keys to the city - but *this*? With a sigh, I gave in and knelt, linking my hands behind my head. A moment later I was unceremoniously shoved face-first to the ground, finding myself eye to eye with the pink Cupid again.

It stared back at me with a smug little smile, even as Dumbass #2 cuffed my hands behind my back.

I sat in the sweltering hot back seat of a squad car, blinking sweat out of my eyes as I watched the store clerk - Naveed was his name, I'd discovered - speaking to the cops. The man kept gesturing urgently from himself to the store to me and back again. From this distance, I couldn't tell if the cops were skeptical, bored, or maybe even... impressed?

But more crucially, I couldn't tell if I'd be getting out of these cuffs sooner rather than later. Sooner would be nice, since I had work to do today. Okay, so mostly I'd be doing paperwork and downloading photos to send to various soon-to-be-ex-spouses... but there was always a chance someone might have called with a bigger job since I'd last checked my phone. Maybe a missing dog... or maybe a background check for a limo company driver.

Yeah - something important like that.

Over by a paramedic vehicle, bandages covering the back of his head, the "Polar Bear Bandit" was being interviewed too. With nothing better to do, I'd occupied my mind thinking up that moniker, and I thought it would make a pretty catchy headline. Though I doubted the attempted theft of a few hundred bucks - plus an improbably large bear - would make the evening news, despite the cutesy Valentine's Day tie-in. Not unless things were going improbably well in the world, and no celebrity deaths / cheating scandals / punch-ups on airplanes had occurred in the last few hours. And come on, what were the chances of that?

The guy looked pretty miserable sitting there, even though - unlike me - he wasn't stuck in a sweatbox with no airflow. Damn, couldn't they have cracked a window?

But finally, after what seemed like an eternity, one of the cops got a call on his radio that seemed to involve me, since it had him glancing across at the squad car. A nod, a few words to Naveed, then he detached himself and headed over. Behind him, the young clerk hovered, clearly torn between coming over to his rescuer - i.e., me - and diving back into his store, from which the departing CSIs had just removed the yellow 'Do Not Cross' tape. With a gesture aimed at me that could have meant anything from 'Okay, back to work!' to 'Hang on, I'll be back!' Naveed disappeared inside.

"Okay, sir." The cop reached the car door, and then mercifully it was opened and I was helped out. "Sorry about that," he continued, unlocking the cuffs. "Had to check you out. We already got your statement, so you're free to go."

I read the guy's name tag and pointedly rubbed my wrists. Not because the cuffs were tight, or my wrists were particularly sore, but just to see if he gave a shit.

To be fair, Officer Murphy gave an apologetic shrug. "Sorry," he said again. "That was, uh, nice work back there. Quick thinking."

Then why'd you leave me to broil in the back of your stinking squad car for half an hour?

But private investigators needed all the cop friends they could get, and I'd already burned way too many bridges the week I'd left the job. "No problem. I know how it is."

Murphy eyed me curiously. "Yeah... my Sarge said you were on the job 'til last year."

I nodded, but he was clearly hoping for more.

"Detective in homicide?" Murphy waited for an answer, eyes flickering over me as if searching for the injury (mental or otherwise) that had led a guy who achieved such a prime gig by thirty to up and resign.

I guessed his Sergeant hadn't enlightened him. Or rather, hadn't passed on the rumors. Only one person other than me knew for sure why I'd left, and they wouldn't be talking about it any time soon. I gave Murphy my blandest expression. "Right."

He frowned and started to ask something else, but mercifully I was spared answering by the hasty reappearance of Naveed. The store clerk wore the air of a papal supplicant as he hurried up to us, a large, gleaming red box grasped in both hands.

"Sir, I cannot thank you enough! This is for you." Naveed thrust the box at me, at which point I realized - yep, the damn thing was shaped like a heart. A giant, shining, red heart. Universal symbol of love and devotion.

Yuck. I took an involuntary step back. Probably not the best time for a lecture on why the media-propagated fairytales of true love and soulmates were just a way to make a few bucks. "There's really no need..."

"Please! You have to - you saved my life!" Naveed interrupted, sounding almost desperate at the idea of my refusing his gift. "It's wonderful chocolate, best you ever tasted."

"I don't really eat the stuff." Not a total lie, since I'd sworn off chocolate following my post-resignation M&M's and vodka binge. Most guys just get drunk, but no: I had to get *creative.* I hadn't felt that sick since I chugged a fifth of scotch after my high school prom.

"Give it to your wife!"

"I'm single."

Naveed grinned. "But it's Valentine's Day - you have a

date, yes? Give it to her!"

I opened my mouth to explain why that wouldn't be happening... for a whole multitude of reasons.

But before I could say a thing, Naveed had pressed the box into my hands. "Trust me," he said, with a broad wink, "you give her this, she will *love* you tonight!"

I could've told him I didn't have a date tonight, and the only thing I'd be getting horizontal with in the foreseeable future was the back seat of my car. And not in a fun way. Still, the guy was trying to be nice. And he *had* just had a gun shoved in his face. Maybe I could cut him some slack.

Meeting Naveed's eager gaze, I forced out a "Thanks."

Then I carried the freaking chocolates over to my car before the damn things melted in my hands.

∂

Five minutes later, the chocolates and I were reveling in my late 1990s air conditioning as I drove down one of the most gone-to-seed, run-down lengths of street in the whole of Los Angeles, right in the armpit of Hollywood. This wasn't 'glitzy, mansion in the hills' Hollywood. It wasn't even 'touristy, cheap-ass' Hollywood. No, this was their coked-up hooker sister.

Only a minute from here, in various directions, you could find some pretty decent office buildings and some nice looking, freshly-painted condos. But in true LA style, these existed as small oases of pleasantness, surrounded by deserts of decay, uneven sidewalks, and disrepair. How was this possible? Because those who lived or worked in those oases never needed to venture into the deserts, other than driving through them in a car. This was LA, after all. Nobody walked. Needless to say, Thatcher Investigations was so far into a desert, if you tried walking from the nearest oasis you'd probably drop dead from heat stroke halfway there.

I parked my car in the small, scruffy lot, grabbed my

stuff out the back, and locked the door. No wheel lock or security system to engage. Frankly, the best anti-theft device in this neighborhood was driving an old beater no one'd want to steal. Even for parts.

I trudged around the corner and skirted a pile of trash someone had left propped against a wall. Then I paused and took a second look.

"Hey, Charlie."

The pile of trash shifted, and Charlie grinned up at me from under two wedged sheets of heavy cardboard, a mop of greasy graying hair, and an ancient Dodgers cap. "Hey, Lyle!" The old guy - he must be in his late fifties at least - had been sleeping next to the building's dumpster on and off for a couple of weeks, so I wondered what had caused him to move. He must've seen my glance over to it, because he scowled and gestured a little drunkenly with the brown-bagged bottle he always seemed to carry. "*Rats*," he said with feeling, and I tried not to shudder.

I briefly considered giving him one of my energy drinks and power bars - not exactly nutritious, but better than nothing, right? - then remembered I'd left them behind in the store. Kind of hard to pay for groceries when you're being dragged outside in cuffs.

I looked down at the heart-shaped box with even more dislike than before, then raised my eyebrows at Charlie. "You like chocolate? It's supposed to be really good." Yeah, I know. My generosity knows no bounds.

Charlie eyed the box with mistrust, then frowned and shook his head. "Nah. No thanks." He patted his waist, concealed beneath an oversized, holey sweater and pair of sweatpants that might have been cream-colored in the last decade. "Gotta watch my weight."

My office was on the second floor, reached by a set of noisy outside stairs and an even noisier landing that made it just a little harder to sneak up on me there. The only downside was I couldn't sneak past my neighbors either, though I gave it a solid try every time.

As I passed the door marked 'Aardvark Bail Bonds' I debated just leaving the chocolates there. Jimmy Morrison was best known for eating donuts, but judging by his size I was pretty sure he wasn't that choosy about how he ingested his calories. On the other hand, I didn't want Jimmy thinking I was hitting on him. That would be... a bad idea, on so many levels.

Wishing I'd just tossed the candy box into the first dumpster I'd seen, I wedged it under my arm while I punched in the code and used my keys. Unlike my car, my office did have security. Lots of it. Meaning it took about fifteen seconds just to get inside if I didn't want to set off an alarm. But finally the door marked "Thatcher Investigations" opened inward, and with a grunt of relief I stepped in and flipped on the AC.

As usual, my desk was filled with paperwork. Well, not just paperwork. There was also a lot of what could more correctly be termed 'clutter.' Old receipts I still had to file. A pile of blank DVDs - sure, courts preferred the originals, but I'd found that formerly loving wives and husbands typically liked to keep the evidence that their spouse was a cheater. A Spanish dictionary, because even after all these years I still wasn't fluent, and the Community College course I kept trying to sign up for either filled up in an hour or got canceled due to low sign-up rates. No, I don't know how those things weren't mutually exclusive. And then there were the half dozen or so stained coasters I never bothered to clean. Or use... which begged the question: how'd they get so many stains on them in the first place?

Also on the same desk - a requirement in these hi-tech times - sat a top of the line desktop computer, high speed modem, and ergonomically-designed keyboard. Which was so encroached upon by the clutter, one keystroke would probably send my treasured-but-fading LAPD coffee mug crashing down to the floor.

Shifting the mug to a safer location, I dumped the candy box on top of the mess. I stared at the garish red heart for a moment, then finally bit the bullet and took off the lid.

Row upon row of heart-shaped chocolates stared back at me. What had Naveed said? *"Wonderful chocolate, like nothing you ever tasted before."* Yeah, right. Call me a cynic, but I figured he'd grabbed the biggest box he could find that wasn't selling. Probably ripped the discount label right off the top.

Still. Couldn't hurt to try just one.

I put a chocolate heart in my mouth. Huh. Not bad. Not bad at all. But then I looked down into the box again, and... holy crap, it was *huge*. It'd take weeks to get through it, and that whole time I'd be stuck with the heart-shaped red satin and the dozens of heart-shaped chocolates. A constant reminder of the dumbest day of the year.

Yeugh. Resolutely, I stuck the lid back on and wedged the whole thing into the trash. Then I stuffed last week's free newspaper in on top of it, so I didn't have to see the red satin edge sticking out.

Just as I finished there was a loud pounding at my door. The door was locked, but after the morning I'd had I was halfway to my back office (and my firearm safe) before I heard Jimmy's muffled voice through it. "Thatcher, you in there?"

I relaxed. Well, mostly.

Sure, Jimmy acted the dimwitted figure of fun when it suited him. Truth be told, I'd never seen much that said different in the nearly nine months we'd been neighbors. But I knew his reputation, and you didn't get to be that successful - or that connected - by being a dumbass. Or by being unwilling to kick the shit out of people from time to time. I wasn't sure Jimmy got his own hands dirty any more, but I'd seen his goons and they'd give The Terminator a run for his money. So whenever Jimmy knocked on the door, I couldn't help wondering if I should be loaded for grizzly instead of teddy bear.

But so far he hadn't done anything threatening - and I didn't want to piss him off - so I backtracked and headed for the door.

"I got a job for you." Jimmy cut to the chase as he waddled in through the door I held open and collapsed into my client chair. To be fair, he'd been waiting out on the landing for a good ten seconds, so between his lack of conditioning and today's heat his usually curly short brown hair was already plastered to his forehead with sweat.

I shut the door behind him and kicked the A/C up a notch, hearing his relieved sigh as the airflow increased to maximum.

Wiping a handkerchief over his face, he glanced around at the junk that covered my desk and shook his head. I knew he thought my operation was unprofessional, given that I met clients amid all this mess. But that was okay. Turned out, we had different definitions of what 'professional' meant. I believed it meant doing my best for the client and respecting confidentiality agreements. That type of thing.

Jimmy thought it meant having a receptionist and nice furniture... then selling client information and photos to a gossip website, or using them to blackmail someone. He hadn't exactly come out and said so. Not with me being an ex-cop. But he'd dropped enough hints that I was pretty sure. Some people might take that as a sign that Jimmy was stupid - or at the very least incautious. Ignoring the possibility that I could be here undercover and this could all be some big set-up.

I took it as a sign that Jimmy was better connected than anyone even gave him credit for. I figured he knew I'd left the LAPD under a cloud, and had a pretty good idea what kind of cloud it was. That didn't mean he knew everything... just maybe a whole hell of a lot more than some of my former colleagues. Which, in turn, I took to mean that I should underestimate Jimmy Morrison at my peril.

I leaned back against my office wall, and watched as he eyed my heavily firewalled and password-protected computer with near-to-drooling interest. Probably wondering if any of my clients were famous enough, or had juicy enough secrets, to bring in serious dough. They didn't, but I guess a guy could hope. I'd have considered moving, but at least the threat of being hacked from the neighboring office suite kept me on my toes. Plus the low rent out here in No-Man's-Land was about the only thing keeping Thatcher Investigations afloat.

"So what's the job?" I asked.

Jimmy pulled his gaze away from my computer with patent resignation. "Bail jumper," he said, leaning back into the chair. "Leroy Baldwin. Missed his court date yesterday." He shifted in his seat, trying to find a more comfortable position. I heard a faint but tortured creaking from somewhere below the faux-leather surface and hoped it held up under the strain. My sanity couldn't take another trip to IKEA this year. "I'm betting the kid's hiding out at his girlfriend's place. I just need you to go bring him in." Jimmy reached into his jacket pocket, then held out a few folded sheets of paper. "Here's the bail piece and her address."

I took a look and saw that Leroy's girlfriend lived in a nice area. "What did he do?"

"Held up a convenience store."

Small world. "Must be going around."

"Huh?"

"Nothing." A thought occurred to me then, and I frowned. "If this is so easy, why can't your guys handle it?"

Jimmy wasn't exactly known for being a man of action, at least not these days. He mostly dealt with things over the phone, or met with clients at his office, or sometimes heaved himself into a shiny black town car, which came with a suited chauffeur to drive him around.

Jimmy's *employees*, though, were a formidable sight. I

didn't know how he recruited, but the workout yard of a prison came to mind. On the other hand, he'd offered *me* work several times now. So maybe that meant I should be worried... or that I should have more respect for his hiring practices.

"They could, if they weren't out of town on another skip." Jimmy's eyes narrowed. "Vegas, on my dime. They better be out lookin' for the guy, not seeing 'Celine' for the third time."

If they were, I hoped his boys enjoyed the show... and getting beaten up. Because only an idiot would assume Jimmy Morrison wouldn't have eyes and ears all *over* that town.

"So - can you do it?"

I wanted to say no, but at the rate money was flowing out of my bank account, I'd be struggling to pay rent on this place next month. No, I wouldn't collude with Jimmy to fleece my clients, or work for any of his other rumored 'enterprises.' And yes, I knew working with him at all probably put me on the slippery slope. Although if that were true, I was already sliding downhill on ice skates, since I'd taken two similar jobs for him before. But at least Aardvark Bail Bonds - the public face of Jimmy's empire - was legit. Grabbing bail jumpers was pretty much the same as arresting people. And frankly, if I did it they stood a much better chance of not getting bruised or banged up than if Jimmy's usual crew was on the job.

But mostly, I really needed the paycheck.

Jimmy knew that too, and looked puzzled by my hesitation. "You got a hot date tonight or something?"

I shot him a withering look. "No."

I expected Jimmy to give me grief for this, but instead he just looked smug. "Oh yeah?" He pointed a pudgy finger over my shoulder. "Then what's *that* about?"

Glancing around, I frowned to see nothing but my barely-used appointment calendar - a free gift from some office supply place - hanging askew on its hook. I was about to ask Jimmy what he meant, when I realized someone had made a bright red entry that spilled out of the space for February 14:

6pm, don't be late! Kaylee.

My heart pounded. "Fuck, that's *tonight?*" I mumbled under my breath.

I'd almost forgotten. Holy crap.

Jimmy smirked at my reaction as he hauled himself to his feet, accompanied by more groans from the chair. "Screwed up, did ya?"

I decided to let Jimmy have his fun rather than explain. Mostly because I didn't want him knowing any more about me than he already did. But also because I owed him. If I'd really forgotten about tonight, there would have been hell to pay. Not that Kaylee would've *let* me forget, surely...? Although, come to think of it, there'd been no texts from her since early yesterday.

Great. That meant this was a test, and one I'd nearly failed.

Nearly? Hell, there was still time for it. "Jimmy, I gotta go." If I left now... yeah, there should be time to do the retrieval and still get there on time. I grabbed my jacket and debated retrieving the chocolates from the trash can. Flowers would be better, but what if I didn't have time to stop for them?

Jimmy was still enjoying himself. "Broke your own rules, huh? So come on, tell me - what's she like?"

"Not now." It wasn't like I'd thrown the chocolates in the *sewer.* I mean, they were still in the box, so it couldn't be *that* unsanitary. On the other hand, I'd already eaten one. And that kind of thing really stuck out. But maybe I could pretend to snag it when she opened the box...?

"So this Kaylee, she's stacked, huh?" Jimmy persisted. "Puts out?"

Anger flooded me before I could stifle it, and I saw Jimmy catch it, his eyes widening as he saw she was more than some bimbo I was screwing. I could see the cogs working behind his eyes as he shut down whatever ribald comment he'd been about to make next, and I felt like kicking myself for giving away anything about my private life. Being around Jimmy was like keeping a big cat in a cage: no matter how much it purred or let you pet it, you better not leave the door open if you wanted to stay safe.

At least he wasn't pressing for more details... yet. Instead he headed for the door, but paused and looked back at me before opening it to the heat outside. "You're still gonna grab Leroy today, though - right?"

I hoped so, but only a fool would promise Jimmy something they couldn't deliver. Plus now I had somewhere I had to be by seven. Maybe taking this job wasn't such a good idea after all.

I reached for the address to hand it back to him, but Jimmy shook his head. "Keep it." I could practically see him deciding whether to threaten or cajole me. In the end he came down on the lighter side, giving the kind of smile a shark wears right before it gobbles you up. "All you gotta do is ID the kid and grab him. How long could it take?"

I sat in my trusty surveillance vehicle, hunched down behind the steering wheel, and stared grimly across the street. On the dash, the clock ticked forward from 4:49 to 4:50 p.m. And still no sign of the master criminal I was here to grab. Until I caught a glimpse of Leroy, there was nothing I could do. The annoying part of doing retrieval work was you needed to positively identify the target before busting into a house or any kind of private property. And even then, it wasn't like I could just bang on the door and yell "LAPD" any more.

Just another way the private sector sucked. Never thought I'd miss applying for warrants so much.

At this point, I wasn't even sure Leroy was in there. But I'd just hung up on Jimmy, who'd still been adamant the girlfriend was my best shot.

I raised my binoculars, studying the large house, the well-kept lawn in front, the look of the whole street. The whole place screamed middle class. Tanya White had to have better prospects than a screw-up like Leroy Baldwin. Or maybe bad boys were just her thing? Love... lust... was complicated as hell. People overlooked or forgave the kind of crap that should have had them running for the hills.

Then again, sometimes people in love were just totally fucking blind to what was going on, even when it happened right under their noses.

I should know.

Ruthlessly clamping down on my meandering thoughts, I focused my attention back on the house... just as my phone buzzed in my lap. Probably Jimmy, checking up on me yet again. I didn't recognize the number, though. "Thatcher Investigations," I said.

As I hung up a minute later, I couldn't help the smile that was spreading from ear to ear. I'd gotten my first referral. As in, someone I'd helped had actually liked my work enough to refer me to a 'pal.'

And what a pal. Gerry Warnock was a record producer who operated in the big leagues. So big that even I, who couldn't have named any of the latest chart hits to save my life (was there even a chart any more?) had heard of him. And he wanted me at his home - as in, his Bel-Air mega-mansion - at ten a.m. tomorrow. He'd been vague over the phone, but it involved delivering papers to some ex-client - a has-been rocker trying to hang on to his faded career. All I had to do was track the guy down. A fading rock star trying to make a come-back? Yeah, I was guessing I'd need all of ten minutes to follow the trail of shameless self-publicizing online. At which point, I could probably just tweet the guy an interview request, casually mentioning that I'd cover the whiskey shots / bottomless mimosas / vegan tacos (depending on where he was on the spectrum of hardcore rocker to cleansed hippie), and the poor fool would come to me.

Personally, I wasn't into exposing myself - in any sense - all over the internet. But social media truly was a PI's best friend. And when it came to the job, I was *all* about new tools and technology, and making sure I had the skills to make very good use of them.

I raised my binoculars as I caught activity at the front of the house. A well-dressed couple approaching the front door... ringing the bell... the door opening to reveal... a silver-haired man in a tuxedo. Looked like the Whites were having a party, unless they took dressing for dinner pretty damn seriously.

As the front door closed, I shifted my binoculars upward to the second floor, noticing a new light on in one of the rooms upstairs. Lucky for me, the curtains were wide open. Now all I needed was for Leroy to be in there, and just walk slowly past the window...

I caught a flash of movement as three women came into the room. Two moved out of view, but the third opened a closet to reveal a large, see-through garment bag hanging inside the door, and -

Crap. I stared incredulously through the binoculars at what the garment bag contained. A high-necked, puffy-sleeved, and - there was no other word for it - *meringue-shaped*... pure white wedding dress.

I cursed again, wanting to wring Jimmy's neck. So much for grabbing the guy when no one was looking.

No doubt about it, this was somebody's wedding day. And I was willing to bet Leroy was the damn groom.

Chapter Two.

"Where's Tanya?"

"Upstairs."

"Because Leroy needs to -"

"Judy, could you take this tray out into the -?"

"Can somebody get the door?!"

I stood on Ed White's porch, listening to the overlapping male and female voices on the other side of his front door. Bracing myself, I rang the bell again.

After a short pause, the door swung open to reveal a woman in her late fifties, wearing the kind of bright, frozen smile that would disappear in a heartbeat the second you stepped out of line. She also wore a designer (or at least designer rip-off) hyacinth pink suit with a complicated matching pink hat, which currently sat a little askew on her expensively styled graying curls. She took one look at my generic beige uniform and the smile disappeared, replaced by an agitated frown. "Can I help you?"

Okay, so much for thinking a delivery person would seem harmless.

I looked past her to see a large group of what appeared to be football linebackers glancing my way curiously. I could have been wrong, of course. They could have been NBA draft picks.

But hey - dealing with a few angry relatives would be nothing compared to the first time I'd pulled the delivery guy routine as a young vice cop. All I'd had to do was drop off bugged pizza boxes to a group of - most likely - heavily armed dealers in Washington Heights. I'd ended up waiting in their living room, shit-scared, for them to get me my tip (their idea, not mine), and almost wet myself when one of them tore into the pizzas and yelled out, "Hey, what's *this*?!"

Turned out he just hated anchovies, but by the time I realized he hadn't found the wire, my life had already flashed before my eyes.

"I got a delivery for a Leroy Baldwin?"

"Gloria? Everything all right?"

The tuxedoed silver-haired guy I'd seen from my car walked out to the door. I was pretty sure this was Ed White, Father of the Bride, and his words made it pretty clear that the woman I'd been talking to was Gloria Baldwin, Mother of the Groom. Towering over her, Ed looked like a *retired* linebacker who'd indulged in the donuts and Buds just a few too many times. I could probably take the guy, but it would hurt tomorrow.

"Ed, he says he has a delivery for Leroy."

I nodded toward the medium-sized van I'd left parked on the driveway, the words 'Epic Events' plastered across its sides.

One of the smartest things I'd done in my first month as a PI was buy it in a sale at an impound lot. Back then it hadn't looked exactly roadworthy, with flat tires, missing paint and bumpers, warped glass in the windows from being parked in too much direct sunlight, and several patches of rust from being exposed to the elements over time. I'd paid a mechanic twice his hourly labor rate to come with me and check over a few vehicles. He'd given it the thumbs up, and I ended up being the only bidder. Maybe because of its decrepit appearance, or because it had belonged to an exterminator company and still bore their peeling slogan, 'We won't kill you *or* your pets!' on its sides. Yeah. Perhaps it was no great mystery why they'd gone bust. There's being clear, there's being blunt, and then there's saying things people just don't want to think about... ever.

Anyhow, their loss was my gain. Since then, I'd used the van in a dozen different ways, sometimes fully loaded for surveillance and stakeout, other times as an undercover or transport vehicle. I'd gotten several magnetic car logos printed up, thin sheets that could quickly be attached and removed from the van's sides, and 'Epic Events' was one of them. Call me juvenile, but I loved the private sector undercover stuff: all the kicks of wearing disguises and play-acting, but with almost no risk. Guess I saw too many 'Mission Impossible' reruns as a kid. The TV show, not the Tom Cruise movies. Well, except number three. Kinda liked that one.

Ed frowned at the van in the growing twilight, as if annoyed by the distraction on his daughter's big day. "Caterers are already here."

I smacked my gum and handed my hastily fabricated paperwork to him. "I'm just delivering a cake."

His frown deepened as he read the printed sheet. "We already have a cake."

"Not like this one." I grinned and nodded over my shoulder. "The thing must be five tiers tall - fills up the whole van!"

I worried I'd overdone it for a second. Then Gloria's eyes gleamed and she patted Ed excitedly on the arm. "It must be from my cousins in Seattle. I *knew* they'd send more than that melon baller!"

I felt a twinge of guilt for ruining her big day. Okay, technically her son and future daughter-in-law's big day, although I figured being TMOTG was right up there too. But hey, I wasn't the one who'd committed armed robbery. If she wanted to blame anyone, she'd have to look to her law-breaking kid.

Ed still looked hesitant though.

I shrugged. "If you're refusing delivery -"

"No!" Gloria grabbed at the paperwork Ed still held.

"I'll sign for it."

I stopped her. "Sorry, ma'am. It's gotta be Mr. Leroy Baldwin who signs for it."

Gloria practically ran into the house. "I'll go find him!"

"And I'll go get the cake." I gave a simpleton's grin, then turned away and ambled over to the back of the van.

Time for phase two.

If they took any longer I was gonna drop phase two. *Literally.*

Dripping with perspiration, I glared yet again at Ed White's closed front door as I shifted my hold on the gigantic wedding cake that tilted precariously half in, half out the back of the 'Epic Events' van. The cake wasn't exactly heavy - seeing as it was mostly styrofoam covered in cracked, uber-elderly pink and white frosting - but keeping it balanced like this was killing my back. Not to mention all the dust was making my nose itch.

I'd borrowed (or more precisely, leased) the fake cake from the display window of a failing Koreatown bakery. I grimaced as I watched a cockroach chew its way through the frosting. Not exactly appetizing. Probably explained their lack of customers and the 'C' rating on the door.

The cockroach gave up on the frosting and headed for my hand instead. I was half a second away from shoving the cake back in the van and going on a cockroach stomp-fest when I finally heard my cue.

"A cake?" I looked up to see Leroy Baldwin standing in Ed White's mercifully re-opened front doorway, frowning at his future father-in-law.

I raised my voice, stumbling theatrically. "Could I get a little help here!"

Sure enough, Ed and Leroy hurried toward me, the prospect of all that pricey pink gooeyness slamming into the unforgiving concrete apparently more than they could bear. They were making this easy. I almost felt bad for them.

Almost.

Ed headed for me, reaching for my end of the cake tray. "I got it..."

"No, it's too heavy!" I staggered again, nodding Leroy toward the opposite end of the cake tray that still sat inside the van. "If you could just..." I panted, "get in there, and pull it back in, we can try again."

"Okay." Leroy sounded dubious, but dutifully clambered up into the van and hauled the other end of the tray inside, taking the 'weight' off me.

"Phew!" I put my hands on my hips and wiped away real sweat as I pretended to glance around. "Okay - I think we can manage if there's four of us. Two on each end." I turned to Ed. "There any more big guys inside?"

Ed frowned. "Well, I guess so, but -"

"Is that a *cockroach*?"

I knew the bluff was over the instant I heard Leroy's puzzled voice. Not missing a beat, I shoved the cake tray deep into the van with him, ignoring Leroy's shout of surprise, then slammed the handily self-locking van door shut on cake and groom both. Ed gaped at me in shock, but I knew that wouldn't last long. Which meant I either made a break for the driver's door or tried to reason with the guy.

I took in Ed's huge bulk and went for option B. "Sir, are you aware that Mr. Baldwin skipped bail yesterday?"

"*What?*"

The shocked reaction confirmed what I'd suspected. This wedding wasn't exactly low key or discreet. I'd figured the poor guy had no idea Leroy was a wanted man.

"Daddy?"

Tanya White came flying out of the house, resplendent in her puffy white wedding dress and almost tripping on its full length train in just those few short steps. Clearly somebody had seen a few too many British Royal Weddings on TV.

"Tanya, go back indoors!"

"But what's going on? Where's Leroy?"

"Tanya!? Baby - let me out!!" Leroy's muffled voice came from inside the van.

"Leroy!?" Tanya practically threw herself at the van's back door, yanking at the handle to no avail.

"Tanya!?"

"I can't open it! It's locked!" Tanya glared at me with a ferocity that said *she* at least knew exactly what was going on, then turned desperate eyes on her father. "Daddy!!!"

I figured it wouldn't hurt to remind the guy that Leroy wasn't exactly a saint. What loving father wants a felon for a son-in-law, anyhow? "Mr. White, do you really want your daughter marrying a man who's headed for jail?"

"What are the charges?"

Good, Ed was being rational. I could get behind that. "Armed robbery -"

"He was framed, Daddy!" Tears flooded down Tanya's cheeks as she clung to the back of the van, still desperately trying to wrench open the door. "He was going to turn himself in tomorrow, I swear! He's only a couple of days late!" She made it sound like he was late paying his cable bill, instead of late showing up to defend himself in court.

I couldn't take this any more. "And you couldn't get married *before* his court date?"

Tanya shot me a glare that said I was a moron, then turned her impassioned gaze on her father. "We wanted to be just like you and Mom, and get married on Valentine's Day!"

Seriously? What kind of idiot risks going to jail, just to get married on the cheesiest day of the year? I snorted, starting to lose sympathy for the not-so-happy couple.

But *I* wasn't the target audience. By contrast, Ed White's face contorted with a mixture of love and sadness, along with a hefty dose of pride in his clearly deranged offspring. It was obvious he was deeply touched by her argument, and I gave bonus points to Tanya for yanking Daddy's heartstrings so expertly. It helped that she was obviously sincere.

Nuts, but sincere.

I should've stuck to playing on those paternal instincts, but I got nervous and pulled out the legal big guns instead. "Mr. White, I have paperwork giving me authority to take Leroy in -"

"And I've waited thirty-five years for my baby to get married!" Ed advanced on me menacingly. "Now where's the damn key to this door?!"

I backed up, fumbling in my pocket as Ed kept on coming. "Okay, okay…" My fingers latched onto something and I threw it toward Tanya. "There it is!"

The way she'd been squinting at me I was pretty sure the bride wore thick glasses most of the time, and as I'd intended she fumbled the catch. She and Ed began scrabbling around for the key on the driveway behind her.

Which only gave me a few seconds to take advantage of them being distracted and drive on out of there. Pulling out the *real* van keys, I launched myself up into the driver's seat and reached out blindly to close the door -

- then jumped like a kid in a horror movie when something smooth and cold grabbed onto my left arm.

Heart pounding, I jerked my head around… to find a very old woman staring at me, her skeletal fingers locked tight around my wrist.

I could have sworn both the driveway and front yard were clear a second ago. Where the hell had she come from?

And what the hell was she *wearing*? Tufts of gray hair peeked out from beneath a huge, feather-strewn reddish-purple hat, which clashed horribly with her nausea-inducing pink and blue Paisley dress. I might have zero fashion sense, but that outfit was just plain painful on the eyeballs.

I glanced back to see Ed lowering himself down onto his stomach. I guess the key ended up under the van, which had bought me a few more seconds, but they'd have it soon. At which point it wouldn't take them much longer to figure out it didn't fit.

Oh, yeah. My father was gonna be pissed at me for using the spare key to his station wagon as a decoy. Not that I planned on admitting it.

"Ma'am, you need to let go," I said, trying to tug my arm away from the colorfully-dressed pensioner.

"I'm sorry, but I can't do that." The old gal sounded genuinely regretful. She also looked like a stiff breeze would knock her over, but she must have been stronger than she seemed because her grip held. Maybe unworldly strength went with the crazy I could see gleaming behind oversized Day-Glo-orange glasses as she moved in closer. Any second now, a couple of orderlies would probably come grab her and take her back to the nice home. I just wished they'd hurry up.

Mentally, I ran through the half dozen ways I knew to get my arm free of an attacker, but even the mildest would probably fracture that bird-like, veiny wrist. "Look, lady, I need to get out of here -"

"Why don't you let them get married first?" she said, sounding weirdly reasonable despite the intense eyes burning into me from behind those psychedelic glasses. "It'll only take five minutes," she assured me earnestly.

"Lady, I don't *have* five minutes!"

It was the truth. Even if I left now, I was going to be late, and I'd rather face a dozen Ed Whites and crazy old birds than the wrath of one Kaylee.

Then I caught sight of what was going on at the back of the van. Tanya had gotten up off the ground and was fumbling the (wrong) keys into the lock, tears carrying mascara down over her pale cheeks. "Leroy! *Leroy!*" she sobbed heartbrokenly.

"It's okay, baby! I love you!" came Leroy's agonized voice from within the van, as Ed clambered to his feet and took the key from his daughter.

Tanya wrenched her veil off her head, pulling apart a careful hairstyle that I bet had taken most of the morning to accomplish, and thrust a hand into her small cleavage to retrieve a pair of thick, unflattering glasses. Watching her pull them on, and seeing her makeup fail altogether under the combined attack of tears, sweat, and reddened cheeks, I realized that I had turned her moment of being a beautiful - or at least pretty - bride into a disaster zone.

Admittedly it was really her *fiancé* who had done that, by getting involved in an armed robbery and then skipping bail... but still, I felt an unexpected twinge of guilt -

Which I stamped down on ruthlessly, turning back to the crazy dame still clinging on to me tight. "Look, I'm doing them a favor. Six months from now he'll be in prison doing a five-year stretch and she'll be counting her blessings she's not stuck faking it through visiting hours."

The old girl tsked unhappily. "So cynical at such a young age." She peered at me more closely. "You don't believe in love any more, do you?"

I thought of the best way to respond, and decided on the truth. Who knew, maybe it'd shock her out of it. "No, ma'am, I do not."

Her gaze softened, holding pity. "What happened, child, to make you this way?"

Enough already. I felt the old anger and bitterness rise up in me and yanked my arm away from her, wrenching it free at last. But the momentum seemed to send her lurching forward, heading for a nasty impact with the van's side, and on instinct I found myself reaching to stop her fall...

At which point, she Tasered me in the chest.

☙

I was happy when I saw Jenny standing on the front porch next to Michael. My heart pumped harder as I strode up the path in my police uniform and caught sight of my smiling mother standing there with them, even as I told myself not to expect too much. But I was just so happy to find the person I loved being welcomed into my family, when I thought something I'd done or said had pushed her away for good.

I told myself it would be enough to find out why we'd gone from lovers who spent every spare minute together to barely seeing each other in the past few months. Of course, my being at the academy and studying all the time, while Jenny tried to get a foothold at work, had been tough on our relationship. But we hadn't split up - we hadn't even talked about it - so I couldn't stop that flicker of hope building that we could get back to where we were before. Back when we were young undergrads at San Diego State, fresh out of high school and ready to change the world.

My brother saw me first... and my steps faltered as I saw a kind of horror spread across his face. Was something wrong with Jenny? Was that why she'd been distant for so long? I pushed the thought away and carried on, forcing myself to remain hopeful -

- until I got halfway up the steps to the porch and saw Michael's left arm around Jenny's shoulders. Because it wasn't the kind of hug you gave a friend; not the way her breasts were pressed up against his side, or the way she had her right arm around his waist, her left hand pressed up against his chest.

I slowed then, frowning, as I tried to figure it out. Maybe Michael had been comforting her or something? What else could it be? I mean, they'd barely met, except at Thanksgiving and briefly around Christmas. I was terrified then that something awful had happened; that Jenny had been diagnosed with cancer and given two months to live. Jogging up the remaining steps, I swore that if she'd gotten sick I would give up the academy to take care of her as long as she lived...

And then I reached the porch, and saw the way my girlfriend was staring up at my brother like he hung the moon. I saw the delirious happiness all over her face; the way she petted him like they'd lain in bed a hundred times together, the action natural and familiar.

Time seemed to slow down as I focused in on Jenny's left hand as it stroked across Michael's abdomen. A hand boasting an engagement ring I hadn't put there.

And that's when the truth finally hit me, like a slug to the chest.

❧

I awoke slumped across the van's front seats, exhausted like I'd just run two marathons, electricity still sizzling painfully across my torso. Yelling and shouting came from outside and from the compartment behind me, but I was more concerned with trying to force my eyelids open so I could see if the old woman was still Tasering me.

Then the pain abruptly fled.

On a burst of nervous energy, I managed to jerk my eyes open finally. I found myself staring along my prone body and out of the driver's side door, where I saw...

Nothing but empty space.

Sitting up in the driver's seat, I peered cautiously out of the window, half expecting to see grandma pointing a damn *gun* at me now... but there was still no sign of her anywhere. I checked the side mirrors, and saw only Tanya and Ed, still struggling with the rear door. It felt longer, but I guessed I'd only been out a few seconds.

Okay then.

Slamming my door shut and hitting the locks, I stuck the key in the ignition and started the engine. Howls of distress came from the rear, even as several burly friends and relatives began emerging from the house, led by Leroy's furious mother.

Time to get out of here.

I put the van in gear and shot down the driveway, turning onto the road with a screech of tires. Pedal to the metal, I accelerated away, feeling like I was leaving the hounds of hell behind me. A quick glance in my side mirrors revealed a horde of angry wedding guests flooding out onto the street, so I guessed I wasn't too far wrong about that.

Putting as many high speed and unpredictable turns as possible between me and them, I rubbed my right hand over the sore place on my chest as my heartbeat slowly returned to normal. It took a few miles, but finally it got there. And the whole time, I had to listen to a litany of pleas that soon turned to wails and then to angry threats from the rear of the van, where Leroy was imprisoned.

At first I tried ignoring the guy. I mean, what could I say? I'd just grabbed him out of his own wedding and had no plans to do anything that would rectify the situation in his eyes. But after... oh, I don't know, maybe the fifth repeat of "You're ruining my life!!! *Please! Please* take me back!!!" the sobs were getting truly heart-wrenching. Either Leroy should be on a daytime soap opera, or this was really tearing him up inside.

"Just for ten minutes! *Please!?* Then I'll turn myself in, I swear!"

Uh huh. Let's say I was crazy enough to turn around and go back. Ed would hold me down while Tanya's crazy aunt - or whoever the hell she was - Tasered me again. Then Leroy would drive off with his new bride, yelling "sucks to be you" out the window, while every bounty hunter in LA - no, the *universe* - rolled around on the floor laughing.

Still, I wasn't going to be a total jerk and let the guy keep begging like that. It was just too humiliating. "Sorry - no can do," I called out firmly.

"But I promised we'd get married *today*!" More sobs were followed by a loud wail. "Tanya's the love of my life! Please - please - !!"

"If she loves you, she'll wait for you to get out of jail." Probably not, but what difference did it make anyway? Chances were she'd have divorced him before he got out, even if they *had* gotten married today. That argument made me feel better.

"B-but I was framed!" Leroy sounded horrified now. "I'm *innocent*! I can't go to jail!"

If that was true, maybe he'd win his case. *Yeah, and flying pink cherubs would throw rose petals at their wedding.* I acted like

I believed him, though. "Great! Then you can get married after all, once this gets cleared up at court. See? No harm, no foul."

I must have sounded less than convincing, because Leroy erupted then in a torrent of howls, coupled with what sounded like him taking out on my van what he'd like to do to me. Pulling onto the freeway, I lowered my window and let the wind blasting past drown out the noise.

❧

"You ruined my life!!"

I gritted my teeth, forcing myself to wait until I'd cuffed the still-struggling Leroy's hands behind his back before brushing the crumbs of desiccated, insect-infested pink gunk out of my eyes and hair. Leroy had erupted like a belligerent bull from the rear of the van. Since he'd switched from pleading and sobbing to yelling "I'm gonna kill you!" by the time we got here, that hadn't been much of a surprise. What I *hadn't* been prepared for was having five pounds of fake display cake and ancient frosting thrown in my face the instant I opened the door.

Guess I'd lost my deposit on that one.

It might have helped if someone else had been there as backup. But no: despite the fact that I'd called repeatedly on my way back, Jimmy - and the bodyguard who accompanied him almost everywhere - had stayed securely indoors until things were safely under control. I'd have chalked it up to some kind of instinctual sense of timing, except I knew for sure that he had a camera on the tiny parking lot. Which meant he'd been biding his time in full knowledge of the slapstick routine going on outside, waiting for a safe moment to emerge from his private elevator.

Douchebag.

"Good job," Jimmy said now, nodding for the mean-faced man at his side to take custody of the prisoner at last.

Thank fuck. I raced back to the van, yanked off my fake delivery guy jacket and threw it onto the passenger seat, then started up the engine.

"Hey, where you going?" Jimmy called out behind me. "Don't you want your money?"

"Pay me tomorrow!" I yelled back.

As I pealed out down the alley that led to the road, I could hear Jimmy yelling after me, "I knew you had a date!!"

I didn't care what Jimmy knew - or thought he knew. All I cared about was getting to the damn theater on time. I glanced at the clock as I pulled the van out into traffic, ignoring blaring horns on all sides as my heart sank.

Crap. I was already an hour late.

I finally sped into the auditorium parking lot at 7:42 p.m., but after slaloming my way around the furthest (and thus likeliest to have spaces) section for a good three minutes, it became obvious that the entire place was full to overflowing. Not an empty spot in sight. Even a few people who'd arrived on *time* had probably had to park a few streets away and hoof it from there.

Since I didn't have time for that, I headed for the auditorium entrance instead. At this point it was either go big or go home, because I was now... I checked the time again... a whole hour and forty-five minutes late. Sure, those prime spots would have been filled by the eager beavers who'd actually arrived early to really show their support. *The way you should have*, my conscience prodded me painfully. But I was desperately hoping that someone had already left, leaving their perfect space vacant right in front of the doors. An early riser, maybe... or a doctor on call... or...?

My burst of optimism died a swift death. Cars were packed like sardines into every available space. Even all eight handicapped spots were taken, though I was willing to bet at least one of those cars wouldn't have a 'disabled' placard on display.

But what was this now...?

I let the van drift forward as I eyed a small, cross-hatched area of concrete right outside the entrance. The little sign post next to it read 'Security Vehicles Only.' I wasn't sure how it was still empty, how every other late arrival had possibly been able to resist. Maybe it was the 'Unauthorized vehicles will be towed' sign underneath... but come *on*, were they really gonna enforce that on a Friday evening?

Still, I hesitated... until I heard the music from inside the auditorium kick up a notch. I might be pretty clueless about musical theater, but even *I* knew I'd miss the big song and dance number if I didn't get in there Right The Fuck Now.

The big song and dance number that Kaylee had been working on for *two months*.

Uh oh. Key change. I had maybe a minute if I didn't want to miss the entire thing.

I yanked the van into the 'forbidden' space, took a rapid last look in the mirror to check for residual crumbs of pink frosting, then threw myself out and ran for the door. And hey, maybe I had a *right* to park there? After all, I *was* in the security business.

More or less.

The strains of 'Hello, Dolly!' swelled as I stepped through the red velvet doors into the huge auditorium. I immediately picked out Kaylee on the distant stage, recognizing her distinctive costume as she was lifted up into the air, and...

I froze to the spot as the person I cared about more than any other living creature on the planet was flung across the stage. *Where the hell was the damn safety net?!* "Holy shit!"

The closest heads in the audience swiveled around to stare at me in shock and annoyance. *Crap.*

"Sir... sir!"

A hand tugged at my jacket, and I dragged my eyes away from the circus act on stage to find the silver-haired head usher glaring up at me. Glaring? More like shooting laser beams out of her eyes. Probably because I'd sworn I'd stand silently in the back until the end of the number if she let me go in.

"Sorry," I mouthed, then turned back to the stage -

- and almost wished I hadn't, as I watched Kaylee being tossed back and forth, swung around, and generally manhandled by two sets of dancers dressed as waiters. Make that two sets of *teenaged males*.

Oh, *great*. Now it wasn't just my fear that she'd be paralyzed at any second. No, *now* I was remembering that skintight bodysuit she'd worn to every rehearsal for the past month. Which begged the question:

How many of those horny boys had groped my *fifteen-year-old niece*?

I glared at the distant dancers as they finally - thank God - lowered Kaylee to the ground so she could join the rest of the ensemble in belting out the final exultant chorus. I joined in the wild applause that ensued when it finished, although unlike most of the audience I'm pretty sure I wasn't wearing a big smile on my face.

I didn't know about Dolly, but my niece wouldn't be going back to that school until *all* those hormonal males got a good look at her six foot two, two-hundred-pound uncle.

And maybe my sidearm, too.

I slid into my fourth row aisle seat - coincidence, or had Kaylee anticipated my sneaking in late? - as the deafening applause slowly faded to merely thunderous. I was still breathing heavily, having just done the five-second dash from the back row before the usher-from-hell could tackle me to the ground and have her crack team of fellow octogenarians drag me outside for a good beating. Or take me out where I stood, and deal with clean-up after the performance... okay, maybe she wasn't *that* pissed at me, but I noticed the carpet and upholstery were the exact shade of reddish-brown that would do a great job hiding blood stains.

Damn. I was having a bad day when it came to little old ladies -

"You missed the entire first half!" a low, terminally pissed-off voice growled next to me.

Make that a bad day with senior citizens in general.

Bracing myself, I turned my head to the left - and looked into the gimlet eyes of my illustrious father, ex-LAPD Desk Sergeant Leonard 'Len' Thatcher. My father had been a towering figure of a cop in his day - I'd inherited my height and build from him - and he'd controlled and terrified generations of perps by looming over them with that exact same glower, over his many fiery years on the job. It had always worked pretty well on me when I younger, too. For the last few years, though... not so much. Maybe because these days I towered over him. Maybe because I'd been a cop too, and the whole 'Dirty Harry' mystique he'd had going on when I was ten didn't quite cut it now.

Or maybe even a really great death stare lost its impact after the first three thousand uses.

Avoiding answering Len, I went back to applauding until it finally died out everywhere, focusing instead on the vision that stood in front of me on the stage. As I stared up at her, Kaylee stayed in character as Dolly Levi, Matchmaker extraordinaire, but still made enough eye contact with me that I knew the sparkle in her bright blue eyes as she smiled held a private message intended just for her unworthy uncle. Something like, "Glad you made it - don't let Grandpa get you down!"

God, I loved that kid. And it was at times like these -

when she looked so very grown up - that I could see so much of her mother in her. Sure, she had the same slender nose and heart-shaped face; even her hair, currently hidden by an ornate wig, was the same sun-kissed, light golden blonde. But it was her smiles and her vivacity that really reminded me of her mom, back when we were in college.

Back before everything changed...

At even that fleeting thought of Jenny and our history, I waited for my body to seize up the way it usually did. But for once, it stayed calm. I wondered if I was finally getting some perspective... then found myself stifling a yawn and realized my eyes had been drifting shut. Guess I was just too tired for the usual emotional spasms.

"You'd better not doze off!"

I shot my father an irritated look. "I've run murder investigations on less sleep."

Fury vibrated from the neighboring seat. If I'd looked over again, I'd probably have seen the smoke rising out of his still-thick thatch of steel gray hair... nah, make that laser beams shooting out of his blue-gray eyes. Had I been too flippant? Probably. Or maybe what had Len so pissed was the reminder that I'd made detective before my untimely departure, whereas he hadn't. Of course, he'd never actually applied. He preferred being a uniformed cop. Protecting and serving on the front line, not like those pussies with gold shields. *Nice thing to say at your son's promotion ceremony, Dad.*

Either that, or it was the reminder that I *wasn't* a detective any more. Len had never made a big deal about it, but I knew that deep down he'd been proud when I followed in his footsteps and became a cop. However, he'd sure as hell shown his *un*happiness with the way things had turned out.

I turned my gaze back to the stage and ignored his scowl. It wasn't like the reason for it mattered anyway - pretty much everything I said seemed to piss him off these days, now that we were back living in the same house.

Why was I doing that to myself again?

Oh, yeah.

I smiled up at the stage, where Kaylee was now sipping tea with the vibrant confidence of Barbra Streisand as she addressed a teenage boy who, sadly, in no way resembled a grumpy, late-middle-aged Walter Matthau. Despite the gallon of talcum powder they'd dowsed his hair in. But honestly, her co-star almost didn't matter. Kaylee was incredible; she could've been sharing the scene with a ten-foot emu for all I cared. And even though it was basically a musical about dating - *on Valentine's Day* - I wished I'd been there for the whole show. I tried not to think how the kid must have felt, coming out on stage and seeing an empty seat next to her grandfather.

Of course, the 'kid' wasn't exactly a kid any more. She was fifteen - and with all she'd had to deal with in the past year she'd had to grow up even faster than her peers, which was really saying something these days. Things that would send most teenagers sulking to their rooms, she took in her stride. Sure, she pouted and pushed boundaries too. But she was reasonable, and she knew what she could challenge and what she needed to accept. Give it a few years, she'd probably be a hostage negotiator. Or maybe working for the UN.

None of that made me feel any better about missing over half the musical, though. Well, at least I was here now. Better late than never, I supposed.

Although... *damn*, I was tired. I hadn't been bragging to Len; I'd run whole investigations on less sleep, and done a damn fine job of it too. Maybe it was the lack of caffeine, or getting Tasered, or maybe the snugness of the auditorium's seats. But whatever the reason, my eyelids kept fluttering closed as I fought drifting off to sleep...

Total darkness enveloped me. Then -

Bright white spheres of lights pinwheeled around me, darting in and out like vicious fireflies on crack. I tried to contort my body to get away from them, but they just kept coming.

As they moved away, I could hear angels singing, but only hazily, as if there were far in the distance. Where in the hell was I?

Then for just an instant, I was back in the aisle of the auditorium, staring down at my own sleeping body as I snored through the big finale, a reprise of 'Hello, Dolly!' featuring the entire cast. I saw Len shoot me a disgusted glare, even as the angelic singing grew louder, still hard to make out although it seemed to pound in my ears... and then suddenly I was back in the darkness... until the lights swirled around me again.

First charging at me, then pulling off and retreating.

"Go away!!"

The lights changed tactics then, swarming higher and higher, as if readying themselves for a dive. My heartbeat thudded faster until they reached their highest point and held for a fraction of a second. And at that instant, the angelic singing became recognizable - someone was never going away again - and I knew it was nearly the last line of the play. I tried to picture Kaylee singing it on stage -

But all I could see were the lights as they finally started down through the darkness toward me. As I backed up slowly, I clung desperately to the singing voices, my only lifeline to reality. Then the lights sped up, coming faster and faster - and I tried to run, but it was like moving through treacle, my legs unable to move fast enough to make my escape.

The musical reached its climax just as the lights reached me. I screamed in agony as they plunged into my invisible body, tearing through my unseen flesh and burying themselves into my pumping heart.

"AAARRRGGGHHHHHHHHH!!!"

I tumbled to my knees - body huddled over, hands clamped to my burning chest - as I prayed for the unbelievable amount of pain to cease.

After what seemed like an eternity, I finally felt it lift. Panting, dizzy, and covered with sweat, I pushed upright,

raising my gaze from reddish carpet that seemed familiar -
- and found the entire auditorium staring back at me.

"Uncle Lyle?"

I turned my head, searching for the sound of Kaylee's worried voice. But the movement was too fast and dizziness rushed to greet me. I'd barely taken in the sight of her, staring down at me from the front of the stage, before the world went black.

Chapter Three.

"Is he on any medication?"

"What, like coke? How should I know?"

I woke to the familiar sound of my father's idea of support. "I'm not a drug addict, Len!" I bit out, then cracked my eyelids open. I found myself staring up at a circle of worried looking faces, half of them upside down. Far beyond, the auditorium's ceiling was covered in angels... or maybe they were Cherubs?

Cupids?

Argh.

I tried to lever myself up, but my head still felt woozy. I sank back to the carpet, deciding maybe I'd stay there a while instead. One of the upside-down faces twisted around, and I saw it was Kaylee.

"Are you okay Uncle Lyle?"

"Just... tired." I hoped that was all it was, anyway.

And here I'd thought the day couldn't get any weirder.

Five minutes later, I'd fended off all attempts to call a doctor, paramedics, or the school nurse, and was climbing into my father's car. My blackout - or, as Kaylee's drama teacher kept calling it, my 'fainting fit' (but since I'd ruined his grand finale I was cutting him some slack) - had been blamed (by me) on a combination of too many all-night stakeouts, not enough food or coffee, and getting Tasered a couple of hours ago.

Len had snorted at that, but Kaylee had looked worried until I'd admitted a crazy old lady had done it - at which Len had downright guffawed. The rest of the small group around us had still looked faintly shocked. Sometimes I forget how much more violence cops are used to seeing than most of the general public.

Good thing I hadn't mentioned the convenience store, huh.

I belted myself into the passenger seat, watching as Kaylee raced about saying goodbye to her various co-stars, and tried to exude the impression of a stable parental figure. As opposed to an unfit guardian who was habitually drunk, high, and/or crazy.

"Need anything from your van?"

Len's thoughtful question surprised me. I considered what I'd left in there. Frosting... cockroaches... "Nope."

"Not even your weapon?"

The old station wagon shuddered as Kaylee pulled open the back door and launched herself in. I ignored Len's question, hoping he'd lose interest.

No such luck. "Well I know you're not wearing it," he pushed, then scowled. "That *fruit* woulda felt it when he felt you up!"

I grimaced. He was talking about Kaylee's drama teacher, also a trained first-responder, who had apparently checked to make sure my heart was beating and I was breathing okay before I woke up.

Kaylee chimed in from the back seat, her voice sunny but firm. "The word is 'gay,' Grandpa."

Len snorted but didn't argue, and - not for the first time - I marveled at the persuasive power of granddaughters. Maybe Kaylee would succeed where I'd failed in persuading him to have a little respect for other people's lifestyles. Or maybe he just loved her enough to fake it.

"And besides, he *isn't* gay," she continued blithely. "He's dating another teacher and she's definitely a woman."

Len started the car. "Probably his *beard*," he muttered darkly.

"No, he doesn't have a beard either," Kaylee replied innocently. But then she caught my eye in the rearview mirror, and I realized she was just yanking the old goat's chain. "He did have a *mustache* once," she went on, "but he shaved it off months ago."

Len opened his mouth to answer, then clamped his lips shut again as he realized he was being teased. I'd give him that, he was still on the ball about most things... when he chose to be, that is. Instead, he grumbled under his breath as we left the parking lot, something about smart-ass kids who should be made to walk home.

I grinned back at Kaylee in the mirror. An instant later she grinned back, but I also saw relief on her face, and realized she'd been worried about me. Despite the way I'd ruined her big moment so embarrassingly. What an amazing kid... and what the hell had she ever done to deserve all my shit? I'd already felt bad for showing up late; now I felt a hundred times worse for letting lack of sleep and over-caffeination do crazy things to me.

I promised myself, then and there, that it would never happen again. No more insane schedules; no more seventy-two hour stakeouts, surviving on power bars and energy drinks. Even if I had to take out a loan against my life insurance and sell every heirloom Mom had left me, I wouldn't let work take over or let Kaylee down again.

My eyes had drifted closed as we pulled onto the freeway, but they shot open as I remembered my big meeting with the music producer tomorrow morning at ten o'clock. If I made a good impression, who knew what lay ahead? Visions of sleek, bright offices on Sunset and a roster of high-powered clients danced through my head.

I'd get a good night's sleep, then show up

professionally early and dazzle him with my expertise, brilliant deductive skills, and sheer confidence.

৯৫

It was 10:09 a.m. by the time I'd finally fought my way through traffic to reach Gerry Warnock's hillside property.

I'd been awake half the night with nausea and a fever, my skin hot to the touch every time I crawled out of bed to throw up in the toilet. And in between those delightful episodes I'd slept only fitfully, my dreams filled with spheres of light that attacked relentlessly. It was a small miracle I hadn't woken Kaylee or Len, but every time I'd felt myself coming to the surface I'd somehow managed to clamp down on the yells that welled up in my throat.

I usually dreamed about crap that was bothering me, something I'd thought about for hours, or - weirdly - something I'd only thought about for a second or two, like catching sight of a news item in a paper. My brain's way of processing something it had taken in recently, I guess.

But flying spheres of light... where the hell had *they* come from? I'd had nightmares about them for hours now, and it was starting to drive me a little crazy.

Was I subconsciously processing being Tasered yesterday?

I still hadn't checked my chest to see if the Taser had left a visible burn on me. Last night I hadn't had the energy to do more than take off my jacket and shoes (and stagger to and from the bathroom), and this morning I'd basically torn off one shirt and flung on a new one as I ran down the stairs. I'd even applied deodorant to my unwashed pits in the car - I'd gotten used to keeping some in there after all my overnights lately.

So much for changing how I did things.

Tomorrow, I promised silently.

I just had to get through today first.

❧

I hastily pulled up to the huge, ornate security gates separating Gerry Warnock's hillside mansion and estate from the public streets below. Separating the entertainment world royalty and their luxuries from the plebeian masses who collectively and voluntarily... nay, *eagerly*... paid for it all. I guessed it was a fairer exchange than with nobility of old. A Baron would show up to collect taxes with some nebulous promise to protect you (which sounded kind of like a protection racket, if you really thought about it); with these guys, at least you got Madonna's latest incarnation, Lady Gaga in a meat suit, or blockbuster 3-D remakes of movies you liked just fine the first time around...

Okay, maybe there wasn't much of an improvement after all.

Minutes later I was accelerating up the driveway in my battered '98 Toyota Camry. In my rearview mirror, I could see the two huge security guards - who'd materialized out of nowhere - still watching me suspiciously. Even though someone up at the house had confirmed by phone that I had an appointment, I think they were still worried they'd let some random homeless guy into their hallowed domain. Hell, even I felt out of place, driving over an expensive road surface that had probably never held a car as old as mine. Well - Vintage Bentleys aside.

For a second, I had the crazy notion that the estate itself was going to classify us both as defective and toss us out. Maybe I needed to think about investing in something pricier if I was going to get more work like this?

Or maybe I should wait and see what Gerry wanted me to do *before* I spent my non-existent savings on a hypothetical BMW that'd stick out like a sort thumb on most of my stakeouts.

But whatever Gerry wanted, I was pretty certain he was

going to be pissed I was late. In my experience, entertainment types like to keep people waiting, not the other way around. I couldn't do anything about that now, though. And given how badly I'd slept, I figured it was a small miracle I'd gotten here at all.

I made an effort to shake off my doubts as I pulled around the massive circular driveway, parking next to a perfectly manicured lawn in front of a huge, Spanish-influenced mansion. Brilliant magenta bougainvillea covered at least half of its walls, and the gardens I'd driven up through just now had been equally impressive. You had to be seriously rich to afford landscaping, legions of attentive gardeners, and the massive water bill that accompanied it all in LA's desert climate.

If I ever got around to buying my own place - and it was a house with a yard, not some first floor condo with a depressing view of a tiny courtyard - I'd probably go for concrete and crab grass, plus big pots of artificial flowers. Maybe I could call it 'eco-chic' and pretend like I was being socially conscious instead of terminally lazy?

As I climbed out of the car, the front door suddenly opened and a terrified looking maid stumbled out. Catching the young woman's eye, I also caught the tail end of a tirade from someone inside:

"...bring milk into this house, when she *knows* I'm lactose intolerant!!"

A second later a vision of loveliness appeared in the doorway. *Physical* loveliness, at least. Around nineteen or twenty, she looked like something out of a Playboy spread. Curling tendrils of long, pale blonde hair swept down her arms and back, and a transparent swimsuit throw-over did nothing to hide the youthfully buoyant cleavage exposed by her tiny bikini, or an expanse of smooth skin and long, slender legs.

The only things ruining the picture were the flashing eyes and furious scowl. The kid was clearly a Bitch with a capital B, and I seriously hoped my job wouldn't involve dealing with her.

"And now she's letting all the cold air out!!" she shrieked to no one in particular, as the other woman burst into tears and literally ran off down the driveway.

Deprived of her subject, Spoiled Little Rich Girl turned her attentions to me. I might not read or watch the entertainment news on a regular basis, and the reality show starlets pretty much all looked the same to my jaundiced eye, but I figured this had to be Gerry's infamous daughter, Bethany. But was Bethany Warnock the over-indulged princess who'd trashed the rooftop pool area at The Standard hotel? Or was she the one who'd made the sex tape with strawberry yogurt, an eighties sitcom star, and a French poodle?

So hard to keep track these days.

"And who the fuck are *you*?!" she demanded belligerently.

"Lyle Thatcher."

Bethany stared back at me blankly.

"I'm a private investigator?"

This time she gaped at me, in an apparent stupor.

I tried another tack. "I'm here to see your -"

"Dadddyyyyyyy!!" Tears sprang into Bethany's eyes, her face creasing into a mask of anguish as she turned away from me and sprinted back into the house.

Cautiously following her, I removed my sunglasses in time to see her run up a huge curving staircase and disappear from sight. I stood uncomfortably in the dimly lit entranceway, wondering what to do next. Go back outside and ring the bell? Where the hell were all the servants? I'd seen one maid run off, but surely a place like this had more. Shouldn't there be a British-accented butler, or some weird shit like that?

As my gaze returned to the staircase, a loudly confident voice came from the rear of the house. "You'll have to excuse my daughter. She's a little high strung right now."

I turned to see Bethany's father heading my way. I

figured Gerry Warnock had to be in his sixties, but he looked about twenty years younger... until he got closer, that is. Despite the lack of overhead light, I could see that his head of thick, wavy hair was artfully teased to look fuller and wavier than nature ever intended, its black color so extreme it could only have come out of a bottle.

The muscle tone in his bare forearms was good, but up close the fabulous tan that probably looked great on camera against his pure white shirt was marred by blemishes that pointed to more than one run-in with skin cancer. I hoped the current tan was fake; that skin didn't need more UV.

"Come on."

Without pausing to shake hands or introduce himself, Gerry strode past me into a massive living room, extravagantly decorated with expensive looking floor to ceiling windows, an eighty-inch flat screen TV, antique furniture, and pure white sofas and rugs over a marble floor. Pure white? I'd never understand that decorating choice. But maybe they only drank champagne, white wine, and light beer. I preferred gray-brown decor myself. All the better to drop Chinese/Mexican takeout and coffee on it.

As I followed Gerry into the over-bright room, I saw the tell-tale signs that said his hair and tan weren't the only fake things about him. Let's face it, there are three types of plastic surgery in LA. The first type is barely noticeable, but those angles in their face are just a *little* too sharp to be real; the skin just a *little* too smooth. The second type looks great on-screen with the right makeup, lens and camera angles, but you can see it in person right away; it's not a horror show, it's just... weird. Then there's the type that's so extreme, makeup only makes it look worse. It's almost like meeting an accident victim; in person, you try not to stare, and even on-screen, no amount of makeup or soft focus can hide it completely. Thing is, though, nine times out of ten they didn't *need* anything done to them; they're victims, sure, but of modern society, not a car wreck.

Gerry Warnock was a type two right now, but all the signs showed him heading for type three at speed. It wasn't so bad - yet - but parts of his face and neck had crossed from suspiciously to unnaturally smooth, and other pieces around them were pulling or sagging. That seemed to be how the downward spiral went: you had to do upkeep, or your face ended up like a weird jigsaw puzzle of old and new parts. I wondered how many of them ended up regretting it.

Hey, for all I knew, some plastic surgery looked so completely natural that even a trained expert would be fooled. But if that existed, then why did so many of the rich and famous end up looking like a cardboard cut-out with skin stretched over it?

As I pondered how Gerry had been sucked down the surgical rabbit hole, he walked over to a huge, highly polished antique table where a sheaf of papers sat next to a large crystal glass of what looked like Scotch on the rocks. "They met at one of my concerts - can you believe that?"

I knew the question was rhetorical. The guy was still basically ignoring me, and yet speaking to me at the same time. Interesting. I'd had a Training Officer who done the same thing, but he'd had trouble connecting to people in general. Whereas I was pretty sure Gerry wouldn't be acting this way around, say, Lady Gaga or Beyoncé. But for the sake of my bank balance, I decided to ignore being ignored, and waited for him to finish telling me what the job was about. At least I hadn't been fobbed off on an assistant. In Gerry-world, a personal audience with the pontiff was probably a great honor in itself. I wondered if he'd expect me to drop to one knee and kiss the opulent (some might say vulgar) pinkie ring he wore, if he ever actually looked me in the eye.

"Fucker's a has-been." He downed half his drink in one gulp. "Fell into a bottle after his band split up, and he's been there ever since. Don't know what he was even *doing* at the damn party. Supposed to be a celebration of my achievements, and those fucking *idiots* invite a *loser* my label dropped years ago and set him loose on my daughter!"

Ahhh.

I pictured an ageing rocker in skintight leather pants taking advantage of a dope- or alcohol-fuelled Bethany, his aura of eighties music debauchery a lot sexier than some pimply boy band member or some rapper with his underpants hanging out.

"And then she fucking *marries* him! With no prenup at all!!" Gerry snatched the papers up with his free hand and turned to thrust them at me. "Annulment papers. Pays to have a tame judge." His gaze flickered up at me then, making first time eye contact, as if realizing he'd just given away something that *maybe* he shouldn't have. Then he gave a facial shrug... at least, as much as his Botoxed muscles would allow... and left the papers in my hands.

It's kind of demeaning when someone powerful openly assesses your worth, and it's clear you register as a nonentity on their scale. Thing is, their idea of 'worth' has nothing to do with being worthy in any true sense, and they'd place oppressive dictators who want to fund their business / movie / concert tour far higher than, say, devoted aid workers. It's actually good - in a karmic sense - to rank low on that kind of scale.

At least, that's what I tell myself at such moments.

Gerry returned to his drink. "He's dropped off the map, though. You find him, get him to sign those papers!" He took another giant swallow. "You do that, you get paid."

Okay, so that part sounded good. But I still had to ask. "And is this what your daughter wants too?"

That earned me another sharp look. "Of course she wants the prick gone! Fucker probably screwed half his dancers behind her back." Gerry glared at me belligerently, as if daring me to contradict him - and for just a second, there was something about him I couldn't quite place.

Defensiveness, maybe? But then he reverted to laying out instructions like he was dictating to his secretary. "Fifty percent bonus if you get it done in the next two days."

The detective in me wondered what the rush was, even as the small business owner in me positively salivated at the thought of more income and told Peter Falk to shut up. "Okay," I agreed. It wasn't my job to be a couples counselor, and it seemed like annulments were the norm for the obscenely wealthy these days. Plus Bethany hadn't exactly seemed stable, and with a father-in-law like Gerry... heck, I was probably doing the new husband a favor.

Gerry downed the remainder of his drink, dropped it onto a grand piano with a varnish-chipping thud, and led me out of the room again. "My office will take care of your expenses and the final check -"

He broke off as we reached the entranceway, swiveling toward the rear of the house with a mildly constipated expression, which I successfully interpreted as a Botox-suppressed frown.

"What the *fuck*?"

I realized then that an eighties-style power ballad was echoing into the formerly peaceful, marble-tiled space through a partly-opened door. It was vaguely familiar, something I'd kinda liked when it came out a few years ago. But Gerry clearly wasn't appreciating it for some reason.

"Mother-fucking *asshole*!"

Gerry strode angrily through the open door, revealing a gleaming, state-of-the-art kitchen beyond and yanking the latest iPhone from his pocket as he went. "Get your asses up to the swimming pool! The fucker's *here*!!" he barked into the phone before heading out of sight around a corner... reappearing a moment later to snatch the papers right out of my hands. "Change of plan - you can go," he barked dismissively, then disappeared again.

I stared after him, pissed as hell. Didn't take a genius to figure out the husband had shown up on his own and my detecting skills were no longer required. So much for my impressing the big music producer and getting more work and recommendations around Hollywood. On the other hand, I didn't see the bodyguards yet, and if the guy had broken into the property he might be both angry and dangerous.

I hurried through the kitchen, following the sound of blasting pop rock music and distant shouting to a set of patio doors. Okay, so I admit my reasons weren't *entirely* altruistic; if I ended up saving Gerry or his kid from some psycho, it certainly wouldn't hurt my business. But I'd worked enough domestic abuse cases as a cop that I was hoping the guy was harmless and had just come to talk. Either way, I wasn't about to leave until I knew.

"Please, Bethany, I *love* you! This is our song, remember?" An impassioned voice cried those words over the pumping power ballad as I emerged into the sunlight.

"You *hack*! *I* had that written for your third album!!" Gerry hurled back across the width of the impressively large swimming pool.

As I came to stand next to him, I realized that his furious words were aimed at a slight figure standing precariously halfway up the sloping hillside against which the rear patio had been built. From the bedraggled state of his torn black jeans and T-shirt, the mud - or blood - streaked on his face and hands, and his messy, twig- and leaf-strewn dark hair, it was pretty obvious he'd defied the Warnocks' top-of-the-line security by clambering over the hillside from somewhere beyond. Not only that, the kid had clearly carried with him the large boom box now perched quiveringly on one shoulder, as it blasted *'I Will Never Leave You!'* to half the neighborhood.

I say 'kid' because this was most definitely *not* the debauched, skeletal, mid-life-crisis-and-then-some fading rock star I'd envisioned, based on Gerry's story. If this was Bethany's ex, he looked barely older than she was - mid twenties at most. He looked kind of familiar, though.

"I shoulda left you doing lame-ass sitcoms in fucking *Canada*!!" Gerry yelled.

Now I knew who he was. Joey Russo, run-of-the-mill child star turned tween pop/rock sensation. He'd been plucked him from the relative obscurity of a cheesy Canadian sitcom about a boy and his lovable dog, after a talent scout caught the episode where the dog got trapped in a building and the kid enticed him out by singing 'Oh, Canada' into the ventilation system.

True story? Who knew, but that was the way Kaylee had told it to me. She loved all that *E! True Hollywood* shit, worrying me that she dreamed of being discovered and getting into showbiz herself. Which - so far as I could tell - almost always led to failure, followed by running out of money and prospects, potentially followed by depression, then addiction, and even death. Or, in *extremely* rare cases, led to success... followed by all the same things, just maybe in a slightly different order.

Anyhow...

I tore my wandering mind back to the present, and realized this wasn't the same Joey Russo I'd been unwillingly exposed to over a decade of his face being plastered everywhere online and in those magazines you find yourself staring at in long checkout lines. No, this Joey was edgier and harder looking, with leather cords around his wrists and neck, rings through his earlobes, and dark brown instead of blonde hair. Maybe it *was* drugs... or maybe he'd just grown up and wanted to ditch the mantle of cute young heartthrob. He still had the heartthrob thing down pat, though; I could imagine Kaylee and her friends swooning over his dark good looks - think Orlando Bloom meets Navy SEAL - all too easily.

Ignoring Gerry, who continued to hurl insults at him, Joey let himself slide further down the muddy hillside, aiming for the pool house roof. "Bethany! Bethany, please, I love you!!"

I looked around at the mansion, wondering if Bethany Warnock was even listening - and spotted her stepping out onto a small balcony, her face a mixture of longing and desperation as she looked across at him. *Romeo and Juliet, eat your heart out.* Despite my reluctance to dwell on yesterday's mess, it kind of reminded me of Leroy and Tanya, too.

Which was actually pretty weird, now that I thought about it. Since I'd started working as a PI, I'd spent most of my time taking photos and video of cheating spouses and bed-hopping boyfriends, in every sleazy situation imaginable. My cynicism had deepened and festered, and I'd never felt more certain that romantic love was a concept invented by card companies and sickos. But for the past two days, it was like I was being stalked by love's young dream.

Almost as if some higher power were trying to intervene...

Right. Like there was anything that could make *me* believe in 'true love' again.

Joey probably *was* boning every female he could, no matter how much he wanted the Warnock powerhouse behind him. And Bethany had probably only married him to piss off Daddy, or because eloping made a good storyline in her reality show. Luxuriating in a comforting swell of cynicism, I shifted my gaze away from Joey and back up toward the balcony where his soon-to-be-ex-wife stood watching. If she was crying now, it was probably because she chipped a nail getting her balcony doors open -

Huh...?

I froze, my mouth falling open, as a small, softball-sized sphere of glowing white light emerged from Bethany's chest right over her heart.

What. The. Fuck?

57

Okay. Nothing to panic about. Just a trick of the light.

I watched the sphere rise slowly into the air, and gulped.

I had to be seeing things. Yeah, that was it. I was just... I was just *tired.*

I squeezed my eyes shut. Hard.

But when I tentatively cracked my eyelids open again, what I was seeing hadn't really changed at all. If anything, now the hallucinations were even *worse.* Because as the first sphere moved slowly away, a second emerged from Bethany's chest behind it... then a third... then a whole *parade* of them, like shiny bubbles erupting from a kid's bubble-maker toy. And the really weird thing was, I felt like I'd seen them somewhere before...

I stopped breathing as it hit me.

They were exactly like the ones in my crazy-ass nightmares.

Involuntarily I backed up a step... and half tripped over a lounger, sending it scraping loudly across the stone patio floor.

Gerry shot me an agitated glare. "What are you doing?" He pointed toward the hillside. "Grab him!"

Almost grateful for the distraction, I looked over at the intruder instead...

And my eyes went wide in shock.

Because the glowing white spheres were erupting out of Joey *as well.*

I squeezed my eyes shut again and shook my head, like a dog shaking water off its fur, hoping to clear it. But when I forced opened my eyelids again...

Yep, the spheres were still there.

Still flooding out of Joey's chest.

My gaze went back and forth between Bethany and Joey, tracking the dozens of spheres as they floated out and up from both their bodies. Yet neither seemed aware they were there, nor did anyone else react to them.

Yeah, because you're having a psychotic episode and imagining this shit!

Still, I couldn't help myself pointing at the air like some crazy person, needing to know for sure if I was losing my mind or if maybe there was some other explanation for it.

"Do-do you see that?" I croaked out to Gerry.

"See *what?*" I heard pounding footsteps from behind me, and Gerry's attention shifted to the newcomer, his relief mingled with ire. "Where the *hell* have you been?! Get up there!!"

One of the huge guards from the gate pushed his way past us, making for the pool house. By now Joey had gained the roof, his feet slipping on its plasticky, faux-tile covering. He lurched sideways, and the boom box dropped from his shoulder. It went sliding gently ahead of him down the gradual slope, then made a graceful arc through the air, still pumping out the hit love ballad... which abruptly cut out as it smashed noisily into a hundred pieces on the patio below.

Meanwhile, Gerry's guard - dodging the impact - had made for the pile of mats and inflatables stacked beside the pool house. He flailed as he tried unsuccessfully to climb up them to the roof, his frustration growing as he perpetuated the stereotype of the brainless heavy.

Farcical though it all was, I barely reacted. My entire focus was on the dozens of glowing white spheres, which had now detached from their owners and were snaking slowly through the air, each group heading toward the other.

I watched, mesmerized, as the stream that had left Bethany's chest wove its way gradually away from her balcony, even as Joey's collection of spheres gradually gained height over the pool.

What would happen when they met?

Nothing! I told myself firmly. *Because they aren't really there!*

Recovering his footing at last, Joey continued pleading with Bethany from his awkward perch. "I promise I'll change! No more clubs, no more partying without you!"

"You didn't just go out partying, you went to *Miami* without me!"

As she threw that back at him, Bethany's white spheres paused in mid-air, spiraling uncertainly and halting their progress toward Joey's.

"I was desperate, baby! The jet was gonna leave!"

As I watched with horrified fascination, Bethany's spheres began to descend toward Joey's once more.

"I thought I'd make contacts, find another backer..." Joey continued, "but I know I should've told you first!"

"You put it on *Twitter* and didn't even *text* me!" Bethany brushed away an angry tear. "Your *fans* knew more than I did!"

At this, Bethany's spheres abruptly came to another wavering, spiraling halt. I stared up at them, amazed by how their behavior mirrored the changing feelings of the two -

Then I caught myself. Those things didn't *have* behavior, because *they weren't real.* They were hallucinations, brought on by extreme, stakeout-induced sleep deprivation, too much coffee and energy drinks, all combined with single-business-owner insomnia. The only thing I should be 'amazed' about was my brain's ability to conjure up crazy shit.

I blinked rapidly again, but the spheres didn't disappear. They didn't fade - they didn't even freaking *waver.* Oh God. I really was losing my mind here.

Gerry pulled me out of my funk by yelling right next to me. "Bethany, get back indoors! You know he's just using you!"

"I'd never use Bethany! I *love* her!" Joey declared vehemently.

"Too late!" Gerry shot back at him. "You already broke her heart by lying to her. By *betraying* her!" His gaze shot back to his daughter. "He just admitted he's desperate. You think he wouldn't do anything to use my connections?

That's the only reason he married you!"

A frantic "That's not true!" came from Joey, but Gerry's words had clearly hit a nerve. Bethany's face crumpled, tears flowing down her cheeks as she turned and ran back inside, the balcony doors slamming shut in her wake.

"Bethany!!"

I switched my gaze back to the air above the swimming pool, half of me expecting Bethany's spheres to have evaporated with her departure from the stage. But both sets of spheres were still there... although they were no longer spiraling in place.

No - to my immediate horror, they'd all changed direction... and were heading right at *me*, like the ghost of some gigantic Chinese Dragon. As I watched in shock, the straggling collection of glowing white spheres drew into a double column... *then picked up speed and came rushing straight at my chest.*

I ducked right -

- and collided with the second security guard who'd rushed up from the gate. His forward momentum threw off my aim, sending me flying across the concrete... and him headfirst into the pool with a gigantic splash.

The wind knocked out of me, I rolled onto my back trying to catch my breath, vaguely aware of Gerry screaming obscenities over what sounded like the pool house being demolished. Hearing a loud yell followed by a second body-sized splash, I forced my head up to see what was happening -

- and let out a high-pitched screech of terror, as the first white spheres *slammed* into my chest.

I writhed on the ground as the flood continued, incoherent with fear as I tried to bat them away, but they were unstoppable. Despite the hits to my rib cage that left me feeling like an overused CPR dummy, my flailing hands met only air - even as the pace increased, my chest trampolining up and down at a speed that left me breathless.

Full blown panic set in then, as I wondered if this was what a heart attack felt like -

Then - as fast as it had begun - the last spheres vanished into my body... and it was suddenly at an end.

I lay there panting on the wet concrete, frantically assessing how I felt, my eyes darting around like I was in some kind of war zone. No, I couldn't see the freaky white globes any more. But were they gone... or were they *inside* me now? I hadn't just seen them; I'd *felt* them flooding into my chest. I knew hallucinations could be sounds as well as crazy visions... but I'd never heard of a hallucination that felt like someone punching you in the ribs. And even if it *had* only been a hallucination: what was to stop it happening again?

I forced myself to take deep breaths, shoving down my terror, and tried to make my arms and legs stop trembling. If I could do that, then hopefully in a few minutes I'd be able to sit upright.

Maybe some day I'd even be able to stand on my own two feet again.

"Get him up! Bring him over here!"

Gerry's angry voice finally did it. However bad I'd screwed up, at least I could save myself the embarrassment of being tossed out the door by his goons.

I somehow crawled to my knees and pushed myself to my feet... then realized Gerry hadn't been talking about me. Although I certainly wasn't their favorite person - the second security guard was soaking wet and kept shooting me angry glares - the main target of everyone's wrath was most definitely Joey Russo.

The kid was dripping wet too; I guessed those noises I'd heard had been the pool house roof collapsing under him, sending him into the pool. The two guards had clearly just pulled him out again, and now held him in what looked to be a painful grip as they half marched, half dragged him over to where Gerry waited by a small patio table.

As they reached him, the older man grabbed a fluttering document off the table and tried to shove a pen into Joey's right hand. "Sign these and get it over with!"

The annulment papers, I assumed.

I sighed inwardly and braced myself to do something about this. Despite the odds - not to mention my weird mental state - I couldn't just stand there and witness Joey signing under duress. I might have suffered a moral slump working for Jimmy, but I still had my limits.

But even as I opened my mouth to say something, Joey spoke instead. "She can't think I married her just to get to you! That's *nuts*!" His desperate gaze went to Bethany's window, voice rising to a yell. "Bethany, I love -!"

The first guard tightened his grip on Joey's neck, turning his cry into a strangled squawk.

Gerry scoffed. "You can pretend all you want; I know what's true!"

"But I don't care who she is!" Joey struggled in the guard's grip, twisting around to stare Gerry in the eye. "What if I swore I'd never ask you for help with my career? I'll sign anything you want!"

"And how are you gonna provide for my Bethany then, huh?" Gerry glowered at him. "You think I'm gonna let her live in some rundown apartment, while you go touring every crap-shit place that still remembers your name?"

"I'd take Bethany with me -"

"In some flea-ridden tour bus with a dozen pot-smoking roadies?! No way!" Gerry stabbed his finger viciously at the annulment papers. "*That's* the only thing I want you to sign for me!"

"I won't!" Joey fought as the two guys holding him tried to force him over the papers, stubbornly tilting his head away from them. And that was my cue.

I cleared my throat loudly.

Gerry looked up at me, and if looks could kill I'd have been a sizzling black stain on the patio floor right then. Despite the Botox smoothing, I could almost see the internal struggle written on his face.

Could I be bribed to keep my mouth shut? Would I make trouble later?

Was it worth the pain?

Apparently, it wasn't. Gerry stepped back, giving a flicking gesture of his hand that had his men releasing Joey, who staggered back from them. The kid had some good instincts at least, because he moved toward me as he coughed and gasped, rubbing at his neck. Then the idiot's eyes went back to Bethany's window.

My cue again.

"Come on," I said, grabbing one of Joey's water-soaked arms and shoving him into the kitchen ahead of me.

As we reached the entranceway and I practically had to drag Joey over to the door, I felt a spasm of pain - or something - flutter through my stomach. Turning the handle with my free hand, I paused on the threshold and felt the sense of wrongness rise rapidly up through my chest... then up even higher, until it formed a tight band around my forehead.

"Don't leave," it seemed to urge me.

I froze, wondering if maybe I was doing the wrong thing by pulling Joey away. I mean, Bethany was right there in the house above us. Shouldn't I be suggesting they sit down together and talk like regular human beings? This was the twenty-first century, not the Middle Ages; it wasn't like she was Gerry's property and didn't get a say.

Perhaps sensing my mood, Joey tried to tug his arm out from my grip. "I need to speak to Bethany! I have to stay here!"

But when I looked around at him, unsure how I should respond, I saw Gerry and his goons only a few paces behind us. Between the cuts and bruises on one - I guess some of the pool house roof had collapsed *on* him - and the water still dripping off the other, the younger men didn't seem very happy. Even Gerry's feelings showed clearly through his largely immobile face, his dark eyes burning with rage.

Yeah. With no Bethany in sight - and I had to face it, she hadn't seemed exactly receptive to marriage counseling anyway - this was definitely one of those times when you ran away so you could live to fight another day. At least Joey hadn't signed the papers. There was still time for him to woo his wife back, if he really wanted to.

Oddly, the ring of discomfort around my skull eased a little at that thought, and I pushed the still-reluctant Joey out onto the driveway.

 ஐ

Joey followed me the few steps to my car like a bedraggled duckling, then hesitated as I opened the driver's side door and got in. I sighed, seeing the uncertainty on his face, then jerked my head to indicate the passenger side. "Get in. I'll give you a ride." As he hurried around the hood of my battered old Toyota, I began tossing all my crap into the back. The door opened before I was ready and I held up a finger. "Hang on!"

I foraged around in the back seat mess and extracted two thin plastic bags, two canvas reusable shopping bags, and an old coat, which I spread over the passenger seat before giving the okay to Joey. It wasn't like my seat covers hadn't experienced a multitude of stains before, everything from mud and ketchup to blood and even (once) urine. Don't judge me: stakeouts are long, I sanitized the area afterward, and *you* try peeing into a bottle in the dark some time. Point is, I wasn't exactly precious about what came into this car.

But water marks were a real bitch to get out. Not to

mention, dealing with something so mundane beat thinking about the crazy-town my life had become in the last five minutes.

Finally, though, I gave him the all-clear, and Joey flopped down into the seat with a loud *squelch* before slamming the door shut.

We made it down the long driveway and back onto public roads without anyone stopping us. I let out a relieved breath I hadn't even realized I was holding, then flinched as I made a sharp corner and water flew into my eyes, flicking off Joey's wet hair.

"Sorry," he said, squeezing out his ponytail, and sending a stream of water over my jeans and the floor on my side. "Sorry!"

I looked down at where he was sitting and sighed inwardly. It was pretty much Waterworld over there. Hey, at least I'd tried. I'd just add new seat covers to my expenses for the month.

Along with the therapy sessions and MRI of my brain, of course.

I felt an urge to at least *try* to get my priorities right. I mean, I could be dying of a brain tumor, yet here I was worrying about car interior design and - now that I thought of it - whether I had funds for a new dust-buster, since the floor could do with a good vacuum after all the sand that got inside, even though I never took it to the beach...

And I was doing it again.

I guessed it was just easier to deal day-to-day trivialities than whatever the hell was going on in my head. The known rather than the unknown... like undiagnosed conditions, or how to pay for treatment (assuming it wasn't already too late), or... shit, making sure Kaylee received my death benefits...

Assuming I'd kept up my insurance payments in the cluster-fuck that had been my life since quitting the job. *Shit -!*

I heard a snuffling noise and quickly glanced sideways. Despite the fact that he was stoically staring forwards, his jaw clenched and eyes fixed on the road ahead, Joey Russo was quietly losing it in my passenger seat. Tear tracks covered his face, his eyes turning red-rimmed as he wiped the back of one hand ineffectively over his cheeks.

Great.

More water to deal with.

I pulled over on one of those massive, palm-tree-lined streets that always made me think of the title sequence from the old 'Miami Vice' TV show. I really wanted to dump Joey out and say adios, then drive myself to a hospital.

Well, no, I didn't *want* to go to a hospital and get confirmation that I was in serious, expensive trouble. But I knew I had to do it. And soon - like, yesterday.

I decided on a compromise - aka, a way to delay the inevitable crap that I wasn't quite ready to face. I'd get Joey some Kleenex, then get back on the road and drive him back to his car first. Another half hour delay wasn't going to make any difference, and I could use the breathing space. And yeah, I wondered briefly if I should be driving in my condition, but I told myself I'd get off the road the second I had a hallucination behind the wheel. Not the most responsible decision, I guess, but I seriously needed *one* thing I could still control when everything else was going to shit.

I felt around under all the trash that had landed in the back seat over the past few days, finally yanking out a nearly empty packet of tissues to shove at Joey. At first he pretended like he didn't need any, then gave in and hastily mopped the moisture from his eyes.

"Where'd you leave your car?"

"I don't drive. I got a ride."

Great. At least he had *one* friend whose shoulder he could cry on, literally and figuratively. "Where does your friend live?"

Joey shook his head. "I took a Lyft."

I started the engine, realizing I'd be driving him further than I thought, and tamping down my stupid relief at postponing my medical reckoning for maybe an hour longer. "Okay, then where are you staying?"

"Sunset Spire."

It took me a second to recognize he wasn't giving me an address, he was naming one of the most exclusive - and thus expensive - hotels in the area. If this was what a 'has-been' could afford in Gerry Warnock's world, I kinda wished I lived there too. Even if the other inhabitants were all assholes. It'd definitely come in handy when the medical bills came due.

Feeling depression and the beginnings of cold fear swarm over me, I pulled out from the curb and headed toward Santa Monica Boulevard.

"Why wouldn't she believe me?" Joey mumbled as he blew his nose, finally giving up all pretense that he hadn't been crying. "I really do love her, you know?"

Much as I wanted a distraction from my other thoughts, I had zero to contribute here. "I'm sure she cared about you, too." Banal platitudes, party of one.

"You could tell, right?" Joey turned in his seat, hope written across his face.

Okay, he sounded *way* too encouraged by my absolute minimum attempt at offering comfort. Maybe what he really was needed a dose of reality, and fast. "I said *cared*, Joey." How best to put this...? "I think serving you with annulment papers is pretty final."

Joey folded his arms and stared belligerently out the windshield. "Bethany believes everything her father tells her. She's too gullible." Wow, he was actually criticizing the princess? For a second there, I thought Joey was finally gonna show some backbone. Then he went and ruined it. "But that's only because she's so sweet, you know? Like, unspoiled by the money and everything."

Were we talking about the same Bethany Warnock? The girl who'd been screaming at some poor maid earlier for drinking *milk*? The girl whose Sweet Sixteen, I now recalled, had involved blocking off Hollywood Boulevard so she and her four *hundred* closest friends could enjoy a private screening of the latest Marvel superhero movie? Okay, so she got points for choosing superheroes over some painful romcom, but that was it.

"She didn't even know I was famous when we met," Joey went on, seeming eager to persuade me of Bethany's awesomeness for some reason. "I mean, I was just sitting at a bar, shooting shit with my band, and she overheard us and thought I was funny."

I glanced over to see Joey's smile twist as he stared sightlessly at the glove box, and felt a weird moment of empathy.

Someone had once had wrapped me around their finger with lies like that, too.

Until she'd stuck a knife in my back and chosen my more successful sibling over me.

"She was probably conning you," I offered cynically.

Joey's head swiveled to face me. "What? Why would she?"

I shrugged, making the turn onto Sunset. "Maybe she liked to sleep with everyone Gerry signed." I was aware I had zero proof, but after all, who knew what trust fund kids got up to? They had to have some amusement, what with not needing to waste time on school, work, and the daily grind the rest of us had to keep us occupied.

But the suggestion earned me an angry glare from Joey. "You don't get it!" He sounded sullenly determined. "We're *soulmates*. It's like we were meant to be together - like the universe wanted us to meet."

Uh huh. Yeah, if there were any kind of intelligent design, I'm sure horny rich kids was *just* the kind of thing it would be focused on.

Not.

I clenched my teeth, resisting the urge to share my views on 'soulmates' and cosmic destiny, which were pretty much the same as my views on most religions, astrology, past lives, and Scientology. And bad movie reboots of classic eighties TV series. Why, Lord - why?

"You think she's just some spoiled princess, don't you?" Joey persisted.

I shrugged, but still resisted saying anything more.

Joey scoffed. "Yeah, well everyone thought *I* was worthless, too. They said I had to be lip-syncing, that Gerry only signed me because I was cute and I knew how to play to the fans. You see? We *both* got treated like we were fakes, like our lives had no meaning, because of what *Gerry* put us through! We bonded over it..." I glanced over to see Joey smile painfully. "Then we realized behind all the glamor and showbiz, we were just two people who wanted someone to really see us - to value us, you know?" He met my eyes, then looked away again, staring out the window. I guess my skepticism must have been written on my face. "We were just two people, sitting there, looking for someone to love."

Huh. *Pretty* sure that was from a cringe-inducing scene in a Julia Roberts movie that Jenny had made me watch with her once.

Joey carried on talking, more to himself than me. "I'm gonna make it on my own. Then Bethany will know it's *her* I want, not Gerry's fame *or* his money."

I figured the chances of him getting back on top - especially with Gerry Warnock gunning for him - had to be somewhere between nil and zero. But at least the idea of winning his wife back gave him something to fight for. However worthless I might think their relationship was.

❧

I felt my heart lurch as I saw the landmark that was the

Sunset Spire hotel up ahead. Once I got rid of Joey, there'd be no excuse not to head straight for the hospital. I considered driving around the block a few times, pretending like I was lost or looking for the best place to drop him off. But in the end I forced myself to simply turn off Sunset into the hotel driveway, and pulled under the minuscule overhang jutting out from the lobby.

Two uniformed valets had looked up at the sight of my trusty steed approaching. They were wearing, somewhat improbably, what looked to be identical Tom Ford outfits (yeah, I've watched the Oscars red carpet a time or two - sue me) and discreet name tags. For a second I thought they would wave me away - perhaps suggest I return after a wash, wax, and trip to a BMW dealership - but finally one of them grudgingly approached my window.

"Relax," I snapped, taking out my nerves and frustration on him "I'm just dropping off a friend." If I'd been in a better mood, I might have laughed at the look of relief on his face. Instead, I just glared and growled under my breath.

Then Joey climbed out of the car, and the valets - rapidly recognizing him as 'Somebody' (and newly classifying me as 'unknown friend of Somebody') - had instant personality overhauls. I'd seen it a hundred times before in this town, but now it pissed me off like never before. Only with an effort did I resist jumping out and punching them both as they fawned over him and became ultra-respectful.

To give him credit, Joey basically ignored it all. Instead he turned around and gestured for me to put the window down. "Thanks for the ride," he said as soon as I'd reluctantly complied.

"No problem," I replied, putting the car in drive, and wincing as a tight band of headache clamped around my skull again.

I needed to forget about Joey and Bethany's star-crossed love life. I had something far more important to worry about, and no more reason to delay it.

Time to get myself to a hospital.

ॐ

"You forget something?"

I stared out of my open window at the burly security guard, who stared back at me aggressively in turn.

"Huh?" I managed incoherently, then blinked in puzzlement as I saw the gates to Gerry Warnock's mansion through my windshield. What the *fuck* was I doing back here?

A second guard pushed past the first, his ill-fitting sweats and belligerent stance confirming him as the guy I'd accidentally dunked earlier. "You gonna leave or we need to do something about it?" And by the way he was glaring at me, I was pretty sure that 'something' wouldn't involve calling the cops.

Even so I just frowned, still too disoriented to think clearly. Last thing I remembered I'd been pulling out onto Sunset, headed for the Hollywood Urgent Care... so how the hell had I gotten back here? A chill went down my spine as I realized I had no memory of at least the past fifteen minutes.

A loud *thump* from above made me jump and reach reflexively for the gun I'd worn at my hip for years. Which was really, really dumb, since it was only the idiot guard thumping the car roof to get my attention, and the last thing I needed was to get myself shot.

Especially since I wasn't even carrying. Again.

Fortunately, Tweedle Dumb and Tweedle Dumber weren't so quick on the draw, and were still stumbling back from my car with their hands fumbling under their jackets when I threw her in reverse and hit the gas. With a screech of tires I hadn't produced in years... and tried to avoid now that I had to replace my *own* flat-spotted ones... I swerved backward across the wide expanse of asphalt, and was careening back onto the main road before they could catch up to me on foot.

My breath came fast and heavy as I drove away as quickly as I could manage without getting pulled over or crashing the car. I took inventory of my body: heart pumping - check; limbs trembling - check; stomach roiling - oh, yeah.

Head spinning - abso-fucking-lutely.

I glanced in the rear view mirror, telling myself I was being crazy and paranoid. They weren't coming after me; worst case scenario they'd report me to the local cops, who would review the security camera footage and basically see nothing.

But fuck it: cops aside, the last thing I needed was trouble with someone as connected as Gerry. As if the earlier shit show hadn't been enough, now I had to come back here and make a fool of myself again.

I sped away from Beverly Hills for the second time that day, feeling like I'd just escaped a nuthouse. Except I was kinda carrying the nuthouse around with me, I guessed.

I tried to fill in the gaps in my memory, but there was nothing there. The last thing I remembered, I'd been headed for the hospital, my mind fixed on what I needed to tell the doctors about my weird and wonderful symptoms. Sure, sometimes we all get so lost in thought we barely remember driving somewhere. But if I'd gone on auto-pilot, I would've ended up somewhere familiar - my office, or home - not somewhere I'd only been *once* before.

So why had I gone back to Gerry's mansion?

And why the hell was I pulling into the Sunset Spire's driveway right now?

I slammed on the brakes, bringing the Toyota to a halt midway across the sidewalk. Someone behind me blasted their horn as they swerved around my rear bumper, barely missing it. One of the valets from earlier was frowning at me from his post, probably wondering what I was doing back there.

I only wished I knew the answer myself.

❧

The wait was comparatively short at the Urgent Care, probably because by the time I finally made it there it was 4 p.m. on a Saturday; most of the little league injuries had come and gone, but it was too early for the drunks and the bar fight casualties to start showing up. Even so, I'd had more than enough time to cool my heels, fill out the paperwork, and even wince through several short videos on topics ranging from irritable bowel syndrome to genital herpes, before I was called into an examination cubicle. Of course, after having my blood pressure taken by a nurse, I waited another twenty minutes for anyone else to appear. But eventually the curtain opened again and a doctor came in.

He was Hollywood good looking, with impeccably cut dirty blonde hair, piercing blue eyes, and teeth that gleamed abnormally white against his tan. "Mr. Thatcher, I'm Doctor Nelson," he said, then glanced down at the tablet in his hands. "You're having some problems with your vision?" He smiled up at me again, with just the right mix of concern and reassurance.

Oh, yeah. With those looks and that bedside manner, this guy would soon be moving on to some lucrative Beverly Hills practice, probably plastic surgery or sports medicine. Or maybe he'd move out to Orange County, where he could sit back more and play golf. The kind of practice where bored, rich housewives would brag about having him as their doctor; maybe play a little hooky with him themselves -

Man, I was *really* seeing the worst in everything today. Cutting off those errant thoughts, I made myself give the doc an answer. "I, um..."

Thing was, I'd been purposefully vague on the tablet

they'd handed me to put my information into, wanting to gauge a real doctor's reaction as I laid out my symptoms. As my initial panic had finally faded in the waiting room, some things had slowly dawned on me. If I *wasn't* dying from a tumor - great news though that would be - I couldn't afford to lose my PI's license because of the side-effects of some energy drink I'd been guzzling to help me stay conscious, or due to some weird allergy to all that icing debris I'd inhaled yesterday.

Bottom line, hallucinations had to be a red flag for all kinds of mental illness, and no way would I be allowed to work as a PI - let alone carry a firearm - if I was diagnosed with something like that. So it was probably best if I worked up to things slowly. "I've been pretty short on sleep lately..." I hedged. "Overdoing it, you know?"

The doc nodded, listening intently. "And what have your symptoms been?" His finger was poised over his tablet.

On the other hand, I could always get another job. I couldn't get another body.

"I've been seeing these bright white spheres, floating everywhere," I blurted finally.

There. I'd said it.

He frowned thoughtfully, peering into my eyes. "These white objects..." he rolled his own eyes up and down slowly, "do they drift up and down when you do this?"

"No, they're not floaters." I hesitated, unwilling to go the whole hog and describe how they'd crashed into my chest earlier. On the other hand, I needed some serious help here, whatever was wrong with me. "I think... I think I might be hallucinating," I confessed.

The doc's hand flew over the tablet before he looked back up at me again. "Any other symptoms?"

"Well, I've been a little... disoriented."

"How so?"

I cleared my throat uncomfortably. "Driving places I didn't mean to go."

He looked puzzled. "And you're feeling well otherwise? Physically?"

I'd been doing my best to ignore it, but now that he asked... "My head's throbbing and my stomach's been cramping too." It had gotten steadily worse, ever since I'd backed out from the Sunset Spire's driveway and driven here, careful to follow the directions of my female-voiced GPS and not let my mind drift off again. Even then I'd probably circled West Hollywood three times before making it into the parking lot.

"Do you often have headaches?"

"I guess so. Tension headaches, mostly." I was definitely tense at the moment, so maybe it was no surprise I felt like crap. "And I passed out yesterday, too," I added, then thought about it. "Twice," I admitted.

The doc looked concerned. "Do you know why? Were you dizzy first?"

My eyes narrowed as I remembered the crazy old woman Tasering me in the chest. Had she left me with some weird kind of arrhythmia? Was *that* what had started all this? "Someone Tasered me the first time," I muttered angrily.

"*Tasered* you?"

I guessed even an Urgent Care doc didn't hear that one often, especially in this part of the city. "I'm a PI. I was bringing in a bail-jumper at the time." No need to get into the humiliating details of how a little old lady had gotten the drop on me.

The doc blinked but took it in his stride. "And the second time?"

No way was I admitting to the crazy nightmare that had preceded my second blackout. Or the fact that it had gone down in front of a few hundred witnesses. "Stood up too fast," I bit out.

Correctly interpreting this as the limit of what I was prepared to go into, Doctor Nelson gave a small but reassuring smile. "All right, well, I'll just examine you to see if there's anything obviously wrong." He took the stethoscope from around his neck. "Please undo your shirt so I can place this on your chest."

Staring at the nearest wall as I undid the buttons on my shirt and pulled it open, I tried to relax so the doc could get a good reading of my heartbeat and lungs, or whatever else he'd be measuring in there. After a few seconds, though, I glanced over at him -

- and found the good doctor staring, with a somewhat non-professional interest, at my exposed pecs.

I frowned at him. "Is there a problem?"

"Sorry," he said, sounding slightly embarrassed. "That's just... well, it's very, uh, *striking*, what you have there."

I frowned harder. I may even have gaped a little.

Now don't get me wrong, I don't hate the way I look. But even though I try to keep reasonably in shape, mostly running when I can free up an hour, it isn't like I work out on a daily (or even weekly) basis any more. And there was no way this place didn't have a stream of fit male bodies parading through its cubicles every day. It was West Hollywood adjacent, after all.

So either the doc had a serious fetish about pale skin and fading muscle definition, or he was talking about something other than my physique right now.

Confused, I followed Doctor Nelson's gaze down to my chest -

- *and got my first look at the huge, colorful tattoo sitting right over my heart.*

Chapter Four.

The tattoo was massive, the size of a dinner plate.

Or maybe that should be *tattoos*.

A dozen warmly hued, overlapping circles covered a wide expanse of my skin, starting just below my left collarbone and continuing almost to my left nipple, colors ranging from rosy pink to bright gold to robin's egg blue. They ranged in diameter from maybe two to four inches, colors merging where they overlapped, and while their placement didn't feel random I couldn't see a pattern to it either. The overall effect was strikingly beautiful, I acknowledged somewhere in the back of my head.

Meanwhile, the rest of me was having a complete and total *meltdown*, because...

What the fuck? It couldn't be real. Obviously. I mean, that was hours of sitting in a tattoo parlor and getting inked, right there.

But I could see what the doc was seeing, which meant... it had to be fake, right? Like, a transfer? Even if I still didn't have a clue how it could have gotten there.

Feeling desperate, I licked my thumb and rubbed it over the closest point of the tattoo like my life depended on it. "Shit!" I rubbed at it again, hoping to see some change - but my efforts caused only a faint reddening of the skin around my 'body art' display. "It's not coming off!" I moaned.

"Should it?"

Doctor Nelson sounded puzzled and more than a little

suspicious. I guess he wasn't buying the idea that anyone could get a tattoo *this* big without noticing it.

Honestly, I was right there with him. It wasn't just about the inking, there was the aftercare, the weeks for it to heal... My old partner had gotten a small tattoo on his left bicep when he made Sergeant, and he'd bitched and moaned about it for days. My huge monstrosity of a tattoo didn't hurt at all.

Only one possible explanation I could think of. Maybe... *maybe* if it was only temporary, Kaylee could've done it when I was passed out in bed yesterday night. Even though I had no idea why she'd have done such a crazy thing - or even *how*, exactly.

"It's gotta be a transfer - you know, a fake tattoo? My niece, she..." really? *Kaylee?* "she must've put it on me while I was asleep." I forced a weak smile. "You know kids," I added, hoping he'd assume she was about five, not fifteen. A fifteen-year-old girl futzing with her uncle's chest while he was asleep? Yeah, that was pretty weird.

Unless it had been Len's idea? Some kind of payback for my supposed irresponsibility?

Either way, *one* of them had to have done it. At least that made some sense.

Raising his eyebrows but saying nothing, Nelson went over to the small container on the wall and squeezed out some sanitizing gel. I figured he was just being extra hygienic at first, but instead of rubbing it into his hands he reached down and rubbed it onto part of the tattoo, then took a tissue from a small box and wiped firmly over the same area.

The tattoo remained as it was, unchanged.

I felt goose flesh rise on my arms as I watched. "Does that mean -?"

"It's real, I'm afraid."

I looked up and met the doc's gaze, expecting him to look either puzzled still, or more likely pissed that I was pulling some kind of prank. But instead of options one or two, a professional mask of detached concern had dropped over his face.

Ah, crap.

Option three - which meant I was headed for a psych consult.

As a cop, I'd seen that look on doctors' faces before, and I didn't want to spend time tied to a hospital bed wearing a straitjacket. Or even sitting on a comfy sofa, in a room where the door just happened to lock from the outside and electronic devices weren't allowed.

I needed to get the hell out of here and go somewhere I could think about this. Up until now, I could buy that I was having crazy visions and imagining shit... but the tattoo made things different. Because now, I wasn't the only one seeing it.

So, while I still didn't know what the fuck was going on here, I *did* know one thing for certain: I wasn't going nuts. Weird crap really was happening to me.

And - brain tumors aside - that was the scariest thing of all.

☙

I fled the hospital like the hounds of hell were on my heels.

The good news was I'd managed to convince Doctor Nelson I was messing with him. I'd startled him by guffawing, then slapping his back as I pretended to crack up laughing. I'd channeled every annoying practical joker I'd ever worked with; the type that used pranks and humor to compensate for being a lousy cop. The doc had been visibly pissed, close to tossing me out I guessed. But that just meant I'd pulled it off.

The bad news was, I'd had to back off on the symptoms I described so he didn't think I was pranking him again. I'd ended up focusing on the headache, and had changed the glowing white spheres to simply 'lights flashing in my eyes' - something I knew would yell 'migraine' to the good doctor. My Mom had suffered from them for about a decade before she died, and visual hallucinations like that were pretty common, I'd learned over time.

I gave Nelson credit, he checked me out thoroughly, even ordered a blood test when I admitted my last 'annual' physical had been almost two years back. I thanked him and apologized - again - for being an asshole at the start. He grimaced a little, but still forced a smile that showed his pearly whites.

What a pro.

Minutes later, I sat in my car with my shirt partway open, trying not to freak out as I felt the goose flesh start up again. There had to be a logical explanation for this. There *had* to be.

I just couldn't think of one.

And worse, every time I touched the livid design that now dominated the left side of my chest, I kept thinking back to the old woman who'd Tasered me. Not only were there no signs that that had ever happened - no redness, no marks, nothing - but the giant tattoo was in *exactly* the spot where I'd felt the electrodes hit and the electricity sparking afterwards.

If it had even *been* a Taser. Because the more I thought about it, the more I realized it hadn't really felt much like the first - and only - time I'd been hit with one during my training. But what else could it have been?

Lost in thought, I jumped as my phone buzzed in my pocket. I checked the number, but caller ID showed 'Unknown' and the caller hung up without leaving a message. Which made the third time that afternoon.

Screw it. If it was a new client, they had bad timing. Whoever it was could damn well leave a message if they really needed something.

I felt worse and worse as I drove back to my office. I clutched the steering wheel so hard my knuckles were permanently white, and fought to follow my GPS's directions to the letter... then cursed up a storm whenever I heard "Recalculating" and had to turn around, since that meant I'd gotten distracted again despite all my efforts. Plus every mild annoyance along the way was magnified. A red light felt like it triggered an ulcer, a driver swerving out in front of me seemed to knot up my guts. I reached the point where I wondered if I should just head home, or turn around and head straight back to the hospital. Why the hell had I walked out of there, anyway?

By the time I neared my block, my head was throbbing in agony, my stomach felt like some alien creature was about to burst out, and every nerve ending seemed to be on fire. Confessing my temporary insanity and losing my livelihood - even for good - seemed a small price to pay for my brain not microwaving inside my skull.

I turned down the alley that led to my building... and impossibly, my headache kicked up another notch when I saw the gleaming, badly parked silver Lexus taking up half the small lot ahead.

"Fuck!" I swore.

Not only was I dying, someone had taken my parking space.

I parked - deliberately blocking the Lexus in - and with difficulty pushed open my door and painfully clambered out. I shuffled toward the stairs, fully expecting to step in dog shit - or on an angry skunk - before I reached them. Maybe a bird would fly over and crap on my head. Not exactly signs of Armageddon, but sometimes it's all about straws and camels' backs. Just one more thing, and -

Through my haze of pain and my deepening misery-fest, I heard an expensive car door slam shut. It made that satisfying *thunk* sound I once read that you actually pay more for. What a world we live in, huh? Even that tiny annoyance sent a shudder of agony through my gut. And that was before the *click-clack* of high heels on concrete - another sound that pissed me off - and the bitchily demanding female voice. "Mr. Thatcher!"

Dammit. Someone clearly wanted to engage me in conversation before I reached the sanctuary of my office, and I still had the stairs to haul myself up. I paused at that thought, picturing not only my collapse at the top, but also the EMTs struggling to carry me back down again. Then the clacking heels came into view, my visitor making it to the stairs before me and blocking my route.

Oh, good.

"Hey, I'm talking to you!" The voice was vaguely familiar, though not the shoes.

Why could I only see her shoes? I realized I was drooped over, staring at the ground as I walked. With an effort I raised my gaze to squint painfully at...

Bethany Warnock? The spoiled little rich kid was staring at me with a mixture of impatience and... was that actual concern on her face? God. I must look worse than I thought. Although... for some reason, the throbbing inside my skull had lessened abruptly when I raised my head to look at her. Must be the angle of my neck, I decided, practically sighing at the welcome respite. Maybe I could stay right here for a while. Like, oh, a few hours.

The pain relief also freed up more of my brain to wonder what Gerry's daughter was doing here, but Bethany didn't keep me in suspense for long. "I need to find Joey," she pronounced, in a tone that said she wasn't used to being refused anything.

I frowned at her, taking in the slight puffiness of her eyes and the places where mascara-laced tears had been tracked through her foundation before she scrubbed them away. I felt an unexpected pang of sympathy for an instant... then squashed it ruthlessly. Call me callous and unfeeling, but I had bigger problems than a socialite who wanted her annulment papers signed. I needed to sit down, lay my head on my desk - at this exact angle - and pass out.

I went to move past Bethany, but she stepped sideways, blocking my route again.

I waited for the painful rage to hit my gut like a sledgehammer, the way my ire at every red light and jerk driver had as I drove over here -

- but to my surprise, nothing happened.

I blinked at Bethany, not understanding it. I took an experimental deep breath, then unclenched my tense muscles and straightened to my full height, waiting for the throbbing and cramping to start up all over my body as it had previously.

But there was still no pain. It was as if the instantaneous headaches, ulcers, acid reflux, and chest congestion had vanished as fast as they'd appeared. It was incredible! I took more deep breaths and reveled in feeling like a normal, healthy man in his mid-thirties again. Pain-free for the first time since... since I'd left Gerry Warnock's mansion, I realized suddenly.

I stood there in the parking lot of my building, breathing in the mild February air and feeling like Lazarus risen from the grave. I'd have grabbed Bethany and swung her around in sheer joy, but honestly? I was still a little afraid to move too much - afraid to even *sneeze* - in case it triggered a relapse. Maybe I'd just stand here for the rest of the day, basking in the warm temperatures and the sheer lack of symptoms...

Bethany interrupted my religious experience, a scowl on her face. "*Well?*"

My expression must have said 'huh?' clear as day, because she followed up with:

"Where *is* he? Where's Joey?"

Joey Russo. Right.

I was inclined to spit out the info, just so she'd go away and leave me in peace to enjoy my reprieve from physical torment. On the other hand... I was betting it was *her* Lexus that had taken my parking spot. Which meant that her leaving would require *me* moving my car... which would first require moving *myself*.

So maybe I should keep her talking. Just for a little longer.

"Your husband?" I asked, playing for time.

"I know you left with him yesterday." She sounded almost jealous, as if Joey had ditched her and run off with a friend instead of being half beaten up and tossed out. Talk about high maintenance. Not to mention wanting to have her cake and eat it.

Wisely, I avoided making any such comments aloud. "I dropped him at his hotel."

"Which one?" Bethany demanded.

"Why?"

"What?" She sounded amazed, stunned even, that I wouldn't just give her what she wanted.

I wondered when was the last time anyone had said no to Bethany Warnock. Kindergarten, maybe? Not that I was refusing *per se* - I'd just seen more than my share of domestic assaults on the job, and one thing I knew was you never helped an irate spouse locate their other half without having a damn good reason first. Just because she was six inches shorter and at least sixty pounds lighter than Joey, didn't mean she couldn't hurt him if she wanted to. For all I knew, there was an ice pick in that oversized, butt-ugly purse hanging off her shoulder.

I tried again, using small words so she'd be sure to follow along. "Why do you want to find Joey?"

"Because I..." Bethany seemed lost for an explanation - or rather, I was pretty sure she had one but didn't want to share it. "It's private," she said eventually, shooting me a haughty look.

But I also saw the way she'd squeezed her purse reflexively before finally answering, and wondered if I should upgrade the ice pick to a revolver. No, this was not looking so good for Joey. Okay, so maybe all she'd brought with her was massage oil and anal beads - no

85

judgment - to make their reunion more special. But I was getting a whole different vibe, and that had my cop instincts on high alert.

I shrugged. "Sorry. Wish I could hel- *YOW!!*"

I yelled out as pain and nausea hit me like a mac truck. Gasping, I grabbed for the stair rail and locked my trembling knees, fighting the urge to drop to the ground and throw up. I'd been expecting the wonderful feeling of wellness to fade when I had to move again, but *this*? This amount of agony, I hadn't been prepared for at all. Maybe I shouldn't have shrugged...?

"What do you mean, you can't help me?!"

I clamped one arm over my stomach, pissed off by her persistence in the face of my agony. "Frickin' leave me alone - *ARGH!*"

Another wave hit, and this time I gave up the fight and dropped to my knees hard, retching violently. I dimly heard Bethany back away in a clacking of heels, probably worried I'd get vomit on her Manolo Blahniks. *Not possible*, I could've reassured her; I hadn't felt well enough to eat since yesterday, so the most that was coming up was bile... even though it felt like I was about to spew up a kidney.

As my eyes swam with tears, agony wracking my belly, I heard Bethany's voice again, more hesitant now. "Are you okay?" To my surprise, she sounded genuinely worried. "Should I call nine-one-one or something?"

I flicked a glance to the side between bouts of retching, and saw her kneel down next to me, her designer skinny jeans and pricey purse making contact with the filthy concrete. I wouldn't have thought the girl of a thousand tantrums had a compassionate bone in her body, but there she was, trying to help. Of course, she did want something from me. Still, I had to admit I felt better about the idea of her tracking Joey down now.

Maybe I should give her the name of his hotel before I died?

As I thought those words, I felt the pain throughout my body abate suddenly.

I slowly sat back on my heels, taking short cautious breaths as I waited for the pain to build again. Instead, though, it continued to subside.

I rubbed hesitantly at my stomach as the nausea slowly dissipated, then clambered to my feet, still waiting for the spikes of pain to return. What the *hell* did I have that made the pain come and go so quickly?

I needed to go back to the hospital and get checked -

At just that thought, a headache clamped iron bands back around my skull. Biting back another cry, I spun away from Bethany's confused expression, trying to keep the growing agony to myself as I made my way slowly back toward my car. But the whole way it was a fight to stay upright, the pain spreading with every step I took.

I heard her following behind me in her noisy heels. "Look, I don't want to sound selfish, but I *really* need to find my husband!"

I reached for the driver's side door... but before my hand even made contact another wave of pain hit me, so intense that I ended up slumped against the side of the car. No way I'd be able to drive like this anyhow.

I felt Bethany push against my side, putting my arm around her shoulder, trying to keep me upright. I had to give her credit, the kid was tougher than she looked. Which gave me an idea.

"Drive me to the hospital," I croaked out, my throat suddenly dry as desert dust, "and I'll tell you where to find him."

⁊

Bethany hadn't been keen on the idea of driving my old Toyota at first, especially when I explained how you had to jiggle the ignition key until the radio came on, or the turn signals wouldn't work. I wasn't sure why she cared so much; most LA drivers never used them at all. But she soon came around when I pointed out the obvious benefits to her - like my throwing up on my *own* upholstery. I left out the benefit to me; namely that this way I'd have my own transportation, if and when I was able to go home.

Pretty soon we were out in traffic and wending our way back to the hospital I'd just left. Bethany drove in silence, shooting me anxious looks but following my directions to the letter, while I was left to watch the road signs and dwell on the fact that my symptoms had completely and utterly vanished.

Again.

It was like my body just couldn't decide how it felt. One minute I was fine, the next I was on the verge of gouging my eyes out from the pain. What the hell was wrong with me that it worked that way? Did I have some crazy virus? Or worms picking their way around inside my stomach and head?

I really wished I hadn't thought of the worms.

"So, why do you want to find Joey?" I asked, more to distract myself from thoughts of them than anything else.

Bethany scrubbed at her eyes with a tissue. I hadn't noticed her crying, but then I'd been pretty distracted there for a while. "I- I think I made a mistake."

"You mean with the annulment?"

Bethany flicked me a glance through eyelashes so thick and black they had to be fake. "Yes."

I saw the approaching intersection half a block away. "Turn right up ahead." As she changed lanes, I added, "Why don't you just call him, ask to meet? He seemed pretty desperate to get you back."

"He's not taking my calls." Bethany stared straight ahead through the windshield as she spoke, her fingers tightening on the steering wheel; I guessed she wasn't used to being ignored.

It seemed weird, though. Joey had literally climbed a mountain... okay, a large hill... to plead his case with her less than three hours ago, and he'd still seemed determined to win her back when I'd dropped him off at his hotel. "Since when?" I asked.

She shook her head, still not making eye contact. "I don't know. I started calling him hours ago but he never picks up."

He'd gotten dead drunk and passed out, I guessed. I pictured how happy he'd be when Bethany showed up, and for a second it almost seemed a shame to make her take me to the hospital first. I was feeling fine now, after all; could barely recall how bad I'd felt before. Okay, so it wasn't like me to be so sappy, but hey, I was having a pretty screwed up day overall.

Then I spotted the turn to the hospital coming up and realized we were practically there anyway. "Pull in here," I instructed, and leaned back in my seat with a sense of resignation, wondering what the hell Doctor Nelson would make of me this time. Probably send me for that psych eval after all.

"Is the hospital, like, inside?" Bethany asked, sounding confused.

And so was I when I took another look outside. Because we weren't back at the hospital. No: we were sitting in front of the Sunset Spire's car port; the same place I'd dropped Joey off at a few hours earlier. I could even see my trusty Toyota's nemesis, the snooty valet, glowering at us from a few yards away as he reluctantly approached Bethany's door.

"What the hell..."

"Don't blame me," Bethany said, aggrieved, "I was following your directions the whole way here!"

Looking back, I realized with a kind of sick horror that she *had* been following my directions. I'd been too distracted by the mystery of my disintegrating pain to think of telling her to use a GPS. But instead of directing her to the hospital, I'd taken her straight to Joey instead.

Worse - and unlike my unintended return to Gerry's mansion earlier - I hadn't been zoned out and lost in my thoughts this time. Until a few seconds ago, I'd *fully* believed we were almost at a hospital that was twenty minutes across town.

Which was just great, since it meant even *more* freaky symptoms to add to the blackouts, night terrors, and extreme hallucinations. Maybe I should just cut out the middle man and have myself committed.

Bethany gasped in sudden enlightenment. "Is this where Joey's staying?"

"Umm..."

She was out of the car before I could concoct a plausible denial inside my head, let alone say it out loud. I hesitated a moment, debating whether I could trust her not to knife Joey in the back... sure, it was highly unlikely, but my dumb sense of responsibility won out in the end. Exhaling deeply, I opened my door, and braced myself for the pain to hit me as I followed her inside the hotel.

The elevator walls were covered with gray protective felt, the buttons showing through a raggedly cut hole in it. The lobby had also looked like it was being refurbished, but I assumed the effect was deliberate since the entire hotel had been this way for the past decade or so. I'd have thought 'building site chic' would go out of fashion eventually, but apparently not.

I'd had to call up to Joey's room to get the number, but Bethany had begged me not to tell him she was with me. So I'd made up some story about wanting his autograph for Kaylee.

Now I was regretting that.

Glancing sideways, I once again eyed the large purse over Bethany's shoulder, which she clutched to her side like she was afraid I'd make a grab for the thing. It was a Versace; I knew because the name was all over it in big gold letters. (You almost had to admire the way those designer brands made their customers pay through the nose *and* provide free advertising too.) But I figured in Bethany-world, the kind of money it cost wasn't even a blip on her bank balance.

Which meant she was being protective of whatever was *inside* the purse. Possibilities included sexy stuff (in case they made up) - which I tried hard not to think about in too much detail - or maybe the annulment papers (in case they didn't). I'd decided the latter would explain her behavior, although since I couldn't rule out it being some kind of weaponry I wasn't letting her out of my sight for now.

In reality, it was seriously nuts for me to be wasting my limited time and energy on these two. Hell, I wasn't even being *paid* for it. I should've waved Bethany off at the car and driven myself to the hospital. Or back to the office; or home to bed.

But honestly, at that moment I didn't care.

I was too busy enjoying how *good* I felt.

No headache. No nausea. No crippling joint pain. It was like the past few hours never happened. I felt great; better than I had in *months*, to be honest. Between all the stakeouts, morning school runs with Kaylee, and late night arguments with Len, four or five hours of sleep a night had become the norm, if not a downright luxury some weeks. But at that moment, I felt rested and relaxed - like I could've run up the ten flights and beaten the elevator.

Which was even weirder, because - as I'd been reminded back at the Urgent Care - I'd slacked off on workouts since I'd lost access to the LAPD gym, and my recent diet of energy drinks, fast food, and coffee weren't exactly what the doctor ordered.

Relishing the lack of pain, I couldn't help stretching my back and sucking in a deep, contented breath as we passed the eighth floor.

"What are you so happy about?" Bethany asked suspiciously. "What did Joey say on the phone?"

I shrugged. "Just told me to come up."

In fact, he'd been almost pathetically pleased to hear my voice, telling me to come up without even seeming to care why I'd stopped by. I'd always figured celebrities - even faded ones - traveled in packs, but at least for Joey Russo that didn't seem to be the case since he'd sounded like he was alone. He'd also sounded drunk and depressed. Maybe not the best combination... or the best circumstances for a visit by your almost-ex wife. But at least she wouldn't walk in on him partying inappropriately, like doing lines with adoring female fans or having sex with a hooker. Or vice versa.

I know. My standards for rock stars could probably be higher.

The hotel room door swung open moments after I knocked, revealing an inebriated-looking Joey. I'd been braced to explain why I'd brought Bethany up without telling him - she'd pleaded for it to be a surprise, afraid he'd refuse to see her otherwise - but I realized there'd be no need when I saw his joyful amazement as he took her in at my side. "Baby?!" His voice was full of hope, longing written all over his face.

Bethany pushed past both of us, moving into the suite beyond.

"Bethany?" Joey followed her in and - feeling like a spare wheel - I reluctantly followed behind. I'd have loved to have turned right around and left them to it, but something stopped me. Maybe it was the way Joey was clearly ecstatic to see her. Not exactly the reaction of a guy ignoring her calls, and it had me smelling a bigger rat than before. Had he been passed out, or turned off his phone... or had Bethany lied about calling him? And if so - why?

Inside, the place was a mess. Either the maid service here sucked, or Joey had basically imploded after I dropped him off. Empty beer cans and miniature bottles of booze were strewn about the floor and furniture (they were gonna rob him blind on the mini bar charges), and an empty full-sized bottle of tequila (room service charges too) was leaking onto the carpet. I'd pretty much expected to see something like this, though.

What I *hadn't* expected? Bethany, going from room to room like she was on some kind of mission. She'd storm into one, disappear for a few seconds, then emerge with an intent look on her face before moving on to the next. Was she looking for something? Maybe she'd had the same idea I had about female fans and hookers.

The whole time, Joey stood in the middle of the living room grinning stupidly after her, not seeming to find this behavior particularly odd. I guess he'd been married to her, so perhaps this was normal. "Baby... does this - does this mean you'll take me back?" His words were slightly slurred, but as Bethany finally gave up her weird treasure hunt and came to a jerky halt, Joey managed to stagger forward to meet her. Reaching out, he ignored the frown on her face and gripped her hands tightly in his.

I was cynically pondering whether he'd done that to be romantic or to keep his balance, when I felt a fluttering around my heart, a strange pushing sensation against my ribcage. I put it down to indigestion, raising my hand to rub against my chest...

And felt something brush over my skin there.

Reacting in panic, I looked down, instinctively batting whatever it was away from me... and freaked out at the sight of several glowing white spheres streaming out through my shirt.

"Yeargh!"

I let out a strangled cry as I flung myself backward, colliding with the wall next to the door and dropping to the floor. I nearly hyperventilated as the flood of spheres picked up their pace, dozens seeming to leave my body at once. I followed their path with frantic eyes... and that's when I realized where the stream of glowing white balls was headed.

Joey and Bethany were both staring over at me, drawn by my yell, but it was obvious they couldn't see the twin snakes of white spheres heading straight for them. Which I knew weren't real - *couldn't* be real. Even so, my instincts were impossible to override.

"Look out!" I yelled, struggling back to my feet and staggering forward.

Joey looked even more confused - almost dumbstruck - but for Bethany, my warning seemed to break whatever spell she'd been under for the past few moments. Tugging her hands out of Joey's grasp, she glared at him, angry tears running down her cheeks.

"Where are they, Joey?!"

Joey looked puzzled. "Who?"

To my relief, I watched the spheres come to a halt just inches from their apparent targets, twisting instead into 'holding pattern' spirals.

Beyond them, Bethany pulled a large manila envelope from her purse and violently yanked out its contents. "Those *bitches* you cheated on me with!"

Joey looked aghast. "Baby, I never cheated -"

"Then explain *these*!" Bethany howled, tossing a sheaf of large, glossy color photos in his face.

He recoiled as they landed on the floor around him, then bent - wobbling dangerously - and managed to pick one up. I was too mesmerized by the motions of the spheres to look, but I heard his spluttering attempts to deny whatever was in them. "But - but -"

"There's no point denying it! I spoke to your girlfriend, *Sophia*," she spat out.

"But... this isn't me! It *can't* be!"

Bethany grabbed the photo Joey held out to her and tore it in half. It looked pretty cathartic to me. "She admitted it to my face!" she yelled at him. "You cheating, lying *bastard*!" Digging into her purse again, she yanked out the annulment papers and threw them at him. "Sign them!"

Joey looked aghast. "But I never cheated on -"

Bethany pulled back and slapped him in the face.

The whole world seemed to hang in place for an instant, then Joey fell back into the sofa, Bethany ran for the door sobbing -

- and the freaky white spheres all did a U-turn and started back toward me.

I gaped in sick awareness of what would come next, as they picked up speed.

No... no...!

Bethany slammed the door at the exact moment the spheres crashed into me, sending me stumbling back as they dove into my chest cavity. I felt something move under my shoe - an empty mini-vodka bottle, I'd discover later - and I lost my footing, flying back toward the wall. My head struck it - hard - and a moment later, everything went black.

ॐ

I came to with a pasty-faced Joey leaning over me.

"Are you okay?"

It took a while for things to come back to me. The moment they did, I jerked upright into a sitting position, causing Joey to lean back hastily. I patted my hands over my body, yanking open my shirt to check the actual skin of my chest, make sure no glowing balls of light were hanging out under there. But I found nothing... except the colorful tattoo I was pretty sure the old woman had left. I was also pretty sure that she - and the tattoo - were behind my weird delusions, since the spheres felt like they went in and out of my chest *right there.*

And now that I'd made *that* connection, I wondered if the tattoo could be inked in some weird derivative of LSD.

Slowly seeping into my bloodstream.

Making me nuts... poisoning me?

Shit. I needed to get back to a hospital, ASAP.

"Hey, man? You're freaking me out here."

I looked at Joey again, saw the worry on his face, and was glad he was still there, anchoring me to whatever reality I had left. I had to admit, I was impressed he hadn't just left me lying there unconscious and bolted after Bethany. Then I noticed the sweat on his face and his heavy breathing. Like he'd just raced the elevator down to the ground floor. So apparently he *had* left me lying there unconscious.

But hey. At least he'd come back.

I got to my feet, Joey helping me, both of us careful to avoid stepping on any of the photos Bethany had brought. Any other time, I'd have taken a look out of sheer curiosity, professional and otherwise. But I was too focused on my goals right now, namely: 1. Get to the hospital; 2. Get every test in the book, no matter how crazy it makes you look; and 3. Pray whatever you have is curable.

I turned for the door. "Okay, then. So long -"

Sharp pain hit me from head to foot, shrouding me in a dark blanket of misery.

I gasped and hunched over, clutching my arm across my stomach as I tried not to puke.

"You're just gonna *go*?"

Somehow I managed to turn back around to face Joey, thinking he could call an ambulance - the paramedics - hell, maybe a *priest*.

And the pain vanished like a ghost in sunlight.

I exhaled on a startled, relieved moan.

Joey was less impressed by my miraculous recovery. In fact, he seemed totally unaware of it, unable to register anything except Bethany and the photos right now. "Well?" he demanded, then thrust one of the glossy pages in my face. "Are you gonna stay and help me, or what?"

I did my best to focus on the close-up image, but it was hard when it was only an inch from my nose *and* my body was still reeling from the joyous, nirvana-like high of not being in pain. "Uh..." I tugged the photo another inch away. As the pieces of it resolved into body parts, I blinked in surprise. "Whoa."

I was less impressed by the sexual content than I was by the sheer number of limbs in the photo. Joey was in the middle of at least three different women, judging by the amount and varying color of skin on display. Only one of their faces was shown, however: a heavily mascaraed brunette, who looked on the verge of orgasm as Joey squeezed her breasts intently, like he was testing ripe melons...

With his wedding ring clearly visible, not to mention a prominent tattoo on his biceps that read 'Joey ♥ Bethany.'

Yeah. No question these were enough to convince his wife that he'd cheated.

I had a question, though: "How did you think she wouldn't find out?"

Joey snatched the photo away and glared at me. "I'm telling you, this isn't me!"

Riiiight. I turned my back on Joey again -

And the agony hit me like a four by four to the chest.

Coughing, feeling like my lungs were about to explode, I found myself turning back to face Joey - almost by instinct, since I guess my subconscious figured it out first...

And the pain was gone again.

This time, I didn't move - didn't speak - just took a moment to examine. To analyze.

Joey - oblivious to the internal workings of my mind - peered at me hopefully, like an eager puppy watching its master. "You believe me, don't you? You'll help?"

"Look, kid, I -"

Even before I spoke the words - words like "need to go to the hospital" or "think I might be dying" - I could feel the sickness bubbling up inside me again, ready to strike. I clamped my mouth shut, keeping quiet, and the feelings subsided.

Joey hung on the promise of more words for a

moment, then seemed to think more arguments were required. "The photos are fake - they have to be." As I said nothing, he continued. "You're a detective, aren't you? I mean, you can help me prove they're fake, right?"

I hesitated a long time before I answered Joey.

Kaylee might accuse me of not 'getting' some things quickly. Like why she absolutely *needed* Twitter and Instagram accounts, or why photos of an ugly, pissed-off cat with a watermelon had become an internet sensation. But I'd been a pretty good detective there for a while, and one thing I'd learned was that sometimes you just had to follow the evidence, even if you couldn't see where it led. Even if it led to crazy town.

'Crazy town' in this case being that, apparently, either I helped Joey get his wife back, or I suffered for it. *Literally.*

I decided on one final test. Whether it was of my theory or my insanity, I wasn't sure right about then.

"I can't help you..."

I felt a band of pain tighten around my temples. I closed my eyes, waiting for the hammer to fall, and spoke again.

"But I know someone who can."

And as I'd expected - as I'd half hoped for, half dreaded - the pain faded back to nothing.

Holy crap.

In a sense, I'd discovered a cure.

The cure just didn't make any fucking *sense.*

Chapter Five.

Joey - oblivious to my horrifying revelation - brightened at my announcement. "Really?"

"Yeah." I bent to gather up a few of the photos, not sure whether to be relieved that my muscles didn't protest at the effort or even more freaked out. In the end I decided to go with happy. If I was gonna embrace the crazy 'solution' I'd come up with, I might as well take the positives along with the negatives.

And talking of negatives...

I studied the photos. If Joey and Bethany were going to make it as a couple - and I was going to get rid of the freaky damn spheres that seemed to be at the root of my health issues - the first order of business was proving Joey wasn't guilty of anything. Problem was, I couldn't see anything wrong with the proof at first glance.

I twisted one of the photos around, trying to ignore the piece of Joey's genitalia in the frame. "You ever pose for shots like these?"

"I never cheated on Bethany!"

"If these are fake," I said slowly, "we're gonna have to figure out how it was done." I sighed and held out one that prominently featured a part of Joey I wished I hadn't had to see. "Does that look like you or not?"

Joey peered closer - winced - then frowned, glancing down at his crotch and back at the photo, as if trying to superimpose one on the other. Like looking at it through his pants would make the comparison easier. Didn't he recognize his own junk? Then again, I guess no guy ever gets a full frontal view of his own partially erect member, unless he likes to masturbate in front of a mirror. (Again, no judgment.)

Finally, he shrugged. "I *guess...*" He suddenly looked desperate again. "But it *can't* be me - I'd never do that to her!"

I suppressed an irritated growl and reminded myself that Joey was still drunk and/or hung-over. "Could it be an *old* photo? Maybe they just added the tattoo and wedding ring."

He shot me a grossed-out look. "Look, man, I went pretty wild when I first made it big - getting drunk off my ass, smoking pot, skinny dipping in hotel pools, whatever - but I think I'd remember a freaking *orgy!*" He moved over to the sofa, slumping down on it, and gestured woozily toward the photo. "Besides, my hair used to be all blonde, and really long."

I checked the photo again, which certainly showed Joey's hair the current color and length. That wouldn't explain it then.

I flicked through all the photos once more, focusing on the women this time around. Something occurred to me as I noticed the same girl appearing again and again: the one Joey was groping in the first shot I'd grabbed from the pile. Squatting down on the carpet, I did a careful check through the entire set. Oddly enough, she was the only woman whose face you could see clearly in any of the shots, which seemed a little too coincidental.

"How about her?" I asked, pointing her out.

Joey leaned over, trying to look, and ended up half-overbalancing, half sitting down. Finally - sitting cross-legged like an over-eager boy scout - he managed to peer at the woman I indicated, and his face creased in confusion. "I *know* her," he muttered, sounding amazed.

Biblically, by the looks of things. "Yeah..."

"No, not from *this,*" Joey shook his head emphatically,

then clutched his head as his hangover clearly began to kick in with a vengeance. "She's one of the new backing singers." He reached for a photo showing her whole face, managing to pick it up after several attempts, then looked puzzled as he stared at it. "I barely remember her name! We only hired her last week. Sonia... Sarah, something -"

"Sophia?" I said, remembering the name Bethany had hurled at him.

Joey shot me an impressed look. "Yeah! Sophia... Sophia Wilde! That's it."

I thought of Gerry Warnock, and how he'd have strong-armed Joey into signing the annulment papers yesterday if I hadn't been there. How far would he go to 'save' his only daughter? "You lose any time since you hired Ms. Wilde? Maybe black out at a party, after a few drinks?"

Joey looked confused, then - as he realized why I was asking - answered with a vigorous "No!"

"You're positive?"

"Yes!" He waved a hand at the empty bottles strewn around him. "Until today, I hadn't had a drink since Bethany left. Too focused on getting her back," he added mournfully, then reached for a huge bottle of water sitting next to the sofa and began guzzling it gratefully.

I glanced back at the photos. They didn't look like Joey was posed and unconscious, or even drugged and unaware. In fact, he seemed pretty damn enthusiastic in most of them.

Which only left Option C.

"Does Gerry know what you look like naked?"

I'd picked a bad time to ask. Water spurted out of Joey's mouth, shooting all over his clothes and the carpet. "What? No!" he finally managed, still coughing. "Why -?"

"If this is a body double with your head on it," I pointed to the body of the guy in the photo, "Gerry had to know exactly who to get."

Honestly, it was a long shot. I'd never even *heard* of

someone trying to pull this kind of crap outside of internet hoaxes, dumb art exhibits, or improbable spy movies. Then again, Gerry *was* in the entertainment business, where body doubles were everywhere. Plus after witnessing him in action yesterday, I could see parallels with certain Bond villains.

And that made me realize I'd asked a dumb question. Gerry Warnock had made Joey a mega-star in the first place, which meant he'd been there through Joey's self-confessed 'wild years.' He'd probably had all kinds of photos lying around for years, just waiting for a good time to use them, whether to boost or burn the kid's career.

"Forget it," I said. "He probably just made a good guess." Joey looked puzzled, but there was no need to freak him out by suggesting his father-in-law had nude photos of him on file. I figured none of it could be *that* bad, or Gerry would've used it as blackmail material to force them apart even sooner.

"So how do we prove it's not me?"

I took a deep breath. "First, you hire me," I said, and braced for the pain to slam my body again.

But nothing happened. Apparently, whatever psychological meltdown / ancient curse / parallel universe I was dealing with here - and right now I wasn't sure which would be better - it didn't mind me getting paid to do what it wanted.

Joey nodded eagerly, getting to his feet. "Sure - whatever you need!"

Talk about being too trusting. Then again, the guy was desperate.

I briefly wondered what would happen if I took another job at the same time... then decided not to think about it. No point in getting ahead of myself. Besides, it wasn't like people were lining up around the block to employ me.

More pressing was deciding what our next move should be. Unfortunately, I only had to think about it for a second before I accepted the obvious. It wasn't like there were many options, and we needed the best.

I blew out a reluctant breath.

"Problem?" Joey sounded worried.

I shook my head. "Nope. Just need to go visit an old friend."

ન્

We reached Boyle Heights in under thirty minutes - pretty good for Saturday evening in LA, although it was still pretty early. Joey had spent most of the drive looking sick and morose, huddled in his seat. I wasn't sure if it was the hangover or reaction to the day's events, but I was glad of the silence; I had enough to think about without listening to his woes.

I'd tried deviating from our route on the drive over, just as one final test. Clutching the steering wheel, I'd moved to the outside lane, even though the exit for Boyle Heights was coming up fast -

- and in the next heartbeat, pain had seared through my skull.

Resisting the urge to claw at my forehead, I'd managed a quick glance at the traffic around me before pulling a classic evasion maneuver, shooting diagonally across all four lanes in one go. We'd made the off-ramp by a mere ten feet as Joey yelled in panic next to me.

His cries, and the horns blasting behind us, had been little more than sweet music to my instantly pain-free self, the endorphins flooding my body making me feel momentarily light as air. As I came down from the high and reality set in, though, I wondered how far I'd go to satisfy whatever was driving me. What rules of law or morality would I break if it meant getting proof of Joey's innocence and ending my pain for good? Even now, I knew I would probably lie, cheat, and steal.

But would I put a gun to someone's head?

Would I literally torture Gerry to make him confess?

Shoving away such dark thoughts, I made the final turn onto the street that held our destination and had to wait for a bunch of kids playing basketball to clear a path before I could proceed. As they reluctantly moved aside, they stared at my unknown vehicle with a mix of childish curiosity and territorial suspicion, and I hoped none of them got a good look at my famous passenger. But if anyone did, they obviously shared Gerry's opinion that he was just some has-been, because they all went straight back to their game after we drove by.

A little way along the street I pulled up in front of a modest single family home and cut the engine. A nearby radio pumped out Mexican pop as I got out of the car and headed for the driveway.

Joey followed me up to the front door, but looked confused. "I thought we were going to see some forensics expert?"

"Don't worry." I told him as I rang the doorbell. "My guy's the best."

I heard soft footsteps a moment before Carlos opened the door. He took one look at me and smiled. "Hey, Lyle."

I grinned back at my old nemesis. "Carlos. How goes the crime wave?"

He shrugged. "Pretty good. We're poised to take over the whole city now." Bold words for one so young. But then, Carlos had always been sure of himself. I guess it was in the blood.

To my right I could see Joey removing his sunglasses - a necessity when hung-over in perma-bright LA - and squinting at Carlos in a kind of surprised dismay. Finally, though, his bleary gaze took in the game controller held in Carlos's hand and the headset around the kid's neck.

"Oh," he said, relieved. "You mean in a *game*."

Carlos raised an eyebrow at me, but limited himself to a smirk as he turned away, leading us inside the house.

At thirteen, Carlos had obviously developed a little

more sophistication and cool than when I'd last seen him. I didn't know whether to be amused, proud, or saddened that I'd lost my chance to hang out with the twelve-year-old who'd ordered me to give him a ride around the back yard after he thrashed me at Halo.

For the third time.

No doubt about it, the kid was a gaming mastermind.

I let Joey go first, staying back to shut the front door before following them inside. We came to a halt in the living room, where a game was paused on a truly massive plasma TV fixed to the wall. The game console sat nearby, as well as an older model. The latter's body had been taken apart to spill its guts on the floor, some bits connected to a sturdy looking laptop sitting next to it. The placement of the soda can and bright orange chips - Carlos's favorites - told me he was one working on the project.

Man, I'd barely been able to keep up with *playing* his video games, let alone understanding how they worked. The kid was barely a teenager, yet already light years ahead of me on a technical level. I suddenly felt past it, not for the first time since I'd hit thirty-five.

But could Carlos solve a cryptic crossword in under an hour?

Oh yeah. Neither could I.

"Hang on," he said, and headed for a door over to one side of the room.

I felt Joey nudge my arm and looked around to see him gripping the envelope of photos tight. "Isn't he a little *young* to see these?" he hissed, looking a little stressed.

I rolled my eyes at his erroneous assumption. "He's not my expert," I said, at the same time as Carlos stuck his head through the door and yelled: "Aunt Reesa, it's Lyle!"

Joey's bloodshot eyes went wide as we followed Carlos down the stairs into the huge basement area. "It's like the freaking bat cave in here," he murmured.

But I was barely listening. My attention was entirely on

the slim, dark-haired woman seated behind a set of monitors, who watched expressionlessly as we came closer.

It had been Hollywood's gain and the LAPD's Computer Crimes Unit's loss when Reesa Fuentes finally quit and turned full time to her 'hobby.' The last time I'd come over, she'd been working on the special effects for some low-budget sci-fi movie. From the looks of the expensive monitors and shiny new computer equipment, I was betting she'd moved further into the big leagues now.

I was sorry I'd missed seeing that, but most of all I was damn happy for her. *And* proud of myself for the small part I played in persuading her to take a risk; to leave the department, when everyone else was spouting doom and gloom, and basically trying to flush her self-esteem down the toilet. If they'd known Reesa better, they'd have known the latter just wasn't possible. But the idea of giving up a solid career with a good pension had made her wary, particularly when she was the main provider for her sister and nephew. Plus even after eight thankless years on the job, she'd still felt she owed the LAPD more.

The night before she'd finally done it, I'd handed her a beer, sat down next to her on the porch swing out back, and told her she'd put enough of herself into helping others. Time to help herself, I'd said.

Reesa had given me a long look and said something I'd never been able to forget. "You better take your own advice before it's too late."

I hadn't known what she meant... or maybe I hadn't wanted to. Either way, I'd changed the subject, and we'd spent half the night sitting out there eighteen months ago, warmed by the Santa Ana winds coming over the mountains from the desert beyond. Warmed, too, by the support and friendship in our hearts.

Then six months ago I'd basically vanished on her for a year. And now suddenly here I was, back on her doorstep... because I needed a favor.

Yeah, I was a dumbass.

As we reached the base of the stairs, Reesa got up and walked toward us, her long hair curling down over one shoulder onto the plain lilac shirt she wore tucked into a pair of old jeans. Jeans that hugged her lithe curves in a way that would have made most guys' hearts beat faster in their chests. She stopped in front of us and smiled...

At Joey.

Me, she ignored completely.

Fuck. Then again, I knew she'd be pissed.

Still wearing the smile, she studied Joey with keen interest, looking slightly down on him from her five foot ten height. "You must be Joey. I'm Reesa." Her voice, as she extended a hand for him to shake, was confident and professional, warmed by her faint hint of a Mexican accent. Yet at the same time, her deep brown eyes flicked over him in rapid assessment - and I didn't think I imagined the flash of fire sent in my direction. As always there was a steely core to Reesa that somehow gave off a clear warning: play nice, or the friendly lady goes bye bye.

"Hi," Joey replied, sounding impressed.

I glanced to my right. It wasn't lust on his face, more admiration, but I knew Reesa had another fan for life. I'd seen her pull this off with everyone from some arrogant banker's prick lawyer in court to a squad-room of male chauvinist cops, and it was always fun to watch. It wasn't a seduction; if anything, it was more an appeal to the little boy who wanted approval from a strict but loving mommy. Mary Poppins meets an eighties-style Jane Fonda fitness instructor. Come to think of it, Reesa could have made a fortune as a dominatrix. I had a sudden, unexpected vision of her in some sex dungeon, wielding a whip and covered neck to toe in black leather...

The real Reesa shot a sharp look in my direction, and I winced.

"Thatcher."

So she was going to acknowledge me after all - albeit in a tone that could freeze hell. Probably still more than I deserved, though. "Rees," I replied, using the nickname her friends used for her. From the slight narrowing of her eyes, I wondered if she was considering revoking that right.

Carlos broke the awkward silence, clearly hoping to take advantage of her distraction. "Can I go over to Chris's?"

His aunt turned her attention on him, and I knew the kid didn't have a hope. Reesa might *get* distracted - sometimes - but she never stayed that way long. "Did you finish your homework yet?"

"No."

Despite everything, the chagrin on Carlos's face as he answered tugged a smile to my lips. I'd missed watching their interplay.

"Then ask me again when it's done."

The battle of wills lasted another few seconds, but then Carlos rolled his eyes expressively and, admitting defeat, turned and trudged back up the steps.

"Might go faster if you weren't playing games at the same time!" Reesa called after him, amusement as well as a mild reproof in her voice.

Carlos glanced back, going for a wounded expression... until he caught my eye and remembered we'd seen him gaming when we arrived. Denial was not an option. Instead, he gave an exasperated sigh. "It's stress-relief!"

"You'll be more stressed if you don't have anything to hand in on Monday." Reesa held out her hand. "Toss me the controller."

"Aunt Reesa!"

"Carlos..."

"Fine!" The kid threw the controller down - it hit the floor, missing Reesa's hand by a mile - then stomped back up the stairs, slamming the door shut behind him.

Reesa sighed then flicked me a wry look. "He'll get over it."

"I know."

I'd been enjoying the brief respite from the freeze-out, but in an instant Reesa's expression changed to something I couldn't read. "Right. You have a teenager at home now, too."

Her words took me by surprise. I hadn't even been thinking of Kaylee; I'd been talking about my memories of Reesa's close relationship with Carlos. Before I could say anything to correct her, though, she turned to Joey and took the envelope from him.

"Okay, let's take a look."

Joey cringed, going from self-assured rock star to humiliated nine-year-old in a microsecond, as Reesa pulled out the photos and leafed through them.

Her eyebrows shot up at all the naked flesh on display, a smirk lighting her face. "So this isn't you?"

"No!"

She shot Joey a bemused look, her gaze skimming the crotch of his pants for *just* an instant before she took in the embarrassment on his face and went back to perusing the photos in a more professional manner. "Well, if they're fakes, they're good." She studied his face critically now, looking between it and one of the photos several times, then headed for some equipment off on a side bench. "But if they stuck your face on someone else's body, it should be easy enough to prove."

Joey followed her, sounding hopeful. "But didn't you say they were good?"

Reesa smirked as she brought a large monitor to life and flicked on some kind of high tech scanner. "Oh baby, I'm better. It's a lot harder to fool an expert than your average person on the street."

I decided to step in here so Reesa could focus on the task at hand. "Reesa does amazing digital effects for movies."

Okay, so maybe I'd wanted to earn some points.

More fool me.

"I handle a sci-fi TV show now, too. I have for six

months," she added, shooting me a meaningful look that wasn't quite angry... but wasn't exactly friendly, either.

I got it.

I'd basically been AWOL from her life for twice that long, and she had every right to be angry at me for showing up now with a client in tow.

It wasn't like I'd ignored her *completely*. I just hadn't called her back when she'd phoned; instead I'd waited a few days then sent her a text message, giving some (lame) excuse for why I hadn't - and still couldn't - call. Eventually she'd gotten the message and the calls had trailed off to one every month or two, and for the past few months only texts.

Yeah, I'd basically left her out in the cold. I'd felt like a heel - but I'd had my reasons. Mostly, the fact that I'd never been able to lie to Reesa well. Okay, make that *at all*. And there'd been a shitload of stuff I couldn't tell her, then or now. In fact, after the past few days I had more secrets to hide than ever before.

So why had I come to her with this?

Don't get me wrong, she was one hundred percent the best person for the job. But I was pretty well connected, meaning I had other contacts and resources I could have tried first. If I'd really wanted to, I could've found another expert to get Joey's ass out of the fire. Maybe not as fast as Reesa could do it, but it would've spared us this awkward reunion.

I watched her start working, scanning in one of the photos, keenly aware that I hadn't needed to come here at all. Not really. But I'd *wanted* the reunion, hadn't I?

Idiot.

Truth be told, I'd been secretly longing to see my best friend again, and the urge had only gotten stronger when I'd thought I had some kind of terminal illness. That kind of shit had a way of focusing your mind. And despite all the risks - despite the fact that it wasn't only my story to confide - maybe I didn't want to die without making a clean breast of things to Reesa. Without letting her know why I'd disappeared from her life.

"How's your niece doing?"

I started at Reesa's question.

"Kaylee? She's... doing fine."

Reesa paused in her work, hand hovering over the mouse as she licked her lower lip in thought. It was an old habit - an endearing one that I'd never teased her about, just in case it made her self-conscious and she stopped doing it. A moment later she glanced over at Joey.

"Hey, uh... Joey... could you do me a favor? Go upstairs and remind my nephew I said homework *then* games?"

Joey frowned at the controller sitting on her desk. "Ahh..."

Reesa smiled. "He has a spare." She saw the reluctance on Joey's face. "I'll do this as fast as I can, I promise."

Joey glanced between the two of us, then nodded his acceptance. He'd have had to be dead not to sense the vibes in this place. "Okay. Just... please come find me as soon as you know?"

"I will."

With a final look at me, Joey turned and hurried up the stairs, copying Carlos by slamming the door behind him. Less of a protest at being banished, I thought, than making it absolutely clear we were on our own so we could talk about the things that seemed to linger in the air between us.

And yeah... with Joey's departure, the tension in the room definitely rose a notch or two. In the silence, I came around Reesa's desk so I could watch what she was doing, seeing her magnifying the scanned-in image on her huge screen. I was just preparing myself for some lame conversational gambit when she finally spoke again.

"You realize I had to find out from *O'Riley* that you'd moved in with them?"

O'Riley. A desk sergeant who'd rivaled my father in terms of how many perps - not to mention newbie cops -

he'd intimidated. Unlike Len, though, O'Riley hadn't been forced into early retirement by his drinking and gambling habits. Which meant he was still going strong at thirty plus years on the job, and consequently knew pretty much everything about everyone.

I realized I'd waited too long before replying. The set of Reesa's shoulders said she was getting angry - and she'd obviously been carrying this around for the past eight months, since that was when I'd moved out of my apartment and back into the 'old homestead.'

But if I apologized, that would open up a whole new can of worms. Better to tough it out. "It was pretty spur of the moment." In reality, Len had been pushing me to give Kaylee a 'proper family environment' for a while, and after weeks of his guilt tripping I'd finally given in. In the old days, I would've complained to Reesa about all of it and asked her advice. But I'd been keeping her at a distance by then.

"Right." She sounded disbelieving. "Just like when you resigned."

This one was easier. "Kaylee lost both parents in that explosion. She was having a really hard time -"

Reesa slammed her mouse onto the desk and swung her chair around to stare me down. "Spare me the bullshit, Lyle." She looked pissed off and fed up. "I know why you quit."

There was no way she knew.

No one did.

I shrugged. "Rees, I'm telling you -"

"Polygraph."

I stilled at that single word, caught off guard. "What?"

Reesa's gaze narrowed on me as she folded her arms across her chest and leaned back in her chair to watch me squirm. "You heard me." As I stared back at her, she held my eyes. "I have a friend in IA, remember?"

"You think I quit to avoid a *polygraph test?*" I went for sarcasm, figuring I still had a chance to throw her off the scent. "What, because of all those payoffs I took so I could buy a Ferrari and a big mansion... oh, wait, I don't have any of those things."

She scowled at me. "I never said you were on the take."

Then what *did* she think? "I quit because Kaylee needed me around. That's it."

Reesa snorted in angry disbelief. "Bull*shit*. You quit because of Jenny."

My heart raced. How much did she know? "What? I don't -"

"Oh cut the *crap*!" Reesa shoved up out of her chair and took an angry step forward, but when I looked into her eyes I saw mostly disappointment. "I *know*, Lyle," she said, slowly and carefully, like she wanted to make something crystal clear. "I knew the minute I saw you together."

Panic seized me, my heart rate speeding, breath stuttering in my throat. How had she -

"Even though you avoided her most of the time," she continued.

I felt my legs turn to Jell-O in relief, as I realized Reesa *didn't* know what I'd feared she might. But then... "What are you talking about?" I asked, not needing to fake my confusion.

"Your sister-in-law, of course." Reesa grimaced. "The one you're still in love with."

Chapter Six.

"I'm not."

And that was the truth. How could I still be in love with Jenny after she'd chosen my brother over me: the detective who was going places, instead of the rookie beat cop with no real aspirations beyond doing my job to the best of my ability? Even though I mostly blamed Michael for seducing her, the way he'd stolen pretty much every girlfriend I'd had growing up. But I'd still had my heart shattered because I'd believed Jenny was different; apparently not.

"But you're still protecting her." Reesa sounded cynical.

She obviously knew Jenny had something to do with why I'd quit the LAPD. I just hoped she was in the dark when it came to the details.

"Look," she went on, "I know you weren't involved with any of the shit Michael did..."

Good. Because truth was, I hadn't had a fucking clue about anything illegal my brother was up to. At least, not until right before everything hit the fan.

"But I think you found out sweet, innocent Jenny was involved too," Reesa said bitterly. "They were making you take a polygraph, so you quit rather than have it come out."

I froze in surprise. She *was* right, in a sense, but completely off the mark too. "That - that's ridiculous -"

"Come on, Lyle. How else did Michael hide his money so well? Why else was she there, on the boat?"

"She wasn't part of it."

"You don't know that," Reesa shot back. "You didn't even know about *Michael!*"

"Yeah - some detective, right? Maybe *that's* why I quit!" In that moment, I almost believed it myself.

Reesa didn't look convinced, but I saw an opening when she winced. "It wasn't just you, Lyle. Nobody else saw it either."

"Yeah, well, I should have. I was his brother."

Plus in retrospect it seemed so obvious. There'd been the big house and the private school for Kaylee; the new cars for both of them every year. But then they'd had two incomes coming in, and we'd all believed Michael when he told us Jenny's realtor business was wildly profitable. For years he'd blamed it for the life they were able to lead, sometimes joking around about being a kept man, always boasting about his brilliant, beautiful spouse.

Jenny had been present on at least one of those occasions, and she'd never corrected him. But she hadn't grown up around cops, so how would she even have known how much a Lieutenant should be making? She'd probably thought he was flattering her in front of their friends and family, modestly giving her more credit and playing up her successes.

Based on all the interviews I'd first offered voluntarily, then been forced to sit through until I finally quit, I knew IA suspected they'd been in it together. Particularly as she'd been on that boat with Michael at the end. There'd also been questions about their finances; how Michael's illicit earnings would have been noticed, if Jenny hadn't been at least *partially* complicit in helping to hide them.

But *I* needed to believe she hadn't known about the deals and criminal activity, or where her picture-perfect life really came from. After all, Michael had fooled both me and Len, not to mention his entire team, who'd been investigated for months and found to be clean. Okay, maybe near the very end Jenny *had* known something, but

I didn't blame her for being too afraid to speak up by that point.

Either way, my brother was the bad guy here. He'd been the one to make the deals with the gang members he was supposed to be arresting; helping to put drugs and guns back on the streets he was supposed to be cleaning up. So the truth was, I shouldn't be blaming Jenny *or* myself. I'd had no real reason to be suspicious of his lifestyle, and it wasn't like we'd ever worked on the same cases, or even in the same part of town most of the time.

"You weren't investigating him," Reesa pointed out, mirroring my own thoughts.

"I'm not saying that was the only reason I quit," I admitted. "I'm just... I'm just not..." *not able* "...not ready to talk about it yet." I forced myself to look Reesa in the eye. "Can't you just let it go? *Please?*"

She stared back at me for a long moment, then huffed out a breath. Turning back to her desk, she busied herself with Joey's photo again, as if a good distraction was exactly what she needed. "It fucking sucks, is all." She just sounded pissed off now, not furious. It was progress. "You loved being a cop..." she glared at me, "and you *were* a damn good detective, Lyle."

"I'm still a detective." I saw the disbelieving grimace on her face and corrected that statement. "Well, some days."

True, hunting down bail skips and cheating spouses didn't have the same kick of purpose and accomplishment as catching a killer. But I did get the occasional case that required more brain power than figuring out the best place to park to take incriminating photos and how soon I'd have to pee.

"And it's really good, the way it's working out." I conveniently blocked out Len's most recent tirade about how I sucked as a co-parent, and the fact that I'd missed more than half of Kaylee's musical. "I'm there for my niece when she needs me -"

Reesa snorted in disbelief. "Because PI work is so nine

to five?"

"I set my own hours." Okay, so they'd been seventy plus hours a week for the past few months, but that was just while the business was getting built up. "I'll be hiring an assistant soon, then I can scale back even more." What the hell was I saying? Hire someone? I'd cancel the damn maid service if it wasn't mandatory in the rental agreement.

Reesa stared at me for a long moment. Then something beeped at her from her desk and she turned to give it her full attention. "I'm gonna be a while," she said, not taking her eyes from the computer screen. "Maybe you should wait upstairs with your friend."

༜

An hour after Reesa kicked me out, I sat moodily in an armchair, watching Joey and his new best pal Carlos play video games on the floor in front of the TV.

Maybe you should wait upstairs with your friend.

Was she trying to say the two of *us* were no longer friends? Or was she simply fed up with the way I wouldn't be honest with her, even about something as relatively trivial as how much my new job sucked?

Yeah, it was probably both. I hadn't exactly been a good friend to Reesa for a while. And it wasn't just that I hadn't been around. Hell, I'd done such a good job cutting myself off from everyone I knew, I might not have heard even if she'd been in serious trouble. And yet here I'd come, waltzing back into her life because... what? Some random client needed her particular brand of help?

Okay, so Joey wasn't exactly a random client... come to think of it, he wasn't technically a client at all, despite his agreeing to hire me, as I hadn't collected the one-day advance I always demanded before I did a thing. Which was pretty dumb of me, since the guy could obviously afford my bargain basement prices if he could afford a suite at the Sunset Spire. I made a mental note to have a little chat with him about it once we were done here, and felt another surge of relief as my own body didn't painfully protest the idea.

I'd felt off kilter ever since I realized that - however improbably - my own health was somehow dependent on Joey and Bethany getting together. Good to be reminded I didn't have to play 'matchmaker' *pro bono*.

Was that why I'd come to Reesa instead of going somewhere else - because I knew she'd help, even if I couldn't pay her? No, I thought immediately; I'd simply wanted a friend I knew I could rely on to help me through this.

Not that I'd told her the truth about what was happening, not by a long shot. Still, it felt really good to have Rees in my corner, even if she didn't know the stakes. She'd always had my back in the past, whether it was offering advice on one of my cases or making sure I didn't down too many beers after a bad shift. To be fair, I'd done the same for her. Even after she quit, we'd played that role for each other... until I'd dropped off the map last year.

Again, guilt shot through me at how badly I'd abandoned our friendship. What if she'd needed *me* for some reason? Oh sure, Reesa could take care of herself physically. She might have ridden a desk in Computer Crimes, but I'd seen her sparring at the gym and she could take down a guy twice her weight without blinking. Still, everyone needed a shoulder to lean on - or cry on - every once in a while, and that's who we'd been to each other for more than half a decade.

Something unpleasant twisted in my gut as I wondered who she'd turned to when I stopped picking up the phone. It wasn't like I'd found anyone to take Reesa's place as my best friend and confidante - mostly because, if I couldn't even tell *Reesa*, there was no point looking for anyone else. No one was smarter or more devoted and loyal... *and great, I was making her sound like a St. Bernard.* But just because I'd drawn into myself, didn't mean she had, too.

I glanced around the living room, looking for evidence of a new person in Reesa's life. At work, neither of us had been big on putting up portraits of family and friends - unlike some detectives, who'd liked to plaster their spouses and kids all over their computer screens and desks. It wasn't that we didn't care, more we didn't like to expose who we cared about most. You put someone's image out there, you had to talk about them, share stories - and that broke the dividing line between work and home. Even if you only *thought* about them, bringing the people you loved into a world where violence and selfishness had led to misery and death... it just felt wrong.

But at home... at home, Reesa was the Queen of Photographs. Maybe because of the hobby that was now her full-time job. Frames adorned pretty much every surface in the living room, except the top of the tall bookcases and the wall behind the TV - but almost none of them held those stiff portraits you saw on most people's walls. Yeah, there were a couple of obligatory ones: the newborn shot of Carlos; Reesa's police academy graduation photo. But the rest were mostly candid shots.

My eyes traveled over them, dreading finding out that the ones of me had been removed... but they were all still there. The one from the day we'd met, when I'd somehow tripped over a wastebasket on the way out of a briefing room, and taken down a desk and a scalding cup of coffee trying to save myself. It had been the closest I'd come to a Three Stooges moment my entire life. With the (relatively) good-natured jeers and laughter of my brethren ringing in my ears, I'd looked up from the pool of hot liquid I was sitting in to see the new 'tech geek' we'd been assigned, capturing the moment for posterity on her phone. You'd have thought that would've started us out as enemies, right?

But while the others had just grinned or slapped my arm as they walked out, Reesa had put her phone down and helped me up, then fetched some paper towels to clean up the mess before the Sergeant got pissy. Pretty soon we were cracking elements of the case together, working through ideas and evidence over midnight coffees at the local diner - and the rest is history. At least it was, until she quit for bigger things and I... well, I screwed up my life.

Searching through the other photos, I saw a lot that I remembered, and only a couple that looked new. Mostly of Carlos or of some outdoor scene Reesa liked. A couple of her with a female friend at the beach or on a hike. None that showed -

I checked myself as I realized I was searching each photo for a new guy.

"They're fakes."

Joey practically leapt up from the carpet as Reesa spoke from the doorway behind us. She looked tired in the better light up here - shadows under her eyes, tiny crow's feet at their corners. Did she have those when I'd last seen her in person? That had been the evening she'd tracked me down to confront me about why I'd really resigned, and I'd lied my ass off to her. I guessed a lot could change in nine months.

Or maybe I'd never really looked for her weaknesses before. Reesa had always had a vibrancy about her that made her seem larger than life; like she could conquer any problem. Something seemed different about her now, though. Maybe it was just the time we'd spent apart, or the different needs of her new job, but -

"You can prove that?" Joey asked, desperate hope in his voice.

I forced myself to focus on the current task. Namely, getting Joey and Bethany back together so that I could - *I hoped* - get on with my life.

"Sure." Reesa smirked and handed Joey a letter-sized envelope. Not me. Joey. Who she just met an hour ago. Of course, he *was* the client, so -

"Really?" Joey took the thing like it was made of glass,

while I fought the urge to grab it away from him, crossing my arms over my chest just to make sure I didn't.

"Yeah - for starters, the specular highlights are all wrong..." Reesa continued, then stopped as she saw Joey's puzzled frown. "Don't worry. I explained it all in my report." She nodded to the envelope then leaned against the door frame. "Someone really has it in for you, huh?"

"My father-in-law."

Reesa made a face. "Well, he must be loaded, because that work was good."

Joey made a face in return. "Yeah, he is."

Much as it was fun seeing them 'bond' (okay, it wasn't), I was acutely aware that Reesa hadn't once looked me in the eye since she'd come upstairs. "How much do we owe you?" I queried, hoping she'd look at me at last.

Reesa shrugged and looked over to where Carlos still lay on the carpet, killing alien gangsters. "I'll bill you." She turned away as if she were planning to go straight back downstairs. "You know the way out." Then she paused, and for a second I thought she'd reconsidered - but it was only to give Joey a quick nod. "Good luck. I have a feeling you're gonna need it."

I chose to believe that had been solely aimed at the father-in-law situation, and not a subtle dig about my abilities as a PI. "Hey, Rees?"

She stopped in the doorway, still not looking straight at me.

"Are you okay? Is... is there anything you could use a hand with?"

I willed her to turn around, but when she finally did there was only contempt in her eyes. "I don't need your help," she said coldly, as if our brief *détente* in the basement had never happened. "I've done just fine without you around."

And that was when I knew - just as surely as if she'd admitted it - that Reesa *was* in trouble of some kind. I also knew she wasn't going to tell me about it, because she no longer trusted me. Not because she thought I'd been a dirty cop like Michael, but because I'd abandoned our friendship like it meant nothing to me.

Fuck.

She must think I'd only come to her now because it was expedient; because a paying job was on the line. And how was I supposed to explain that this 'situation' was more than just a job to me? That - even though I'd only just admitted it to myself - I'd come to her seeking a friend more than anything else?

Dammit. The secrets I couldn't tell her had kept us apart this long, and now I was desperate to share another one. Except I knew she'd never buy my story - heck, I'd *been* there, and I still wasn't sure I believed what I'd seen.

Yep. If there were higher powers at work, they were royally screwing with me.

"Rees, I'm sorr-"

"Just leave."

Reesa turned away and went back through the basement door, slamming it behind her.

"You should probably go now."

I looked over to see Carlos staring me down from where he stood in the middle of the carpet, game console hanging loosely from his hand. Behind him on the huge screen, someone's - I was guessing his - unattended avatar met an ugly death, the screen flashing warnings about lost lives. It was good to know Reesa's nephew had his priorities right.

Still, I couldn't just walk out of there without trying.

"Is she all right?"

"She's fine." I thought that was all I was getting, until Carlos shrugged and added, "But maybe she'd be better if you were around more." He turned his back on us too then, going back to his place on the floor. I wondered what other profound, Yoda-like words would come out of his mouth... but he just started up his game again, cursing under his breath when he saw his player was down.

He was only thirteen, after all.

ॐ

Joey wouldn't stop bugging me on the way back to my car. "So... you and Reesa, are you like -?"

"Nothing's going on." I shut him down hard. Or at least I tried to.

"But something was before?" he persisted. "When you were both cops?"

I glared at him over the car roof. "You think just because two people work together they're gonna end up sleeping with each other?"

"Of course not." He waited until we were backing down Reesa's driveway before adding, "They usually do, though, if there's any kind of vibe."

Don't ask. Don't ask... "You think we have a vibe?"

Joey smirked at me. The bastard. "Kind of reminds me of my dad and stepmom. They worked together too... before they hooked up," he added slyly.

I scrambled to change the subject. "What line of work?"

I'd unwittingly picked a good distraction topic, because Joey's smile died. "He's my manager. Mostly he deals with the acting side though." He cracked his knuckles noisily; a nervous tick, I figured, and hoped he'd stop since we'd be stuck on the road together for another hour at this time of the evening. "He and Gerry never got along once I got into music more. Dad thought Gerry was pushing me to do too much."

"Like what?"

Joey made a sound of disgust. "I was a fifteen-year-old virgin, and he wanted to make people think I was sleeping with another of his 'stars' because we both had albums coming out and it'd be good PR."

I shot Joey a quick glance out of the corner of my eye, taking in the distressed denim jeans and designer shirt under an expensive leather jacket. It suddenly struck me that - while he was rocking the whole rock star look - he never played the part. No pushy demands or acting like he was too precious to open his own car door. At Reesa's place, I'd even found him helping Carlos with his homework when I came upstairs from the basement. And he'd gotten right down on the carpet to play video games, keeping the kid happy and entertained while Reesa worked, whereas I'd just sat there on the sofa feeling sorry for myself.

For the first time, I found myself hoping we succeeded for Joey's sake, not just to save my own ass or because I didn't like to fail. Even if personally I'd rather slit my own throat rather than be stuck with *Bethany* as my wife.

Of course, I felt that way about marriage in general, so -

I felt my phone buzz with an incoming text in my pocket and pulled it out, unlocking the screen then handing it over to Joey since I was driving. "What does it say?"

"It's from someone called Alex..." Joey grew excited as he read the message, "he says he's found Sophia!" A pause, then: "What do we need dirt on her for?"

I wanted to grab the phone back and see for myself what Alex had written. The type of search he'd run for me was the kind I'd run a thousand times myself, but with everything else going on I hadn't had the time - or focus - to do it myself, so I'd called in a favor from a fellow investigator who'd owed me. "What does it say? From the start."

Joey still sounded uncertain as he read the text aloud. "Sophia Wilde, 625 Culver Avenue, Hollywood. No dirt on her yet. Still checking." He paused, then said "There's another text: How did the big date go? Jimmy."

I braced for more interrogation about my love life, but fortunately Joey was too stuck on the Sophia Wilde stuff.

"So? Why's this guy trying to find stuff on Sophia? We

can just show her the proof the photos are faked, and she'll cave - right?"

How could Joey have spent nearly his whole life in the entertainment business and still be that naïve? I wondered. Oh, right: he was from Canada. Poor kid was just too nice. "Gerry's a powerful, connected guy. We need leverage to get Sophia to admit he was behind those photos, so she's more worried about us than about him retaliating."

I half expected Joey to ask how Gerry could be vile enough to do something like that... but I guess there was naïve and then there was just plain stupid.

Instead, I heard him sigh. "I just don't want Bethany hurt."

Yep. Definitely too nice.

&

It wasn't until I pulled my Toyota up behind Len's station wagon on the driveway that I realized I'd zoned out again. I'd meant to swing by the Sunset Spire hotel to drop Joey off... although maybe this time I'd just conveniently forgotten, since Hollywood wasn't exactly on my way home to Silver Lake from Boyle Heights.

"This your place?" Joey looked out at the hillside community just starting to light up in the growing dusk.

"Yep." Oh well. At least this time I hadn't shown up where anyone wanted to punch me out. I sighed and climbed out of the car, Joey following suit. If he wanted a ride back to his hotel, he could Lyft it again. Or Uber it, or whatever other noun-verbs there were. And at least he'd give the driver a thrill, assuming he got recognized.

"Oh. My. *God!* Joey Russo?!"

An ecstatic - yet also totally freaked out - Kaylee stood by the recycling container at the rear of the house, clad in her favorite Hello Kitty pajama bottoms and a ripped Led Zeppelin T-shirt she'd stolen from me, despite (I was pretty sure) having zero clue who they were.

She definitely knew who Joey Russo was, though.

"Why didn't you *tell* us you were bringing someone home?"

I could hear the edge of something in her voice, and from the quick glare she shot me I knew I was in trouble. I wasn't sure exactly why as yet, but I might've counted my chickens prematurely about not getting beaten up tonight.

"I'm not even *dressed*!" she added with hissing emphasis on the last word, and at that point even my dumb male brain finally got it. I guess no teenage girl dreams of meeting a young, handsome rock star with a large white cat stuck all over her bottom.

"You're kidding, right?" Joey stepped forward, looking suitably awed. "Those pants are low-key retro, and that T-shirt is *lit*."

I barely understood what Joey had just said, but when Kaylee blushed and grinned I could've kissed him on the lips.

Thankfully, before I could act on any such impulse, Len threw open the screen door and peered out at us from inside. "What're you all doing out there? Dinner's getting cold in here!"

Thank crap I'd auto-piloted it home.

Dinner in the Thatcher household had been a big production when we all lived together, my father kicking up a huge fuss if it wasn't on the table - or if we weren't all there, ready to eat - when he got home from his shift. Most of my elementary school years had involved doing homework and maybe going across the street to hang out with my friends, but always - *always* - being back in the house, washed up and tidy, by six forty-five. Even if Len had called at the last minute and said he'd be late - which happened more and more once the heavy drinking started, the excuses going from genuine to total bullshit to, eventually, nothing - Mom, Michael and I always sat down and started eating then, just in case he showed up and threw a fit.

Or maybe sticking to his schedule had helped Mom pretend things were fine in their marriage, even though he was getting home drunk and stinking of other women. He'd tell her he had "one drink" to unwind with his squad, and passed the perfume off as badge bunnies coming on to him.

Of course, after Len had cheated on Mom for enough years that she finally had to admit it and threw him out, things were bound to change. For a few years it was still the three of us, so the basic format was the same. Except, without our father there to 'scare us straight,' Michael and I would play hooky from time to time. And once he was fifteen and dating, we'd barely see Michael for days.

Then Mom first got sick the year I started high school, and Michael made more of an effort to be around - even though by then he was in college and had a lot of other stuff in his life. She got better that time, but it made us more aware that family dinners were important - especially since we didn't want Mom having to cook and tire herself out. So Michael and I took turns making the food, or - just as often - took the lead to order in pizza or Mexican food or something else. Dad was never around, but at least the alimony and child support paid for it.

And then there were the years when we all kind of drifted apart again. Michael was a young cop, living in a sweet bachelor pad in Venice, and I was getting my Bachelors in Criminal Justice down in San Diego. But even so, we'd try to meet up every other Sunday - and we always got together for the big holiday meals.

I had bittersweet memories of our last Thanksgiving before Mom died. She'd wanted to make it special - a real celebration - since Michael had just made it into vice, and my first serious girlfriend Jenny would be there too.

The next month, Mom finally told us the cancer was back.

Once Mom was gone - and Michael and I had fallen

out over Jenny - there was no family left to have dinner together. Sure, once Kaylee was a toddler, Michael and Jenny had started asking me over every so often, and then Dad had started AA and shown up from time to time. But there'd never been any kind of formal day or time.

Except... after Kaylee and I had moved back in with Len, it was like we'd reverted to my childhood. Now every night was Family Dinner Night again, and I was in deep shit if I forgot to call by mid-afternoon and say I'd be missing it, even if I had a last minute stakeout or some place I needed to be for a job.

If it had just been Len I might've blown it off more... but I wanted to do right by Kaylee. Plus my father was always a *major* pain in the ass whenever I screwed up his precious dinners. Pretty ironic for a guy who'd never appreciated his wife cooking for him every night and had skipped those meals whenever it suited him. But then, fairness was never a big thing with Len.

Last month I'd sinned big time by missing the big one - a Sunday night - because I had to spend forty-eight hours straight on a surveillance job. I'd gotten home only a couple hours before dawn... and the fucker had taken it out on me by using a chainsaw outside my window at *seven in the morning.*

So bottom line, even though it was weird as hell to be sitting around the kitchen table, trying to eat my father's dry beef lasagna while Kaylee and Len stared obsessively at Joey (albeit for different reasons), it was *way* better than the alternative if I hadn't shown up.

Honestly, though? The way my remaining blood relatives were acting right now gave me a whole new empathy for women and gay men everywhere, who had to watch their new boyfriend get the third degree after they brought him home. I'm pretty sure Len wouldn't have glared at a woman the way he was eyeballing our male dinner guest, and as for Kaylee... let's just say it was the first time I was *glad* that Joey was Bethany-obsessed.

"So how long have you known Uncle Lyle?" my niece asked sweetly, fluttering her eyelashes in a way I hoped was more fangirl than flirty, even as she worked her powerful arm muscles to saw through the solid layer of burnt pasta at the top of her bowl. I might be more of an 'eat to live' than 'live to eat' kind of guy, but it didn't take Gordon Ramsay to know Len's cooking was awful.

Joey sent me a nervous glance, and I guessed he wasn't comfortable spilling the painful details of his failing marriage with a teenage fan he'd met less than fifteen minutes ago.

Some people are weird introverts that way.

I jumped in to answer for him. "Just a couple of days. I'm helping him out with some... um... contract stuff." A marriage was a contract, right?

Len shot me a narrow-eyed look that said he wasn't buying it.

But before he could open his mouth to interrogate me, Kaylee beat him to the punch. "Cool!" She put down her knife and fork and leaned forward eagerly, revealing *waaay* more of her cleavage than I thought appropriate. I really wished she'd stuck with the Led Zeppelin / Hello Kitty mash-up, but in the time it had taken for Len to serve dinner she'd snuck upstairs and changed. A complete contrast to the 'teen pajama party' outfit of before, this one seemed more appropriate for a night out in West Hollywood... during the annual Halloween Carnaval. I'd mentally dubbed it 'Teen Elvira' and would've sent her back to her room to change again, except I knew Joey wasn't a problem and I knew Kaylee would be mortified if I tried.

Plus I had to admit, I was kind of interested in how much the vein on Len's neck could pulse before it blew. Of course, he was probably torn between thinking Joey was gonna steal his precious granddaughter and figuring Joey was another 'fruit' - in Len world, any guy who wore eyeliner was gay - so most likely the old man didn't know if he was coming or going...

Even better.

"So are you gonna, like, reinvent yourself for your comeback?"

I tried not to openly wince at Kaylee's question, since a comeback basically implied you'd faded away.

But Joey took it in his stride, shrugging his shoulders. "You think I should?"

"Well..." Kaylee shot me a nervous look.

Yeah, you started it, I thought. I raised an eyebrow, which seemed to encourage her to go on.

"I mean, you were just a kid before, right? But now you're all grown up." She gave Joey an appraising look that sent a shiver down my spine. When had my baby niece turned into a young woman? When had she started looking at *guys*? I cleared my throat, unwilling to hear more, but before I could make some dumb comment about the food or the weather, she continued, "You could have a whole new image. Like, I don't know: hot bad boy punk rocker..." I groaned inwardly; was *that* what she'd been picturing? "...or sexy crooner..." this was just getting worse, "...or even, like, *country singer* if that's what you wanted."

Joey grinned. "Yee haw."

Kaylee blushed. "Maybe not..."

"No! No, you're right." Joey gave a twisted smile. "It's kind of what Bethany says, too." Then his smile abruptly died and he stopped talking.

I opened my mouth to change the subject, but Kaylee spoke before I could, asking innocently, "Who's Bethany?"

Urgh. Letting Kaylee know the rock star at our dinner table was married was probably a good thing, but I didn't want Joey getting drunk off his ass again tonight.

But he sounded okay, almost defiant, as he answered. "She's my wife."

Kaylee's eyes went wide - and to my relief, she looked pleased not devastated. "OMG, you got *married*? *When*?!"

"A few months ago." Joey tried to smile but it didn't reach his eyes, and I could tell Len had noticed too. Even now, his cop brain was probably putting together unhappy marriage with PI and coming up with sleazy divorce case stakeouts. Hey, if only it were that easy.

"Whoa!" Apparently oblivious to the signs, Kaylee plunged on. "I mean, you must've kept it *so* quiet or, like, TMZ or Perez would've totally had it by now." She paused, reconsidering. "Although, I mean, they did completely miss Alexis and Mila being pregnant, like, *twice*."

The mere fact that I knew what Kaylee was talking about told me I'd been spending waaay too much time browsing the internet on stakeouts. It makes you wonder what previous generations put in the brain space we give up to celebrity news crap, viral blog entries, and cute cat videos. Probably stuff like an in-depth knowledge of world history, or learnings from ancient books of philosophy. Maybe a foreign language or two.

But hey, we got Wikipedia and Google translate, so at least we can still look shit up. Here's hoping the power never goes out for good, right?

"So... what was your wife's advice?"

I tensed at the further reference to Bethany, but Joey surprised me by cheering up a little. "She likes the songs I write myself; thinks I should focus on those."

"What kind of songs are they?"

I sat back and chewed on my mouthful - Len's food always took a lot of chewing - as I watched Kaylee prying info out of Joey like he was an old friend. He, in turn, looked pleased by all the questions - which seemed kind of weird, given that this was his line of work and surely he must have better people to discuss it with than a teenage fan and a couple of tone-deaf ex cops.

Joey looked slightly embarrassed. "Mostly ballads - you know, love songs, that kind of thing."

Kaylee sighed. "Ooh, I *loved* 'I Will Never Leave You'."

The one Joey had been blasting from the top of the poolhouse.

Joey practically swelled with pride. "Yep, that was one of mine."

I frowned, though. Hadn't Gerry said he'd had that written for him? I decided not to embarrass Joey by pointing this out, but in the end it wasn't up to me because the doorbell rang at that moment.

Len grunted in annoyance and shot an aggrieved look at Kaylee, who leapt up from her chair and practically ran for the front door. A bad thought hitting me, I jumped up too and followed her into the hall, catching her just as she reached it.

"Tell me you didn't invite friends over to meet Joey."

Kaylee frowned up at me as she reached for the peephole Len had trained her to always use, genuine hurt in her expression. "My friend Jason comes over sometimes to borrow one of my books. He only lives across the street." Pulling her eyes from me, she turned to check who stood outside. "Grandpa hates it when he just shows... Oh."

Letting the peephole swing shut, Kaylee stepped back from the door with a shrug. "Don't think it's for me." She lowered her voice as if they might be able to hear her from outside, which didn't seem likely; ex-cop Len was nothing if not anal about home security, and he'd insisted on some pretty solid doors and windows being installed. "Looks more like one of those church ladies."

Church ladies?

I moved to look through the peephole myself, as Kaylee continued, still in almost a whisper, "You know, the ones who come around on Sundays?"

As I took in the woman standing outside under the porch light, I could see what Kaylee meant. In her prim, dark gray dress and small feathered hat, a large gray purse hanging from one hand, she looked just like one of the Jehovah's Witnesses who seemingly never gave up on trying to convert my father.

Except for the fact that the feathers were bright purple.

It was the crazy old bat from the wedding. The one who'd Tasered me, or... *something.* The one I was pretty sure had given me nightmares, hallucinations, and an inescapable compulsion to play Cupid.

I'd wanted to find her... hell, I'd wanted to *throttle* her.

I just hadn't planned on her finding me first.

Chapter Seven.

I sent Kaylee back to the kitchen before I cautiously opened the front door.

I don't know what I was expecting, exactly: maybe for the old woman to light me up again, zap me into another dimension, or reveal herself as some kind of demon.

Instead, I found myself staring warily at the epitome of Harmless Little Old Lady. Which, after a second or two, made me feel pretty damn stupid.

"Yes?" I demanded nervously.

HLOL smiled up at me, blinking behind her glasses... and yeah, they were the same freaky ones as before, although at least this time their bright orange glow didn't clash with everything else she was wearing. That didn't make me feel any better, though. "I'd like to hire you," she said happily, as if it were the most normal thing in the world for clients to show up after 8 p.m. at the front doorstep of my home.

"How did you find me here?"

She blinked again, seeming puzzled. "You were in the Yellow Pages..."

Yeah, right - like I'd put my home address in the -

"See?" Beaming, she thrust a folded up sheet of paper into my hand.

I unfurled the yellow sheet, checking down it until I reached the pen-circled advertisement, and... *what?* My home address was right there, front and center.

I thought back to the week I'd placed the ad. Too many

stakeouts, juggled priorities, and late nights. Could I have screwed up and typed in the wrong address on auto-pilot? Although... *wait a second...* how had she even known my *name* to begin with...?

Realizing I was letting myself get distracted, I crumpled the sheet of paper in my hand. Her knowing my name and address was odd, sure, but her doing something weird and witchy that left me with a big-ass tattoo on my chest and the recurring sense that I was dying in agony - now *that* was where I should be focusing.

Eye on the prize, Lyle.

Eye on the prize.

"Okay, lady..." I folded my arms and loomed over her - which wasn't difficult, since she was about five two to my six feet, not to mention I was standing on a higher step. "What the *fuck* did you do to me when you hit me in the chest?"

"Language, young man," she said reprovingly.

"So you're not gonna deny it?" I wasn't exactly thinking it through as I yanked my shirt up and gestured angrily to the tattoo underneath. "And what the hell is *this*?!"

Across the street, two runners catcalled and wolf-whistled as they jogged past.

"Nice abs," my visitor commented, raising her hand as if she wanted to have a feel.

I backed away, jerking the shirt down over my torso again. "Don't touch me, you crazy old bat!"

But as I glared at her, it struck me. The crazy I'd seen in her eyes before, the loopiness that said she was one sandwich short of a picnic... it wasn't there any more. Instead, there was a quick intelligence in her gaze; a wicked amusement in her barely hidden smirk. She sighed regretfully as she lowered her hand again... and I noticed that now it didn't shake at all.

"Who *are* you?" I murmured, feeling a chill run down my spine.

As I waited for her answer, there was a moment of

doubt; a moment in which I wondered if I'd become the kind of ageist asshole who sees someone with gray hair, someone stooped over, and just assumes they're mentally deficient. Had I dismissed her as 'not all there' when really she was just a little eccentric?

But then she grinned... and there was a twinkle in her eyes as she visibly - *and completely* - shed the distracted old lady persona she'd used up until that point. "Wouldn't you like to know."

I'd been conned, I realized.

By a pro.

I still struggled to understand what was going on here. "You did something to me," I stated, determined to take my chance to get a straight answer out of her now that she'd dropped the act.

She simply smiled back. Then she stepped past me into the hallway and trotted unerringly toward the living room.

I closed the door to the street and followed her in there, closing that door behind me too -

- then blinked, wondering exactly how that had happened. For one thing, I'm pretty broad-shouldered, which meant I'd been effectively blocking our small front entrance. So how had she 'stepped past me' at all? And why hadn't I stopped her or called out, instead of blindly following her in here *and closing the door*?

The shock to my system somehow made me angry instead of scared. "Who *are* you?" I demanded.

"You may call me Mara," she said.

"Okay, *Mara*, what did you to do me?"

"Do?"

I took a step forward, putting myself well into her personal space. Right now, I just didn't care. "You shocked me in the chest..." I forced myself to go on, "and I didn't have this crazy tattoo until then!"

Mara sent me a conspiratorial grin. "Trust me; in the end, you'll appreciate it!"

Huh?

"I don't 'appreciate' a giant tattoo I can't explain!" I was building up a real head of steam now. "Especially when my fucking *health* is tied to the screwed up love lives of *total strangers!*"

Mara smiled delightedly and clapped her tiny hands together. "Oh, clever boy!" She suddenly reminded me of a scheming, slightly deranged Bette Davis, smiling wide-eyed at her victim in one of the old black and white movies I'd watched with my mom growing up. "I *knew* you'd figure it out!"

"Figured *what* out?" I yelled.

She waggled a finger at me, smirking. "Now now," she admonished, "settle down." Even as I glared back at her, Mara's attention drifted, becoming fixed on a photo sitting atop our ancient TV set.

"Hey, answer me!"

Totally ignoring my wrath, Mara trotted over to the photo, smiling as she picked it up for closer inspection. She was so fucking smug, it drove me nuts. Gritting my teeth, I had the urge to grab her by the shoulders and shake her until she lost that smirk. But I wasn't into violence except in self-defense, and it wasn't like she was actually attacking me, even if she had assaulted me at the wedding.

Instead, I just glared at her as she continued to amble around the living room, peering at the photos and knickknacks on the mantelpiece; the books on the shelves.

Had she Tasered me, then hit me with some designer drug that made me hallucinate crazy shit for the past twenty-four hours? Sure, I felt completely myself - fully in control of my mental faculties - most of the time. But maybe it was some kind of timed release deal?

I mean, let's face it.

It was either that, or Mara was a *witch*.

The woman in question swung around to face me, her eyes glinting with humor. "I assure you, I'm no more supernatural than you are." She paused as if considering. "Well... perhaps that's not saying much any more."

I took a step forward, unable to restrain myself. "What the hell does *that* mean?"

Mara waved her hands. "Oh calm yourself. I'm simply saying that we're both gifted with certain... *abilities* now."

"*Gifted* with abilities?" I stomped another step forward, barely preventing myself from looming over her the way I *reaaally* wanted to right now. "Are you kidding? I'm *cursed!*"

She seemed unperturbed. "It might *feel* that way, until you're used to it -"

"I'm a fucking Genie in a bottle!" I raged, pissed off beyond belief. I'd had enough time to think by this point, and it had become increasingly clear to me that I was basically Joey and Bethany's very own love-life wrangler, regardless of the fact that I was unpaid, unwilling... and let's not forget, utterly *unsuited* to the job. Why the hell had *I* been signed up for this anyway? And what made their lives so much more important than mine? I felt my anger build as I remembered each time one of them had asked for my help and - no matter how much I'd resisted - I'd been compelled to give in.

Would that be my life from now on? A dog either one of them could call to heel any time their relationship was on the rocks? Oh shit. I thought about it: a spoiled princess and a rock musician - they might *never* be stable. I pictured years - no, *decades* - of putting my entire career and personal life on hold every time Joey smiled at a backup dancer and Bethany felt insecure. I'd never be able to run a business - hell, I'd barely be able to function. If Joey went on tour, would I have to go too -?

A sharp *crack* filled the room as Mara's slender palm connected with my jaw.

I stumbled back in surprise, almost tripping over the sofa. I collapsed onto it instead, like a puppet with my wires cut. Only then did I realize my heart had been beating out of my chest, my inhales and exhales more pants than breaths. I'd regularly been in in dangerous, stressful situations for the past fourteen years - I'd even thrown up after my first undercover stint. But never before had I come close to hyperventilating. I guess it's like they say: loss of control really is the scariest thing of all.

"Good *gods*!" Mara stood over me, exasperation in her voice. Then she seemed to soften. With another sigh, she sat down next to me, reaching out a hand to pat my thigh. "Some big tough police detective *you* are."

But she sounded fond rather than critical, and for the first time... for some reason... I didn't see her as the enemy. I met her eyes, all bluster gone; deep into desperation territory. "What did you do to me?" I asked quietly.

"And you see, that's just why I came here," she said reassuringly. "To put your mind at ease. Explain how all of this works and what you need to do to end the link with your couple."

End? Ending it would be good.

"And I will..." she brushed an imaginary piece of lint from her skirt; was she finally nervous about something? "...provided you do a *tiny* favor for me first."

I ground my teeth. So much for not seeing her as the enemy. Maybe it was my cop instincts telling me doing favors was never a good thing. Maybe it was the way she was suddenly acting coy. But something told me whatever she wanted wouldn't be small, or easy. "What is it?"

"I need Leroy out of jail so he and Tanya can get married."

I nearly laughed in her face. A prison break. That was the 'tiny favor' she wanted?

Maybe she really *was* crazy.

Mara scowled at me before I could say anything. "Oh come on," she snapped, her tone implying I was an idiot, "I'm not asking you to do anything *illegal*."

I frowned, realizing this wasn't the first time she'd seemed to read my mind. But then, probably she was just good at reading people's expressions.

Most con artists were.

"Then what *do* you want?" I asked suspiciously.

"Leroy claims to be innocent. And I'm inclined to believe him." Mara smiled at me. "I just need you to prove it." She stood up and adjusted her neat little purse where it hung over her shoulder. "For a detective like you, it should be easy."

She headed for the living rom door - and I was up and in front of her in a flash, blocking her exit. "Hey! What happened to explaining what you *did* to me?" I glared at her. "And more to the point, *undoing* it?!"

Mara regarded me thoughtfully, her owlish gaze behind those huge glasses reminding me uncomfortably of the first time I'd met her. "I decided an incentive would be useful. But don't worry: once Leroy is free to be with Tanya, I promise I'll give you what you need."

"So I do what you want, or you leave me stuck like this?"

Mara blinked back at me then gave a little shrug. "I suppose so," she admitted, her voice tinged with apology.

Ugh! How could she act so mild and harmless then turn into some kind of senior citizen version of Mata Hari? Even now I couldn't tell if she was genuinely regretful or inwardly laughing at me - or maybe it was *both*. Mara certainly seemed to have multiple personalities.

I wanted to rail at her, force her to undo whatever hex she'd put on me. Hell, I wanted to get her arrested, see her cuffed to a table in one of those cells where the lighting made the walls look sick and everything smelled of stale coffee. Go at her for hours until she broke down and gave up everything.

But who was I kidding? No cop in their right mind would believe my story. So unless I was willing to tie her up in Len's basement and see if she cracked after a few days, I was shit out of options. And even if I was crazy enough to do that, I wasn't about to apply interrogation tactics to anyone her age... although I figured Mara was a *lot* tougher than she looked.

"Fine," I snarled eventually. "I'll check into Leroy's innocence for you -"

She held up a cautioning finger. "*Prove* his innocence."

"What?" I fought to keep my temper. "You just said it yourself - you're not even sure he *is* innocent!"

"But I have wonderful instincts about people." She smiled wickedly. "I chose you, didn't I?"

The implication in those words distracted me briefly... and in that instant she stepped around me, heading for the door. I moved to intercept her again, but she was surprisingly fast and made it out into the hallway before I could.

"I'll expect a report on your progress tomorrow morning," she said as I followed her out, moving toward the front door. Acting like she was just another client - which pissed me off even more.

"Hey!" I snapped "I didn't even say I'd do it yet!"

Hand on the doorknob, she turned back to me with a half amused, half pitying expression on her face. Yep, there were those dual personalities again. "There really is no alternative."

I fumed at her audacity. "Look, lady, I -"

"You done with your business meeting then?"

I looked around to find Len glaring at me in his usual disparaging manner from the foot of the stairs. "Can you give us a sec?" I bit out, annoyed at getting it on two fronts now.

Len looked puzzled. "I thought your lady friend left."

Huh? I gestured to the old woman standing behind me. "Does it *look* like she left?"

My father frowned past me, then stared back at me like I was nuts. "Yeah."

I spun back around... and realized Mara must've fled when I turned my back to speak to Len. *Pathetic.* I stormed toward the front door and yanked it open. If she thought leaving mid-argument would secure her victory, she was acting like a twelve-year-old kid -

I came to a stop less than a foot outside the door, my head swiveling in confusion. I had an uninterrupted view of the driveway and the sidewalk for about fifty yards in both directions... and there was no sign of her there. Unfreezing my feet, I hurried down to the road in case she was hiding behind one of the cars - then peered through a few windows in case she was actually *in* one of them - but still nothing. I even got down on the ground and peered under them... nothing but air.

Okay, that was impossible.

Unless...

Grinding my teeth, I went back into the house and stalked my way toward the living room, unsurprised when the play of light under the door signaled movement in there.

I wasn't sure how she'd doubled back on me, but -

Len looked up as I burst in. He was over by the desk, studying a piece of paper in his hands. "At least she's paying you good money," he grunted, then handed it to me as he left the room.

Still trying to wrap my head around things, it took me a few seconds to focus on what I held. It was a check, made out to 'Lyle Thatcher Investigations' in the amount of Five Thousand Dollars.

Five Thousand Dollars?

My eyes flicked over to the account name in the upper left corner - which read simply *Ms. Mara K. Thetchem*, with no address. Gritting my teeth, I checked the memo line next. In neat writing sat a single short phrase: 'Leroy is innocent.'

I glared around the room, like I was expecting her to be hiding somewhere. But no, it was empty. I had the urge to check the entire house then, the logical part of my brain insisting she must have doubled back and gone out the back way or something. After all, she couldn't have just disappeared off the front doorstep. And I knew damn well that check hadn't been sitting on the desk when I'd left. Maybe Len had been in on it - yeah!

But the whole time, a cold feeling was gathering in the pit of my stomach. Because deep down I knew she hadn't pulled some kind of Ninja move to evade me, or done a deal with my father to mess with my sanity. Just like deep down I knew I didn't have brain cancer or some other illness that was making me see and feel things that weren't there.

Deep down, as I gripped that small piece of paper so hard I almost ripped it, I knew that the whole world had suddenly changed around me. Crazy as it seemed, my new normal was a world in which the old rules didn't apply. And as out of control my life had seemed just a day ago, it was a thousand times more screwed up now. Like, in what universe did I hold a check for *five thousand dollars* and wish that it would disappear?

I found myself staring at the bottles in Len's old-fashioned drinks cabinet, mounted on the wall over by the window. God only knew why he still kept it stocked with booze, since he'd been in AA for years and I was the only one who drank anything at all.

Maybe a shot - or two - would help.

Instead, I forced myself back into the kitchen, seeking out a shot of familiarity and normalcy instead.

Of course, this risked running into another episode of being baited by my father, but luck was with me for once. Len sat next to Kaylee, mercifully distracted as he peered over her shoulder at something on her laptop.

"See?"

Len frowned in at Kaylee's screen and wrinkled his nose. "No."

"Grandpa...!" Kaylee looked beyond frustrated. No doubt she was trying to teach him something related to social media again. "It's right there - right after the w-w-w!"

"Ohh." Len made a slightly ashamed face. "Sorry."

Kaylee looked guilty and twisted around to kiss him on the cheek. "You're doing great. Just remember: if you can't figure something out, Google is your friend."

"I will."

He seemed so earnest.

Little did Kaylee know, Len was faking his inability to master modern tech. Sure, he'd been stubborn at the start - like me - and still maintained a flip phone for show. But I knew he had Tinder on the smartphone he kept hidden in an almost-never-used winter jacket, and I'd had to talk him out of installing spyware on Kaylee's phone after he'd spent a solid week researching what was out there.

Okay, so we installed *one* tracking app, but it was in case of emergencies only.

Anyhow, given all that, it was pretty obvious he was feigning cluelessness simply to get more bonding time with his granddaughter. Wasn't like he could offer to take her ice-skating or for ice cream any more. Teenage girls were *way* too cool for that.

It suddenly occurred to me that something else was missing.

Well - other than Mara Thetchem and my sanity.

"Where's Joey?"

Kaylee looked excited. "He was tired, so -"

"I gave him your room." Len smirked up at me. "Figured you'd sleep on the pull-out sofa in the living room."

Gee thanks, Len. Although I had to admit, I was a little shocked he was willing to risk having a strange man sleep in the same house as his precious granddaughter, even if it did give him the pleasure of evicting me from my own bed. "Weirdly trusting of you," I said, moving to make myself a coffee before I headed for the sofa-bed's lumpy mattress and a night of unrest.

"I locked him in," Len replied smugly.

I swung around in annoyance - Len had told me he'd

lost the key to that door years ago - but before I could comment, Kaylee cackled in glee and burst out, "Yeah, take that, bitches!"

"Language, young lady!"

I shot Len an aggrieved glare. Funny that he'd always been the one swearing in our house when I was a kid. Of course, he'd usually been drunk back then.

Kaylee bit her lip and tried to look obedient and apologetic, but I could see the way her eyes kept drifting back to her laptop screen, and the delight dancing in them.

"What happened?"

She turned her laptop around so we could both see the screen. Oh, right. In this era where nothing could be allowed to go undocumented, *of course* she had updated her Facebook page to report that she currently had rocker Joey Russo sleeping in her house, and for good measure had posted a selfie of herself and Joey making faces at the camera.

"Did you -?"

"Ask Joey for permission before I posted?" Kaylee looked offended. "Duh. Of course. He said it was the least he could do to thank us for being so nice to him."

"Uh huh." I sighed, hoping our house wouldn't be surrounded by eager fans by tomorrow - then winced as I pictured Bethany finding out about it too. It'd be just my luck if she took it into her head that Joey was screwing my teenage niece now. She'd probably come over with a shotgun.

Kaylee had turned back to her screen - clearly not wanting to miss the 'OMG's, 'I h8 u!!'s, and indecipherable emoticons that would doubtless be streaming in very soon - but swung back around in excitement. "Oh, and do you know who his father-in-law is?!"

"Yes," I bit out, not enjoying the reminder of Gerry's influence.

"He's like the *king* of tweets!"

After Trump, I assumed.

Len make a disgusted noise. *"Tweets."*

Leaving Kaylee and Len to duke it out over the concept of self-expression versus privacy - the opening salvo started with Len complaining, "And how can you have three hundred and nineteen *friends?*" - I turned back to my coffee, spooning instant granules into a mug as the kettle boiled. Yeah, some people only drink ground coffee from beans imported from Outer Mongolia via a yak's ass, and that's great for them. My taste buds - not to mention my bank balance - genuinely prefer good instant. I let my thoughts drift, tuning out the familiar argument going on behind me as I tried to plan out the next day in my mind.

Alex had come through for me on getting reliable contact info for Sophia Wilde and her agent, but I knew I'd have to play it smart if I wanted her to flip. I was betting Gerry had offered her something - and/or threatened her with something else - for her to stick to the story that those photos were real. Which meant my special brand of persuasion - or deception - would be needed.

I pulled Mara's check from the back pocket where I'd shoved it and stared at the amount with a sinking feeling. I couldn't afford to turn down five thousand bucks... assuming the check didn't bounce. I took out my phone and deposited it, so I'd know by morning if it went through. Not that it would change anything, really, since my need to know more about what she'd done to me was a far more pressing concern than my sinking bank balance right now. On the other hand, not having to split my worries over bill paying too would be a nice reprieve while I figured the rest out.

Yep: Mara had me by the short and curlies, no question about that.

Which meant that tomorrow, in addition to helping Joey with Sophia Wilde, I'd *also* need to look into Leroy's conviction and see if his claim of innocence held any merit

I hissed and clamped my hand to my skull as pain

sliced through it at just the idea.

What the fuck?

I tried again, thinking about how I should probably start by visiting Leroy in -

Arghhh!

I leaned over the counter as the waves of pain slowly dissipated, glaring at my own reflection in the side of the toaster for lack of being able to wring Mara's scrawny neck. So let me get this straight: I was gonna get spanked for letting Leroy's case distract me from helping Joey and Bethany, even though Mara had set me *both* tasks?

How was that fair AT ALL?

"Uncle Lyle, are you okay?"

I forced myself to mask the pain I was still feeling, turning toward Kaylee's concerned face. "I'm fine." I dumped hot water over the coffee granules then took the mug over to the refrigerator to grab milk. "Just gonna have this then turn in."

Not that I expected to sleep much tonight. If I knew myself - and I did - I'd spend the whole night trying to figure out how I should split my time tomorrow without having a complete physical breakdown. Which would, itself, cause a shit ton of pain just to think about. *Unless...*

Grabbing my coffee and kissing Kaylee goodnight, I felt an unexpected surge of gratitude to Len for sticking me on the living room sofa overnight.

At least I'd be in the same place as the drinks cabinet I'd so nobly ignored earlier.

Enough Scotch, and I'd be out like a light.

ૐ

The next morning dawned bright and early.

Much too bright and much, *much* too early.

I groaned and winced as my alcohol-soaked brain had to deal with stuff like getting up, washing, and getting dressed, even as I relived the plan I'd come up with in the two hours between opening the bottle and finally knocking myself out.

The plan itself was pretty simple. The clear priority was getting Sophia to confirm she'd set Joey up, then taking all the proof to Bethany. I already had a pretty good idea of how to con Sophia, and as I sat in the kitchen guzzling down my third coffee, I set things in motion with an 8 a.m. phone call to her agent. Who was already in the office and sounded like she'd been awake for hours. On a Sunday. Whoever says entertainment people are lazy schmucks never saw a filming schedule.

I'd already spent thirty painfully hung-over minutes searching Gerry and Bethany Warnock's recent press releases and social media feeds, trying to figure out the best way to get to her. The bad news was they were both going to be attending some music awards show in Europe on Wednesday. The good news was they weren't leaving until tomorrow. But unless I wanted to deal with my current symptoms - not to mention a lovelorn Joey - for a lot more days, I needed to wrap this up fast.

Fortunately, my research had mostly convinced me that they - and their devoted fans - would collectively tweet, blog, post, and basically *barf* their whereabouts in enough time to let us catch up to Bethany before their flight. My one concern was that Gerry might keep their plans for today a little more under wraps than usual, if the idea was to keep Bethany away from Joey until they left the country.

I figured with all the wealth and power the guy had, he had to be at least that smart -

My phone buzzed on the table and I glanced at the screen.

Or maybe he was dumb as a box of rocks.

I'd set up an alert for the Warnocks' various social media feeds... and look at that. Gerry (or an assistant) had just tweeted where he'd be that evening. An album launch party for a group called 'The Birdies' - which sounded like a bad Beatles / Byrds mash-up, but what did I know. That didn't mean Bethany would be there too, of course, but at the risk of wanting to poke both my eyes out I'd checked both their Instagram pages plus a few celebrity websites, and she seemed to have been at all his recent events. Even if she'd looked less dazzling than her usual toothpaste-commercial, paparazzi-magnet self.

"Lyle?"

I looked around to see Joey stagger into the kitchen, looking like death warmed up himself.

"Coffee?" I offered grudgingly, indicating the almost empty pot. Okay, so I was lazy enough to drink the crappy 'real' stuff when it was just sitting out, especially if it would piss off the person (Len) who'd set it on timer the night before. Being able to blame Joey was a nice side benefit, though.

Joey's eyes lit up, and he was at my side, ready to suck it out of the spout, before I grabbed him a mug. Close up, I could smell him over the coffee - B.O., not booze, although I bet there was still some of the latter coming out of his pores too from earlier yesterday.

I suddenly realized he must've slept in his clothes all night. My fault, I guessed. I hadn't exactly thought past "he's taking *my* bed" to making the kid comfortable. I tried to picture Len being considerate to a guest - nah - or Kaylee offering her sexy music hero some of her uncle's pajamas and maybe underwear... yeah, she was precocious and confident, but not *that* much.

Thank god.

"We'll swing by your hotel for a change of clothes," I said.

"And a shower," he mumbled into the mug as he lovingly swigged it dry.

I guess no one offered him any towels either. Damn, I really sucked at being a host, and I couldn't fault Joey for not being the perfect guest.

Well, except for the little matter of lying to my niece last night. "I know you didn't write that song," I said. Was

I being petty? Yep.

Joey turned puzzled eyes on me.

"*I Will Never Leave You*. Gerry said he had it written for your third album."

Joey pulled a face. "Yeah. By *me*." He sounded fed up now. "I kept telling him I had my own stuff, but he never believed me. Refused to listen to anything. In the end, I sent in the demo anonymously." He gave a short bark of laughter that sounded anything but happy. "Good thing too; at least people still wanted to hire 'Jared Reese' as a songwriter after Gerry dumped Joey Russo." My face must have conveyed the question in my mind, because he continued. "I was pushing for more control over my career. So he dropped me from his label, and told everyone I was hell to work with and needed to be *auto-tuned*."

Jeez. Not that I was about to start feeling sorry for the guy with all the platinum records, but I guess even the rich and famous don't always have it easy.

"Who wants waffles?" Kaylee's bright, cheerful voice made me envious of her youth as she entered the kitchen. Namely that she was too young to get legally drunk like an idiot.

"Uhh..."

She shot me a suspicious glance. "Are you hung over?"

"I'm fine."

Her gaze went between me, Joey, and the almost empty coffee pot, and I saw a kind of grim resignation come into her eyes. Not the kind of look you want to see on someone you love, let alone a fifteen-year-old child, and I felt guilt settle around me like a cloak. Without saying a word, she made a beeline for the fridge and pulled out milk plus a stick of what looked like asparagus, then raided the freezer for the frozen berries she kept in there to make smoothies with. Plucking a banana from the bunch hanging off a novelty Statue of Liberty that had randomly appeared when I was a kid - Mom had loved a good yard sale - Kaylee headed for the one kitchen appliance capable of filling me with fear right at that moment:

The blender.

"Kaylee," I pleaded, as she shoved the items into it and I noticed Joey surreptitiously backing toward the doorway, "could you make your smoothie a little later?"

"Sit down!"

I jerked reflexively before realizing I was *already* seated, then glanced sideways to see Joey, also suitably cowed, return to sit at the table too.

Kaylee poured a load of milk into the blender, added a generous helping of something from a dark brown bottle - was that Worcestershire sauce? - then stared between us meaningfully, finally fixing her gaze on mine. "This is for *you*, dumbass!"

I'd barely had time to take in her unexpected language when she hit the button - and my head exploded. Over the deafening, pain-inducing jackhammer noise, I just about caught Joey's stifled whimpers next to me. I thought I'd become used to being in agony, but this was even worse -

- although mercifully briefer, as Kaylee shut down her instrument of torture and started pouring a thick, brownish concoction into two tall glasses. My eyes widened in horror as I felt Joey stiffen in his seat next to me too. She didn't expect us to *drink* that, did she?

The two glasses clunked down onto the table in front of us.

Yep.

Kaylee retreated to the far side of the kitchen table before sitting down and eyeballing me coldly. "You need to take better care of yourself." The statement was more a command than anything else.

My heart sank as I looked into her eyes. I sighed heavily and reached for the glass. Suppressing my stomach's urge to roil at the mere sight of the stuff, I closed my eyes, plugged my nose, and forced myself to gulp it down.

I felt like crap, and not just because my body and brain were conspiring to kill me right now. For the past year I'd done everything I could to make my niece feel safe and secure with her parents gone... and in the past thirty six hours I'd collapsed in front of her (in the most dramatic way imaginable), admitted to being Tasered on the job by a little old lady, and now was nursing a hangover first thing in the morning. She was bound to put two and two together and come up with Addict.

And the last thing I wanted was Kaylee worrying about whether I was turning into her parents.

Maybe it was an inevitable side effect of working with drug dealers, or a way for Michael and Jenny to deal with the stresses at work and at home, but the department's investigation had revealed their perfect life wasn't so perfect after all. For Kaylee's sake, and my own need to know, I had dug even further. Between party animal reps at various bars and clubs, stashes in their home, and even one short stay in rehab for Jenny, it turned out they'd had more addiction issues than any of us realized before that boat exploded...

Except Kaylee, it seemed.

That hangover remedy - which I could feel (don't throw up; do *not* throw up!) slithering down my gullet even now - hadn't magicked itself up out of nowhere. She'd made it before, and not just once. Was that where her smoothie habit came from? Mixing up Mommy and Daddy's morning pick-me-up? Or had it started out as strawberry milkshakes, and only switched to adding the hangover aids later on?

Shit. She'd had so much to overcome already. Which was another reason, if I even needed one, that I wasn't about to tell her - or Len, for that matter - what was really going on with me right now.

Added to the fact that they'd probably have me committed if I said it out loud.

I lowered my now empty glass, realizing Joey had

followed my lead and drunk his down too. I had to admit, I didn't feel any *worse*, and it was probably good to put something in my stomach aside from coffee.

I opened my mouth to thank Kaylee, but at that moment the kitchen door swung open to reveal Len in the doorway. "Visitor for you." I expected him to look at Kaylee, but instead his eyes fixed on me. "I left her in the living room."

Her?

Getting up hastily, I went around the table to plant a quick kiss on my niece's cheek. "Thanks for the smoothie," I said, then added in a murmur I hoped Len wouldn't hear, "but it's not gonna be a regular thing, okay?"

"Okay."

I was disheartened by the expression on Kaylee's face - more humoring than believing me, I knew - but I promised myself I'd prove it to her. After all, the only reason I'd gotten drunk was because of the freaking pounding in my skull, and once I'd settled this mess I'd be back to normal.

Yep, I'd be back to being happy ole me, with my failing company and lack of prospects. But at least I hadn't started drinking about *that*. Not yet, anyway...

I shoved the depressing thought aside and ruffled Kaylee's hair, drawing a light squawk of protest, then marched toward the living room and my visitor. Whatever she had to say to me, there were a few things I'd be saying to the elusive Mara K. Thetchem *first*.

I burst into the room... and came to an abrupt halt. Because it was Reesa, not Mara, who turned around when I entered.

"Reesa?"

Considering the last time we saw each other she'd slammed a door between us, I hadn't been sure she'd ever want to see me again. Having her here in my house, standing right in front of me... it made me realize how much losing her forever would hurt.

It also made me realize how much I'd hurt her by pulling away over the past year, and I felt like a total bastard for expecting her to forgive me when I showed up out of the blue yesterday.

"Hi." She cleared her throat uncomfortably, then dug into her purse for something. "I was in the neighborhood, so I thought I'd, um..."

Stop by to clear the air between us?

She held out a small manila envelope. "Drop off your invoice."

Oh.

I took it from her reluctantly. "Thanks." A moment passed and Reesa made no move to leave, which was fine with me. "Do you have time for a coffee?" I asked finally.

"Sure." She hesitated. "I mean... maybe." I'd never seen Reesa look so uncertain, but then suddenly she exhaled a loud breath and blurted, "I came to apologize, okay? You happy now?" Glaring at me like I'd somehow pissed her off again, she continued, "I kept putting off calling, and finally I knew I had to get in my car and drive over here."

I couldn't help it. I grinned in sheer relief.

Reesa scoffed. "Oh great, now your ego's gonna be sky high."

I forced the grin away, needing to be clear how much I appreciated her making the first move. "Rees, if you hadn't come over, I'd have been at your door later today."

She looked mollified. "Really?"

I fingered the invoice in my hands. "Yeah. I was gonna use this as an excuse, too." Okay, so I was pretty sure I had a packed day ahead of me, but I'd planned on heading over to her place with my checkbook by the end of the night.

Reesa looked slightly embarrassed. "If you need more time -"

"Actually I can pay you right now," I said quickly. Even

though it still freaked me out a little, Mara's check *hadn't* bounced, so my bank balance was looking good for a while. Plus I was planning to bill Joey for whatever Reesa charged, of course. Assuming his rock star quarters at the Sunset Spire were something he could actually afford, he had to be doing pretty well for himself now, no matter how much Gerry derided his 'comeback' attempt or how desperate things might have looked earlier.

"That's good. I'm really glad."

I could hear the relief in Reesa's voice, and tried not to focus on that. It didn't mean she thought I was incompetent or couldn't manage out on my own, she was just worried for me. Like any good friend would be.

I smiled into her eyes, feeling glad we'd reconnected after all this time. "And you're doing well too, right? I mean, all those new projects you have going..."

I trailed off as I realized her warm gaze had cooled, a shadow forming behind her eyes.

Yep, Reesa was definitely in some kind of trouble.

"Rees -"

"Uncle Lyle... oh, hi."

I jerked out of my reverie at the sound of Kaylee's hello, and turned to see her looking in through the open door.

"Kaylee!" Reesa's lips curved upward, the smile crinkling her eyes at the sides. "Wow, you've grown up so much since I last saw you!"

It was weird, but I'd somehow forgotten they'd even met before. But yeah, there'd been a few times. A couple of barbecues Michael had thrown for the department at his house, plus one memorable family dinner Reesa had come to when I'd needed a friend at my side. And I could see that - whatever Reesa thought of Jenny, Michael, and the situation they'd left me in - she was genuinely pleased to see Kaylee again.

Even so, Kaylee hesitated, but I realized she was looking at me to see if I was okay with her intruding. Any other time I'd have been delighted. Truth be told, I couldn't think of much I wanted more than the two most important women in my life striking up a friendship. Reesa was great with kids - take Carlos for example - and Kaylee could use a female role model who wasn't a pop diva or reality show starlet. Or a mother who'd turned a blind eye to what her husband was doing and gotten drunk or high instead.

But right now I felt like I was onto something with Reesa and I wanted to see if she'd confide in me about it. I opened my mouth to tell Kaylee we'd come find her in the kitchen in a minute, but Reesa beat me to it.

"It was the Fourth of July party, right?"

"Yeah." Kaylee's grin was wide, only a trace of pain at the memory behind it.

It had been the year before last - the year before everything blew up in our faces. Michael and Jenny had gone all out, splurging on a lavish, catered party in their huge, newly-landscaped rear yard. It seemed like half the LAPD had come out, including Michael's team from vice and most of the cops he'd ever worked with. I'd invited Reesa and her family, and Kaylee had hung out with Reesa's sister and Carlos for a couple of hours while Reesa and I shot the breeze with other cops, reminiscing over old stories and sharing new ones. Between entertainment, catering, and booze, the entire thing had probably cost more than my car... or maybe my car and my van... but of course, back then we'd all thought Jenny was just celebrating another great sales year.

Now we knew better, of course. But I was glad Kaylee could still enjoy those memories of her parents, even though they'd been spoiled for me once I figured out what paid for it all.

"You know Carlos never stopped talking about that game you played together?"

Reesa encouraged Kaylee to come in and sit down, and I knew I'd lost my chance to talk about whatever I'd seen in her face earlier. Even if Kaylee left, Reesa would be on her guard now; she wouldn't spill until she was damn good and ready. I'd be better off giving them time to catch up and inviting Reesa to go out with me some other time.

But not like out on a date or anything.

Obviously.

I headed for the door. "Can you keep Reesa company while I get my check book?" I asked Kaylee.

"Sure."

I dug my spare check book out from under my briefs - no, I'm not a total slob; no home office means I have kind of a dual purpose filing system in my bedroom - and headed back down the stairs as fast as I could. But even so, out of habit I avoided the ones that creaked. Call it instinct, I guess; most situations in my line of work, you don't want people to hear you coming.

Unfortunately, that instinct was gonna screw me over this time.

"So, are you seeing Uncle Lyle now?"

I froze on the fifth stair from the ground, my foot dangling in the air as I clutched the railing for balance.

The wait before Reesa replied seemed to go on forever, but was probably no more than a second. "No. We're just friends."

I put my foot down softly, wondering why her saying it out loud bothered me, when I'd told Joey the exact same thing two days ago.

"Really?" I could hear the hopeful note in Kaylee's voice.

"Um, the thing is..." I found myself straining to hear Reesa's answer, "I think we're better off that way."

I suddenly realized I'd been hoping she wouldn't rule it out.

Which was screwy, because hadn't I *just* been thinking the same thing, literally two minutes earlier? I didn't date. Didn't do relationships. And Reesa was sexy as hell, but hooking up with her wasn't worth ruining our years of friendship.

Clearly, I was just out of practice at ignoring the impact she made.

"So you don't like him that way at all? I mean..." *why was Kaylee still probing*? "...like, don't you think he's good looking?"

Okay, I did *not* need to hear the answer to that.

Quickly leaping back four stairs, I proceeded to pound down the staircase like a hungry quarterback who'd been promised a porterhouse steak and five cheerleaders, landing with a *thump* on the floor below.

Needless to say, by the time I re-entered the living room the conversation had shifted away from whether Reesa was interested in me sexually or not. Even if I hadn't heard anything, the guilty looks on their faces would've told me they'd been up something, so I faked turning suspicious, like any half-decent detective would. "What were you guys talking about while I was gone?"

Kaylee covered with an ease that actually worried me. "I was just confessing my crush on Joey."

"You do remember he's married, right?" I said casually.

It was a cheap shot, but I needed a distraction and Kaylee's reaction was exactly as I'd predicted it would be. "That's why it's called a *crush*!" She turned to Reesa, annoyed. "It's like he thinks I'm going to go out and attack every hot guy I see!"

"She has a point," Reesa added, with a smirk that looked forced to me. I could tell she was trying to get us back into our comfort zone, but it seemed Kaylee's questions had left us both a little uneasy.

I forced a smile, then made a show of grimacing. "Reesa, I hate to do this, but I have... uh... plans today." Sure, I could've said 'work,' but I wanted her to think I was meeting a hookup. Was I being juvenile and petty? Maybe. Did I immediately regret being such a dick? No. "Could we catch up more some other time?" I could see her stiffening up, thinking I was giving her the long-term brush-off again, so I added, "How about a drink one evening next week?"

Reesa's shoulders loosened a little as she realized I was serious about it. "Make it at McDougall's, and you're on."

I suppressed a shudder at the thought of my father's favorite cop bar, but for whatever reason Reesa had always loved the atmosphere, filled with its scent of ancient testosterone and beer-stained billiard tables. "Great," I forced out, then added more honestly, "I'll look forward to it."

Reesa smiled. "Me too."

Joey and I left the Sunset Spire hotel ninety minutes later, him freshly - albeit quickly - groomed and dressed, and me fresh from another staring match with my nemesis the valet downstairs. Good thing the guy never seemed to take a day off, or I'd have missed out on that pleasure.

While I'd waited in the car, I'd put up with the brain ache and made myself examine the ideas I'd come up with overnight for dealing with the Leroy situation.

Here were the two possible hypotheses I had to work with: Number one, he was guilty, which meant no amount of digging would help. I wasn't framing some other poor schmo just so Mara would spill the beans about whatever was happening to me. I tried telling myself she talked in riddles most of the time anyway, so it wasn't like I was losing much. But truth was, she was the only one who knew *anything*, so without her help my goose was pretty much cooked. If Leroy turned out to be guilty, I'd have to figure out something else she wanted, and fast. Or maybe get ready to go down on my knees and beg.

Or number two: Leroy didn't do it... in which case, I had to be able to prove it. Lucky for me, Jimmy's file on him would have all the info I'd need to investigate.

Unluckily, when I'd told him I needed to borrow it for a case (omitting certain supernatural details), the fucker had gone and *charged* me.

So much for being neighborly.

But at least now I knew the basic facts, which were as follows: On November 8th, at 10:33 p.m., four guys in stocking masks (rocking it old school) had held up a liquor store in Burbank, two of them carrying handguns. The crew of geniuses had gotten away with a measly hundred and fifty two dollars and a case of Patrón. Unbeknownst to them, there'd been a camera where they'd parked their (also stolen) getaway vehicle. It had caught the four of them climbing back in... and the driver *removing his mask* before they drove away.

Maybe he worried some off-duty cop would see him back out of a parking space with pantyhose over his face? Or maybe he'd been too drunk to think straight? Either way, one database check later and the detectives had a name: Hector Robinson. And pretty soon they had two more. The stolen car belonged to the owner of a restaurant where Hector had been an hour earlier, with a couple of other guys from the neighborhood who also had sheets a mile long. Eric Jenkins and his brother Jerome had kept it together under questioning... until a search warrant revealed the case of tequila under a tarp in their back yard, with two store employees' prints all over it.

So that was the story: three guys get wasted on tequila at a Mexican joint, get tossed out for being drunk and disorderly, make a half-assed plan to go rob more of the stuff from a nearby liquor store, and - to pay the restaurant back for kicking them out - steal the owner's Honda Civic as their getaway car.

But none of them would give up guy number four.

Which was where the detectives had gone digging into their records some more, turning up a fourth member of their old crew: Leroy. He'd been out of the life for a while and seemed to be getting things together; he was going to school, engaged to a nice girl, no arrests in over three years. But phone records showed he'd at least been in the area, and he hadn't been able to provide an alibi. Hector, Eric, and Jerome had all denied it was him but refused to give another name, and Leroy matched the physical description of the guy who'd been with them.

The clincher, though? His prints were on two bullets in a gun found in Hector's car when they picked him up. He claimed he must have handled them years earlier, when he first joined the gang and did menial tasks like passing ammo around... but the detectives weren't buying his story.

Which meant that *if* Leroy really was innocent, I had my work cut out to prove it.

Either way, I needed to speak to him and get a feel for the situation. Sure, I'd had him yelling his innocence at me through the rear of my van for twenty minutes, but I'd get a better read on it if I could see him at the same time. And if I decided he might be innocent... well, maybe he knew who the fourth guy actually was, or he had an alibi he wasn't remembering. Something as simple as driving through a red light or stopping for gas could do the job, although I figured his attorney would already have covered that with him. Of course, it all depended on how much time his attorney had spent with him and his or her level of motivation.

I might be short on time, but I was *highly* motivated.

Unfortunately, getting in to talk to Leroy wasn't going to be easy. Partly because the last time I'd seen him he'd been trying to kill me. But mostly because even the *thought* of diverting from my main task to visit the jail made the pain in my head get so bad I wanted to vomit -

"You're sure she's gonna be there?"

My thoughts were interrupted - yet again - by Joey's version of 'are we there yet?' I forced myself to answer calmly, even though I wanted to punch him in his too-good-looking face. "Yes."

"But how do you *know*?" he persisted.

We'd just started up the steep road to the hilltop filming location in Griffith Park, and I somehow resisted the urge to pull over and throw him off the edge.

Screw it. "Well, I guess she might not be," I said. "She might have overslept, or Woody Allen might've offered her a part in his latest movie..."

Out of the corner of my eye I saw Joey's fingers clutch around the small but powerful state-of-the-art video camera he held in his lap. He'd better not break my favorite piece of equipment (body parts aside), or I'd be billing him for that, as well as my daily rate. "So you're saying we could *fail?*"

Of course we could fail, dumbass!

Anyone who says "Failure is not an option" is an idiot. Failure is *always* an option, because life isn't a dumb movie script. You know, the kind where the hero gets shot at a bazillion times and never gets hit - other than the obligatory flesh wound to make him look more heroic - but nails every bad guy with a single bullet. In the real world? Most plans go to shit - and *no* plan survives contact with the enemy. That's why you have plans B, C, D... all the way down to 'S' for 'seat of your pants' - or just plain '*shiiiittttt.*'

I decided not to wax philosophical with Joey, though. I needed him distracted, not freaking out even more. "Hey, can you grab the map?" I pointed to the mess on my back seat. "It's under there somewhere. Just want to check this is the right way."

Five minutes later, we were parked next to a couple of massive Star Trailers. I glanced around as I climbed out of the car and spotted Gary right away, waving to me casually from the bottom of a taped-off pathway. I waved back, then pointed Joey toward a small hillock I knew would be a great place for him to wait. "Okay, over there's a place you can be out of sight but still get good shots and audio."

Joey squinted at where I was pointing. "Where?"

I checked the time then hurried Joey over to where I meant. We didn't have long before Sophia was due - if I'd learned anything, it was the bigger the lure the earlier the mark arrived - and I still had to get ready to meet her myself.

We rounded a couple of larger boulders and found the hiding place I knew about from jogging up here. I know, it doesn't exactly go with the hard-boiled private eye stereotype, and I'd been slacking off the past couple of months anyway. But in theory I needed to stay fit in case I had to pursue a target on foot, even though my recent jobs had mostly involved playing couch potato for hours in a parked car or motel room. And if I was gonna break a sweat I preferred getting outside for some air, instead of going to some dingy, smelly gym where half the guys were channeling Rocky or reliving their days in prison. Or - even worse - being cooped up in some mirror-walled fitness place with everyone checking me out as potential boyfriend material and 24-hour news blasting everywhere.

Or maybe I was just afraid to find no one checking me out at all these days. I shut that thought down quickly; I'd worry about it again when I hit forty.

Positioning myself behind Joey, I got him to kneel down so he couldn't be seen from the path. "See? You stay here, wait 'til she comes past you, then film us through there." I pointed out the gap in the grasses that would be perfect for it.

Joey frowned up at me, no doubt starting to suspect that I *may* have been up here a time or fifty before. In which case, I probably hadn't needed the map I'd urged him to find on the back seat, until he'd almost barfed in the car from being twisted around that long.

I ignored this and gestured for him to get set up with the camera, the way I'd shown him before we left the house. "She could get here any minute," I reminded him, then added, "And remember, don't let her see you or the camera. The light could catch on the lens -"

"I won't do anything until she's looking away."

I started to leave, but I wanted to be sure. "You're *sure* you're good with this?"

Joey looked exasperated. "Shit, Lyle - I'm not gonna forget to press 'record' or yell at her and ruin it!"

Yeah, but what Sophia had done to him would test the most measured guy's temperament, and I still had visions of Joey on that pool house roof, yelling at Bethany while holding a fricking *boom box* over his head.

I must've looked skeptical because he glared at me in annoyance. "I'm not a complete moron, you know. I want my wife back more than I want revenge." His expression turned dark. "Plus I'm not gonna blow our one chance to nail Gerry."

And I could tell he meant that.

All right then.

Reassured, I headed back to the car to get both my disguise and my game face on. Still, if I'd had longer to plan this out I'd have brought someone else I could absolutely guarantee would keep their cool. But Thatcher Investigations' budget didn't stretch to having a cinematographer on call, and at least Joey had experience with a camera. Back in the day, Gerry - Mr. Social Media - had been worried about Joey's 'digital footprint,' so he'd had Joey film 'behind the scenes' content at concerts and put it on his own YouTube channel. I liked the irony that Gerry himself had given Joey the skills to screw him over. At least, if things went to plan.

Which they probably wouldn't -

I felt the twinge of a headache and decided to think more positive.

⁓

Thirty minutes later I was letting Gary set the scene while I waited inside one of the trailers, the window open a crack so I could hear the show.

Officer Gary Barawski had been three weeks from his twenty years when a tweaked out pimp shot him point blank during a routine traffic stop in Hollywood. Five years later, Gary was retired with a good pension and still working the Hollywood beat, but in a different sense. He'd had to give up the job; the damage that had been done to his lungs meant he'd never pass a physical that involved running for more than a bus, and he'd never wanted to be stuck behind a desk. But being a film location security guard was another thing. Gary had always been fascinated by the movies - not just the glitzy stuff, but the real grime and elbow grease of the industry - and now he got to be a part of it. He'd even gotten some parts here and there and I'd heard he was a pretty good actor, as his current performance was proving to me.

"I'm, uh, I'm really not supposed to say -"

"Please?" I could practically see Sophia's eyelids being batted at him. "Just give me a hint."

A pause. Then, "Okay. Well, you know those 'Avengers' movies?"

Sophia's voice was breathy; excited. "Yes?"

And that was my cue.

I moved quickly but stealthily down the length of the trailer -

- then slammed the door open, phone held to my ear, as I went into my full-on 'slick-dick producer' routine. "No!" I ignored Sophia and Gary entirely as I headed for the taped-off pathway next to them. "Cut him in on the back end, but tell him we won't go over two mil."

Out of the corner of my eye I saw Sophia watching me worriedly. She was dressed in a figure-hugging pale blue dress that emphasized her dancer's slim musculature and wearing enough makeup for a screen test.

"And if he pulls that crap one more time, he'll never..." I caught myself in time, "work for me again!"

I'd almost said 'he'll never work in this town again!' - but I wanted to appear powerful and charismatic, not sound like some mustache-twirling movie villain.

I reached out with my Armani-covered sleeve - the suit was from a second-hand store in Burbank but it had still cost *way* too much - and lifted up the caution tape blocking me. Shit - if I really walked down that dusty path I was gonna ruin these Gucci loafers (which also hadn't been cheap), so I hoped Gary stopped me pretty quick -

"Uh, Mr. Turner?"

"What?" I swiveled around, glaring at him.

"This lady's here to see you?" Gary looked nervous, like he was doing the wrong thing and risking getting fired. Man, he was *really* in character here.

I let a smooth smile sweep over my lips, switching from entitled asshole to caring friend of the *artiste* in a millisecond. You know, just like most regular producers. "You're Sophia Wilde?"

Sophia - who'd been watching our interaction with barely concealed anxiety - preened under my favorable regard. Even so, somehow her energy was off. Sure, she exuded sexiness and confidence, but at the same time there was an edge of desperation to her. She wanted all of this *way* more than she was trying to let on.

Which could only work to our advantage.

Neglecting to thank or acknowledge Gary at all - like the asshole I was pretending to be - I turned a gleaming smile on Sophia and extended my hand. "Stuart Turner." These days no one showed up to a job interview without Googling the heck out of whoever they were meeting, so I'd picked the name of a producer with a few decent credits but no photo on IMDb, and no contact info anywhere that I could find online. Just in case, Gary had run the name past his own agent who'd confirmed the guy wasn't in the big leagues, so Sophia's own people weren't likely to have a direct line to him either.

Sophia's confidence was clearly boosted by my warm greeting. I could see her nerves fading, her face glowing as she turned the charm up to high. Next to us, Gary gave a good impression of a dismissed junior employee. Did Sophia care how her potential boss treated people? If she did, she hid her concerns well... or maybe she just lacked empathy and figured she'd be treated better than some lowly security guy. I assumed the latter, given what she'd done to Joey.

"Thanks for meeting me all the way up here." I gestured around with the hand that still held my phone. "Hope you didn't think I was some kind of serial killer."

"Of course not."

I strode away from Gary, Sophia following dutifully at my side. "Don't worry, I won't bury you alive." I shot her a smirk. "Well, not until we're shooting at least."

Sophia looked interested at first, then acutely disappointed. "I'm... I'm playing a *body*?"

I laughed. "Of course not! I never waste talent, Ms. Wilde. And I hear you're really something."

Even as she preened under my compliment, I could practically see Sophia's thought processes racing behind her eyes. She was a backup singer and dancer with only a couple of acting credits since she'd left Tallahassee: one on stage and one in a dog food commercial where she'd been cut off at chin level. Her agency had few ties to anyone, and even they had more or less dropped her six months ago from what I could tell. So who the hell had referred her to me?

I didn't leave her hanging for long. "Gerry Warnock's one of our producers, and he said you'd be perfect for the role. He said a recent performance you turned in for him was 'Emmy-worthy' - and that's a direct quote."

Sophia's expression shot from seductive to horrified so fast I could practically see her skin wobble in response. A second later she forced a smile back to her lips, but they were pressed together so hard they were nearly white.

"Maybe you could tell me how you prepared for the part?"

"Uh... I..."

I let my smile fade a little, my eyes narrowing. "Gerry said it was challenging - required some improv...?" I encouraged.

Behind Sophia's eyes I could see her brain whirring. "Um... yes, I..." she stuttered.

"You don't know what I'm talking about, do you?" I let my happy mask fall away completely, ignoring her to scowl at my phone as I tapped the screen. "Fuck." I raised the phone to my ear. "Brittney? So much for doing Gerry a favor - you called the *wrong* Sophia Wilde! Sort this out!" Turning away from Sophia, I headed for the taped-off pathway again, tossing an insincere smile over my shoulder. "Sorry for wasting your time."

I let my eye catch Gary's; he gave a little nod and started meaningfully toward her.

"Wait!"

I forced myself not to grin as Sophia ran in front of me to block my path.

"I'm her! I'm the one he was talking about!"

Moment of truth time. Pouring every ounce of skepticism I possessed into it, I said, "*You're* the Sophia Wilde Gerry Warnock hired to lie about sleeping with his son-in-law?"

"Yes!" Then her eyes went wide as she realized what she'd said. "Uh... I mean..." Sophia lowered her voice, glancing around nervously. "He said I wasn't supposed to talk about it. To *anyone*."

I regarded her faux-sympathetically. "Right. Yeah, I can see that."

The lines of tension around her eyes remained, even as she forced a smile. "So can we just pretend he saw me on stage or something?"

I pretended to consider it for a moment, then said. "Nah." Turning away from her startled expression, I yelled, "You can come out now, Joey!"

If there'd been horror on Sophia's face before, it was nothing compared to the moment a grim-faced Joey stood up from his hiding place and marched toward her, video camera still pointed at us despite how emotional I could see he was. "How could you lie to Bethany, Sophia? I thought you were cool!"

"I-it wasn't my fault!" Sophia backed away from Joey as he strode toward us. "He said he'd kill my career if I didn't help!"

"Oh, so you did it for free, then?" I asked. One look at her face and I knew. "No? How much did he pay you?"

I saw her lips tighten and knew she was finally done incriminating herself. But just to put the cherry on top of her nightmare sundae, I held up my phone to show her I'd been recording us too. If this were a TV show, I'd have somehow managed to rewind it to *exactly* the place where she admitted her misdeeds and played it back to her, but the visual seemed to be enough. With one last frantic look at Joey, Sophia turned and sprinted for her car.

"Whatever it was, it wasn't enough!" Joey yelled, starting to go after her, but I caught him by the arm.

"Let her go. We got what we needed."

I could see by Joey's expression that what he 'needed' was Sophia tied to a chair for about an hour so he could berate her some more. But we wouldn't win this thing by getting arrested on a kidnapping charge.

"You sure liven up my retirement job." Gary gaze was amused as he strolled over to watch Sophia's rapid exit with us. A flurry of stones was kicked up as she first spun her tires then fishtailed her fashionably sporty Jeep back onto the main roadway, before disappearing from sight in a cloud of dust. Looked like she'd spent her pay-off on a new car; shame she'd just ruined the paintwork.

I reached over and shook hands with my former superior. "Thanks for the assist, Sarge." And no, I didn't hand over an envelope with a few hundred dollar bills inside. Gary came from a time when more cops were on the take - not that it didn't still happen, hell, my own brother was proof of that - and no way was I insulting him by making him feel like he was taking a pay-off. I'd be paying him as a part-time consultant, IRS-declared, all legal and above-board.

Okay, so I also needed to keep my own dealings squeaky clean in case IA or anyone else came sniffing around, maybe deciding I'd known more about Michael than I'd let on. Even the jobs I took for Jimmy risked looking bad to those guys... but Jimmy was smart enough to keep things legit when he wanted and it hadn't bitten me in the ass yet.

Gary grinned back at me as he released my hand. "Any time. Although..." he glanced down at his uniform, "next time you might need to use me in a different capacity." As I just frowned stupidly, he filled me in. "I'm going full time. Quitting the security gig and aiming for more roles. I'll always help you out though, any time I can."

I smiled broadly, although inwardly I sighed. I'd been secretly hoping I could persuade him to come work for me full time some day. But undercover PI jobs wouldn't exactly work if he started getting recognized.

As if he read my mind, Gary gave a wicked smile. "Don't worry. If I get too famous, I'll wear a disguise."

Joey was silent as we walked back to my car, so I took a moment to check my phone for messages... and lo and behold, my contact at the sheriff's department had come through big time on the massive favor I'd asked of her.

I had an appointment to meet with Leroy Baldwin at Central Jail at noon.

Maybe things were finally starting to go my way -

"Now we take this to Bethany, right?"

I peered at an agitated Joey across my Toyota's dust-streaked dark blue roof. How to phrase this... "Sure." I broke eye contact and reached for the door, slipping my sunglasses on as I got behind the wheel.

I heard the passenger door open and slam shut about a second later, the car's suspension shuddering at the enthusiasm with which Joey had jumped in. "Right now?"

I let out a reluctant breath and braced myself. "I just gotta do something first."

Owwwwww! Like someone had taken an ice pick to my brain, my 'curse' told me how it felt about that idea. Which - again - sucked goats, because it was crazy lady's fucking fault I had to multi-task *anyway*.

"What do you *mean*?!" Joey looked like he'd be right there with a second ice pick if he had one available. "She's leaving the country *tomorrow* - I'll never see her again!"

I struggled to fumble the key into the ignition as I fought waves of pain, wishing I'd kept that particular nugget of information to myself. "It's Europe, Joey, not the moon."

"But -"

"We know where she'll be this evening - I got everything planned out."

"Yeah, but -"

As Joey spoke, I felt something pressing against the side of my skull, as if it too were pushing back on my argument. I glared up at the car roof, mentally addressing whatever planet or spiritual plane Mara lived on. "Oh, holy *fuck*," I yelled at full volume, "will you just *trust me* that I got this covered?!!"

To my amazement, it worked.

Kind of, anyway.

The excruciating agony dimmed down to a background buzz of pain, like a nagging tension headache.

"Okay!" Joey sounded weird so I glanced toward him. He was sat against the passenger door, looking a little freaked out. "I believe you."

How loud had I screamed? I looked out through the windscreen to see Gary staring at us from his post, one hand on his belt like he was making sure it was near his service weapon... even though I'd noticed they only issued Tasers at 'Security to the Stars.'

Yeah, I must've been pretty loud.

I raised my hand in a friendly wave and saw Gary relax a little, then started us moving slowly toward the park exit. My car was an automatic, but I still needed to get my brain in gear. Or rather, I needed to work on convincing it I had my eye firmly on the Joey-Bethany prize, even while I dealt with the Leroy situation.

Maybe I could find a good hypnotist.

Or a Jedi.

We were down the hill and approaching the freeway before I noticed Joey hadn't said anything for a while. Looking over at him when we hit a line of cars at a stop sign, I saw he was hanging onto the video recorder and shooting me occasional glances like he was trying to tell if he was better off in the car or jumping out.

I sighed. "I'm sorry I yelled. That was, uh... unprofessional."

Joey's gaze flickered up to meet mine and I could see receding tension mix with determination in his eyes. "Do what you promised with Bethany, and we're fine."

"Everything'll be fixed by tonight, I swear. I'll pick you up at six, okay?" I gripped the wheel tight between my fingers, trying not to dwell on all the things that could go awry.

I flinched when I heard a cracking sound. Dammit, I'd liked that steering wheel cover.

In the seat next to me, Joey made a sound of disbelief. "Man, you are *seriously* tightly wound."

Chapter Eight.

The Los Angeles Central Jail was literally on the wrong side of the tracks, situated on the far side of the train lines from Union Station, next to Downtown LA.

The area around it was a real mix: within about a mile lay one of the city's few wineries, a major art museum, and one of the best jazz venues in the state... as well as a shit ton of empty buildings, trash-covered streets, and Skid Row. As I drove through those streets toward the main gate of the jail, I spotted more bodies in sleeping bags huddled against the sides of buildings than I'd seen before on my trips here. Were there really more homeless people in the LA basin, or were there just more in the downtown area now, making the most of the growing foot traffic as more and more condos were built?

Not that this particular side of downtown seemed to have benefited from that resurgence as yet. It still had the same run-down, abandoned feel it had always had, the only difference being that in the recent past the whole area had felt pretty much deserted after a certain time of day, other than around the core of hotels, restaurants, and bars to the west of Pershing Square. These days, though, you had the sense that the whole place was regenerating... except here.

So maybe I was wrong.

Maybe the people sleeping on these streets just wanted peace and quiet, and to be left alone.

As I showed my ID, stowed my things in a locker, and went through security screening inside the jail's visitor center, it was both the same and different to my last visit when I'd still been a cop. Sometimes there'd be a general rivalry or vague sense of mistrust between LAPD officers and sheriff's deputies. But I'd always hated that schoolyard crap and tried to take people how I found them, and I'd personally never had much of a problem. The most irritating were the deputies with chips on their shoulders because they'd tried and been unable to get into the LAPD for whatever reason; the worst, though, were the LAPD jerks who referred to deputies as 'jumped up security guards.'

Since 'security' was practically the definition of running a jail, I'd always figured the deputies here got that kind of harassment more than most, so I'd gone out of my way to be accommodating and courteous. Of all the times I'd gone through this same process - except then I'd been stowing my service weapon in a special secure box - I'd never seen anyone act less than professional. Of course, I'd also had my visit expedited; no arriving sixty minutes early then twiddling my thumbs in a waiting area.

Now, though, I was just another visitor who had some kind of association with an inmate, and while I wasn't treated badly the differences were another stark reminder of how I was no longer a cop. No greetings; no updates on the wait time. No special treatment, in short. *Welcome to the rest of your life*, I thought, not for the first time over the past nine months. I wondered how long it would be before it didn't keep hitting me anew that I was no longer on the job.

I tried to shove my self-pity aside as I sat in the visitor room waiting for Leroy to be brought out, focusing on how at least I wasn't homeless or locked up in here. Yeah, I really was cheering myself up by thinking about how much worse other people had it. Didn't make me the Dalai Lama, but oh well. If it worked, I'd take it.

He finally appeared on the other side of the glass partition, and although I'd been braced for whatever angry reception I got, Leroy didn't even make eye contact until the officer escorting him had undone his handcuffs and walked off. When he finally looked up, I saw he was sporting a black eye that must have been inflicted not long after he got here. Either that or Jimmy's boys had 'fun' settling him down for transport, an idea that settled badly in my gut since I'd taken off the second I handed him over.

Since when had I forgotten what men like Jimmy were capable of? Maybe I should worry more about that slippery slope.

I could see Leroy wasn't going to speak first, so I jerked my chin toward his eye and asked, "How'd that happen?"

I was rewarded with a glare as Leroy clenched his jaw. But just as I feared I'd been right about my suspicions, he dropped his gaze to the table and muttered, "Got into it over my new tattoo."

Not uncommon when opposing gang tats were involved, but somehow I didn't think that was the case here. Not if the ink was new... I rubbed unthinkingly at my own fresh 'artwork.'

Leroy suddenly glared at me again, tugging his jumpsuit open to reveal a bandage over his chest. "I got Tanya's favorite poem tattooed over my heart before the wedding."

I frowned, peering at the small square. "Must be short."

"It's a haiku." He closed the jumpsuit again, muttering, "Idiot," under his breath.

"Says the guy who got married when he should've been in court," I shot back, then regretted it as Leroy's gaze turned dark. What the *fuck* was I doing, baiting the bear? I was here to get Leroy to talk, not make him want to charge me through the glass. "Look..." I raised my hands, going for calm. "I'm not here to fuck you up. I've been hired to find evidence that you were set up."

Leroy's eyes widened, and I couldn't tell if it was in shock, delight, or horror... until he slammed his fist down on the table so hard the whole assembly shook. Which cost us another two minutes of precious visiting time when a deputy had to come over and lecture him about managing his anger before putting him back into cuffs. Oh yeah, that was *really* gonna help.

"Who hired you?" he demanded the second we were left alone again. "Was it Tanya? Her dad?"

"Yeah," I said, hoping he didn't speak to either of them for a few days, since the last thing I needed was an irate Ed White tracking me down and punching me. Then I cut to the chase before anything else could go wrong. "Look: we have about thirteen more minutes before I'm outta here, so if there's anything, *anything* at all that you can tell me about who was really in that car, or where you really were that night, let me know."

Leroy glared back at me mulishly, so I tried another approach.

"If you're keeping quiet to protect someone, think of Tanya. Think of what *she* would want."

He got a conflicted look on his face at that, so I figured I was on the right track. Way I saw it, he knew who the fourth guy was but he was feeling torn between loyalty to his old friends and gang mates, and to the woman he loved. *If* he was innocent, of course. But I was still clutching onto that theory with both hands.

I persevered. "Don't think about the guys who did this, the ones letting you take the fall. Think about your *own* life, your own future with Tanya. Don't you owe it to her to tell the truth?"

"Tanya knows I didn't do it," he mumbled.

"You sure about that?"

Leroy swung his head up, startled. "Of course!"

But I could hear the uncertainty in his voice. Time to play dirty, I decided, mentally crossing my fingers it'd work. "I don't know. Last time I talked to her..." I sighed, "I hate to say it, but seemed like she had some doubts."

Leroy gasped like a kid who'd just been told Santa wasn't real. "No! No, she wouldn't -"

"Think how it looks, Leroy." I gave a helpless shrug. "You say you didn't do it... but you claim you were in bed at ten thirty on a Saturday night?"

"Yeah. I was tired." He folded his arms defensively, glaring right at me... and I knew he'd just lied. Sometimes too much eye contact was overkill, compensating for a need to look away. No wonder they'd arrested him, if it was that obvious he was lying in the interview.

Still, something wasn't adding up quite right. "You sure you weren't stepping out on Tanya? Doing something you don't want her knowing about?"

Jackpot.

Leroy's whole body froze up, pupils dilating like he was having a panic attack... which I guessed he basically was. "No! I'd never do that!" he said too quickly, his voice pitched way too high.

Holy shit. Chalk one up for the cynic. But even so... how had nobody seen this before? Detectives and Public Defenders weren't exactly known for their wide-eyed naïveté. Or maybe they *had* guessed the truth, but Leroy had just denied it like he was now and they'd been forced to go along with it. Either way...

I cleared my throat and took out a pen and notepad. "Okay, what's her name and address?" When he didn't respond, I looked up to see Leroy staring at me in horror. We did *not* have time for this. "You're a terrible liar," I said succinctly. "Now tell me about the girl you were with that night." I paused, realizing there could be other reasons Leroy was lying. "Or was it a guy?" I held up my free hand in protest. "No judgment here."

177

"I wasn't with a girl *or* a guy!" Leroy hissed angrily, eyes darting around as if he were afraid someone might overhear. At least he seemed equally upset about either suggestion, which I had to give him credit for; hard enough doing time without the other inmates thinking you're gay or bi. "I'd *never* cheat on Tanya!" he declared.

"But...?" I probed, hoping we were getting somewhere. I could see his lips quivering, like he was considering spitting it out but still needed another nudge. "Look," I said, "anything you tell me... it's privileged." Total lie on my part, but we were running out of time. "I couldn't tell Tanya, even if I wanted to and thought it was in your best interest. Talking to me..." I stretched the truth even further, "it's like talking out loud to yourself." Did that even make any sense? No... but I could tell Leroy *really* wanted to spill, so I was basically just giving him the excuse.

For a long moment I thought it hadn't worked... then he bent low over the table, almost pushing his face through the glass. "Swear to me you won't tell Tanya!"

"I won't -"

"Swear to God!"

Hmm. Awkward, since I was pretty damn agnostic about any gods or goddesses... or Easter bunnies or tooth fairies, for that matter. But I figured I was batting a thousand on lies already, so I raised my hand and proclaimed solemnly, "Swear to God."

Leroy slumped back in his seat, chin to his chest and looking forlorn, and muttered something under his breath.

"Didn't quite catch that," I prodded.

"I said, I went to *Boobies*, alright?" he hissed, then darted his gaze back and forth to make sure no one had overheard us.

O...kay. Finally, the situation was becoming clear.

'Boobies' was... well, it was exactly what it sounded like: a joke of a titty bar on the outskirts of Glendale, as classless as they came. It wasn't so much famous as a neighborhood landmark that had been around since well before my time, the bright neon sign emphasizing the two 'O's in the name. Bottom line (no pun intended), it was the kind of place where young-to-middle-aged guys like me went for cheapskate bachelor parties, and middle-to-old-aged guys like my father went to escape their families and get drunk. Len probably had a seat named after him. Maybe a whole stage.

"So... you went to a strip club, and...?" I encouraged.

Leroy shot me a distraught glance. "I fucked up."

I knew it. "You screwed one of the strippers. What happened, you get cold feet about committing to one woman for all time?"

I could've gone on about how monogamy was a social construct and no one *actually* fell in love for life, but his eyes widened in surprise. "No! I told you, I'd *never* cheat on Tanya!"

I glanced up at the wall clock, since I'd had to leave my phone in the locker. "Leroy, you gotta start telling me the truth now, we're almost out of time."

"Okay."

I watched as he bowed his head, wondering what the hell he could've done that made him look like he was confessing to a priest right now, if it didn't involve actual sex. Lap dance? Motor-boating? *Golden shower?*

My ideas were getting more depraved - and frankly, less credible for a strip club setting - the longer he stayed silent, but finally he spat out in a hoarse whisper, "I was helping Moonbeam with her Bermuda Triangle."

I blinked a couple of times, trying to parse that sentence, and figured I'd go with the most obvious part first. "And Moonbeam is...?"

"My ex-girlfriend. That's her stage name," he added - surely unnecessarily. Although you really never knew these days... "She called me up, all upset she was gonna get fired." His gaze pleaded with me to understand. "All the other girls were busy, and she'd lost her contacts so she

179

couldn't see to do it right."

"The Bermuda Triangle?" Which was what, a cocktail? Lap dance position? "So you went over there and...?"

His voice dropped into an even hoarser whisper. "Applied the hot wax in the right place."

I reflexively clenched my thighs as I pictured Leroy - who seemed generously hairy - applying hot wax to any part of his anatomy... then realized what a "Bermuda Triangle" had to be. "You gave your ex a *bikini wax*?" I asked incredulously.

Leroy groaned and dropped his head into his hands. "Tanya'll never forgive me if she finds out!"

I was grinning when I left the prison - and before you call me heartless, bear in mind that I stoically resisted chuckling, laughing, or even smirking while I was in with Leroy. I might have snorted initially at the surprise, but after that I held it together long enough to get every detail of that night.

Moonbeam - whose real name was Candy (no kidding) Atkins - had been Leroy's girlfriend for a year when they were both the grand age of fourteen, after which she'd dumped him for a boy on the football team. But they'd still lived in the same neighborhood, so when her latest boyfriend had started beating on her, Leroy had come back into her life and - as he put it - 'sorted shit out.' They'd been nothing more than friends since, so calling her his 'ex' seemed a stretch to me, but I guess he worried that was how Tanya would see it.

Anyhow, he'd never introduced the two of them - he'd wanted to, but after a bad home life and a prostitution arrest, 'Moonbeam's star had declined and she'd worried about messing things up with his new girlfriend. And when she'd offered to come forward with an alibi for him, he'd lied and told her the cops knew but wouldn't accept it.

I couldn't believe he'd just *assumed* they wouldn't without even trying, but he managed to convince me in the final minutes before I had to get out of there. After all, aside from his long-time friend, his alibi consisted of the two other strippers who'd seen her smuggling him in the back door of the place. In Leroy's mind, what was the point in ruining his engagement when he knew no one would accept their story?

I didn't think that was true, but I guessed he had reason to think so. A good alibi didn't *always* mean a case got dropped, although in my experience it would unless there was damning eyewitness evidence that put the accused at the crime scene, too. On the other hand, not all alibis were 'good.' The quality of the witnesses made a difference, as did their connection to the accused - so yeah, a nun and a couple of retired judges who'd never met Leroy before would be better than three 'Boobies' lap dancers, one of whom worshipped the ground he walked on.

But regardless, *I* now firmly believed Leroy hadn't been the fourth man in that robbery. Unfortunately, my opinion didn't count for shit in a court of law, so I needed to get out there and prove it -

Dull pain thudded into my skull at the thought. A little reminder from whoever was controlling my shit show of a curse that Joey was my main priority. Like they were jealous I was cheating on their pet project or something.

I grunted in frustration, pausing in my trek across the parking lot to glare up at the heavens. "For fuck's sake, I have six hours to kill!"

As I climbed into my trusty Toyota, I ignored the stares from the other departing visitors and the guard near the exit speaking into his radio. I guess I was getting used to it by now.

I'd only worry if he closed the gate before I could drive out.

༈

"Boobies" looked positively depressing as I pulled up

and parked a few feet from the door. I'd driven past it before, after dark, but now the neon glory of the evening was replaced by the sunlit revelation of faded paintwork and shoddy building repairs, while the small parking lot revealed its massive potholes and cracked tarmac. I'd looked Candy up online and had her contact info, but it made sense to check out the club in person anyhow, just in case there was another way to prove Leroy was here that night. A stripper ex-girlfriend might not make an ideal witness, but time-stamped security footage would do very nicely.

On the plus side, the matinee performance was discounted and well drinks were three bucks off. I'd discovered those enticing facts when I'd called from the car to find out when Moonbeam/Candy would next be on stage. It turned out she wasn't performing until eight that night, but the guy I'd spoken to had generously volunteered the information that she usually showed up on Sunday afternoons to try out routines in front of a smaller audience. No doubt a strip joint would be the opposite of a diner in terms of attracting the after-church crowd.

Maybe he was telling the truth, or maybe it was just part of his sales technique. I wasn't sure. But I'd made some other phone calls too - prepping for our infiltration of Gerry's launch party this evening - and one contact had promised me what I needed from a Jewish wedding at the Burbank Marriott. It was only a couple of miles from here, so I figured it wouldn't hurt to stop in at "Boobies" for a drink en route.

Scanning the exterior, I spotted surveillance cameras covering the front and rear entrances. Although who knew whether the tapes were wiped every day or every week, or if the cameras were even working at all. I had to believe a place like this taped the customers entering, for their own protection... but in my experience, most business owners were cheap unless they'd had problems before. Sad to say, Leroy's freedom might depend on at least one dancer having been assaulted in the past, or one client having sued the club for tripping on a crack in the parking lot.

At the door I was met by a bored bouncer who stared at me moodily. "Cover's fifteen dollars." He sat on a stool that had seen better days, the black plastic cover torn half off. Not exactly classy, but it probably didn't show up at night and I guessed the daytime clientele weren't that picky.

I pulled two twenties out of my wallet and saw a glimmer of interest in his eyes. "You know if Moonbeam's around?"

He scowled. "Why?"

"Why'd you think? That girl can *move*." I was going for suggestive but not sleazy; the guys who worked these places could either be assholes or be pretty protective of the girls, and I didn't need to be barred before I'd even spoken to Candy.

This one just stared at me impassively for a long moment, then produced a phone, holding it sideways like it was a flute instead of putting it against his ear. "Hey Ro, Moonbeam on stage right now?" I bet he held his weapon sideways when he pulled it, too. Moron.

A growl came back over the speaker. "Yeah. Why?"

The bouncer's eyes met mine.

I handed the two twenties over.

"No reason." My new friend stepped aside, ushering me into the darkened cavern that lay through the door.

I reclined against the faux leather of the rear booth and tried to look at least slightly interested in the ladies of 'Boobies' undulating on the distant stage. In reality, I was wondering if I'd been conned by both the guy on the phone and the bouncer at the door, since none of the women on stage matched the Facebook photos I'd found of Candy. I wasn't sure whether to be pissed at the bouncer for taking my bribe then lying, or pissed at myself for offering it at all.

"Hey, baby. You want a lap dance?"

I looked up to see two bikini-topped and thong-clad women standing next to my booth, glistening hips tilted suggestively toward me. I almost declined automatically, a reflex trained by having been propositioned numerous times as a cop... then realized with a jolt that the woman who'd spoken was none other than Moonbeam herself.

I hadn't recognized her at first in the dim strip club light, the heavy eye makeup and long fake eyelashes throwing me. Not to mention the miles of sleek skin and vast cleavage that definitely hadn't been exposed on her social media sites. She licked her lips temptingly, running one manicured hand slowly from her waist to her thighs. "I'm Moonbeam, and this is Cheri-Pie."

I sent out a silent thanks to the taciturn bouncer at the door, who'd clearly passed on my interest and delivered Moonb... no, I refused to call a grown woman after a My Little Pony... *Candy* into my lap. Literally, if I bought a dance. All I had to do now was go through with it, and I'd have her undivided attention without drawing her bosses' notice or ire. Yet still I hesitated, because there was one *tiny* problem:

I was a lap dance virgin. While I'd been on calls in clubs like this one, I'd never actually been out there on the floor or paid that much attention to what one involved. My few undercover assignments had been in other types of places, and ironically my distaste for matrimony meant I'd never been to any strip club bachelor parties either. Plus I'd basically been celibate since Michael and Jenny's boat exploded, apart from one drunken hook-up with another lonely cop the night after the funerals and my own hand in the shower from time to time. 'Pent up' didn't begin to cover it.

So I was a more than a little worried about keeping the interview professional, if it involved a stripper sliding up and down my 'pole' and stuffing my face in her boobs. What if I got hard?

What if I did *worse*? Sure, I wasn't exactly in the mood right now. Not only was I majorly sleep-deprived, it still felt like my mind and body weren't my own.

On the other hand, stress had a tendency to make me need release more than usual, and I was definitely feeling it now...

My internal debate was cut off as Candy leaned over me, arms resting on the seat either side, her impressive chest area filling my field of vision. "Say yes, baby," she said huskily, leaning in further as if she were about to lick a stripe up my cheek.

"I'm here for Leroy," I said, hoping to head off any tongue contact.

It worked. Maybe a little *too* well.

Candy ricocheted back like I'd just called her mother a goat-fucking whore. Across the room I could see the two bouncers by the door react, clearly trained to spot problem clients and deal with them before the women got hurt or the disturbance spread to the whole floor.

"I'm trying to prove his innocence," I said quickly.

Candy and Cheri-Pie exchanged glances, then Candy's gaze shot to the steadily approaching bouncers. I don't know what she did, but the two men subsided into watchful glowers as Candy moved in to drape her ample curves over my thighs.

"You want a dance - right?"

I forced a smile for our audience. "Sure."

As Candy began to undulate, the music pounded even louder - or maybe that was just my heart pounding in my ears - and I felt instantly uncomfortable. Sure, she knew how to move, but it just felt off somehow. Both clinical and dirty at the same time, if that were even possible. It was gonna take me a moment to -

Abruptly, Candy's boobs thrust into my face, forcing me back against the rear of the booth. I figured she was angling our bodies to make talking easier without being detected, so I leaned back and made room. She followed me down, still shimmying over my lap with a kind of hypnotic grace. Before she cut off my vision altogether I caught sight of a waitress walking past with something amber in the glass on her tray, and found myself suddenly longing for McDougall's and their single malt scotch; the very antithesis of this place.

If I hadn't brushed her off earlier, I could've been there right now with Reesa -

Ohhh, no.

No no no... I was *not* thinking about Reesa when I had another woman draped all over me half naked. And I most definitely was *not* comparing my best friend's body to Candy's more voluptuous frame, or imagining what *her* long legs could do if they wrapped around my thighs the same way...

I barely held it together as Candy whipped off her bikini top and began to gyrate, my mind still distracted by the Reesa fantasy that seemed to have come out of nowhere. My little brain perked up in interest, even as my big brain was signaling a red alert and telling me it needed to go into shutdown mode...

Ask your questions, dammit!

"I know he was here that night," I managed to squawk out. See? I could stay professional...

I retracted that thought as Candy began to grind her pelvis against mine. I just wished I could retract certain pieces of my anatomy too.

Fuck.

I was never gonna hold it together. Doesn't matter if you're playing good cop, bad cop, or whatever, you need a certain level of detachment when you're conducting an interview... and that's pretty hard to achieve when the interviewee is grinding her pubic bone all over you and slapping your cheeks with her nipples.

Still, gamely doing my best to keep my mind focused, I tilted my head back and attempted to make eye contact with the woman above me. "He needs an alibi!" I said, pitching my voice so it rose just above the volume of the throbbing dance music.

"You shouldn't be here!" Candy hissed back at me, and despite the apparent abandon of the lap dance I could sense her anxiety. At least it had the effect of dousing most of my interest; fear isn't usually a turn-on unless you're a sexual predator. Even as she increased the speed of her swaying/grinding motion across my lap, her pert breasts undulating up and down in front of my face, Candy's eyes flicked toward the side again. "My boyfriend gets jealous."

I glanced over discreetly and saw a shorter guy watching us intently. I'd seen him come out of a room marked 'Office' soon after I arrived, and I'd noticed him because he held himself with authority and not a little swagger, even though he wore the same plain black uniform as the other security around. "Of lap dances?" I asked, surprised. Given her job, that had to be unfortunate for the guy.

"Of Leroy!"

Huh? "I thought you only dated in high school." For all of two months, according to Leroy.

Candy huffed in annoyance. "Yeah, well, I was a dumb kid then!" She bucked forward and writhed against me to the beat of the music. "I never shoulda let him go." She pumped her pelvis and belly against mine with each thrust. "Leroy's the love of my life!"

I guessed her routine was so choreographed, she didn't even register the disconnect between what she was doing to me and declaring undying love to another guy.

"So you'll give him an alibi?"

Not answering, Candy leaned back, tightening her calves against my legs and raising her arms to sweep her hair up above her head. The effect made her prominent nipples stick out like matching binkies. Mesmerized, I wondered what would happen if the lap dancee leaned up to suck on them... but seeing movement from my right, I was pretty sure it'd earn them a black eye from Candy's boyfriend. Apparently the guy also had limits unrelated to Leroy.

I waited until she returned to the 'normal' bump and grind before pursuing my question further. "Just tell me: was Leroy here the night of the robbery?"

"Uh huh." Candy gazed over my head as she did some workmanlike but unfortunately effective swivels over my groin. I felt myself harden again against my will and fought the urge to pull her off me. "Got here at nine, didn't leave until after midnight."

I frowned, my gaze darting involuntarily to the minuscule bikini bottom Candy still wore - thank fuck. "I thought he was just waxing your... uh..."

"Bikini line?"

I jerked, realizing the voice had come from my left side. Cheri-Pie was perched there, apparently eager to get in on the action before her own dance commenced. Her expert tongue delved into the whorl of my ear as I tried to form a sentence. "Were you there too?" I managed to get out.

"Uh huh," she murmured, leisurely continuing to lick.

I wasn't sure if Candy was pissed by me getting distracted, or just gearing up for the big finish, but as Cheri-Pie kept working on my ear, Candy started some serious twerking right up against an even more erogenous region. I now fought the urge to forget about the case entirely.

Then Cheri-Pie removed her tongue, and for a brief moment I could think more clearly. "We were all kind of pissed at Candy for letting him backstage, so..." I turned my glazed eyes toward her in time to see her shrug, "she made him stay to do all of us."

Despite the coils of guilty pleasure darting through me - *I would not come in my pants, I would not come in my pant*s - my eyes went wide at this. No fucking wonder Leroy hadn't wanted his fiancée to find out! Hell, most guys wouldn't want *anyone* to know about it. Being backstage with strippers was one thing, but trimming their bushes half the night did not sound manly or sexy in the least - not unless you had very specific masochistic tendencies.

Candy scowled down at me as if she could read my mind. "Hey! His mom runs a beauty salon. Leroy used to help out all the time when he was growing up."

Jeesh. And I thought *my* mom had been embarrassing the time she picked me up from school and announced - in front of the entire football team - that I'd have to tidy my room if I wanted to watch 'Sabrina the Teenage Witch.' I pictured the hulking Leroy Baldwin as a teenager, applying wax to various parts of the female body, and cringed.

On the other hand, this could only be good for his case.

"So how many of you can give Leroy an alibi?"

With a final double plunge of Candy's hips, it seemed my time was up. She swung herself off my lap in an expert dismount, then - still glaring at me in disfavor - moved to recline elegantly on the seat to my right. As Cheri-Pie saddled up for her ride on the Thatcher Merry-Go-Round, I caught sight of Candy's boyfriend glaring at us, maybe wondering what she was still doing there.

But back to the matter at hand... I twitched as Cheri-Pie unerringly grabbed my nipples through the thin shirt I wore, hoping she wasn't about to add pain to my pleasure. I guess that worked for some guys, but I wasn't one of them; too many nip twists from Michael when I was a kid.

I rephrased my question, hoping to distract her. "That means more than one of you can give him an alibi, right?"

Cheri-Pie rolled her eyes, and for a second I thought she was making the universal sign for 'obviously,' but as it morphed into a full blown simulated orgasm and she started vibrating on top of me, I realized she might be out for this round of the conversation. And oh, man, what she was doing was making my body light up with all kinds of reminders about how much sex it should be having. And not those limp-ass courtesy email reminders; we're talking collection agents standing at your door, ready to tow your car and sell your plasma TV.

I realized I was gonna be hobbling all the way to my car, if I even made it past the men's room, unless she stopped with that undulating. *Wow*. Talk about embarrassing. I can honestly say that, up until that night, I never *once* got hard during an interrogation.

It was Candy's answer that saved me. "We already tried. No one believes us."

Leroy was right about that? "With multiple witnesses?"

"I have a record for..." Candy sounded reluctant, "a few things."

I focused on the woman writhing above my lap like she was having her own personal orgy. "What about you, uh, Cheri?"

Cheri-Pie began doing a rippling body roll, working thigh and abdominal muscles that looked like they came straight from the Olympics. "I kind of... gave my boyfriend... an alibi... last year," she moaned out rhythmically to the beat of the music, before starting to swing her lengthy hair across my chest in some kind of sideways head-banging move.

"A fake one," Candy added before I could ask. "And the other girl's illegal, so she ain't talking."

"So there's..." I spat out some of Cheri-Pie's hair, "nothing that can prove he was here? Not one of the bouncers? Not security tapes?"

I caught Candy looking away guiltily, and caught her by the wrist to get her attention.

"Which is it?"

"No touching!" Candy's boyfriend's voice floated over the music as he took a threatening step toward us.

I released Candy's arm and held my hands up apologetically. He still looked pissed, but subsided back as another guy muttered in his ear. I didn't know if it was just a reminder to stay cool, or if I should worry about getting jumped in the parking lot when I left.

We avoided conversation for a few moments after that - better safe than sorry - and I focused on pasting a dumb grin to my face and controlling my reaction to Cheri-Pie's enthusiastic assault on my groin and chest, while some rapper vented about tapping asses and getting down with his 'ho's. Usually that kind of music at that volume would make my head ache, but I'd take the distraction if it got my attention off my other head and stopped me doing something truly embarrassing in my underwear.

Finally, as Cheri-Pie went into her finale, Candy spoke again. "They keep video of all the entrances for at least a year."

I stared up at the ceiling to cover my reaction, at last blessedly oblivious to the physical stimulation I was receiving. "Why the *hell* didn't you tell the cops that?"

Candy sounded upset. "'cos Gun'd delete them if he knew it'd help!"

I risked glancing at her again. "Gun?"

Candy inclined her head, indicating the guy still shooting me hate stares from a distance.

Probably because I was paying more attention to the stripper who'd tagged out than the one still in action. Turning my attention back to Cheri-Pie - who had saved the 'best' for last and was now twirling actual *tassels* from her pierced nipples - I hissed out of the side of my mouth, "They'll come in with a warrant - he won't have time." Besides, from the looks of it, I doubted that cretin could even figure out how to program his DVR.

"He set up the whole system," Candy hissed. "Controls it from an app on his smart watch. He gets any idea Leroy was here that night and that evidence is *gone*."

As Cheri-Pie flopped off me with a faux-satisfied sigh, she breathed into my left ear, "He's part owner here."

I twisted my head to take another look at 'Gun.' *Really?* But then why had Candy been worried about getting fired because her bikini line was off? Something wasn't adding up here...

And I was rapidly losing my chance to ask more questions, as Candy and Cheri-Pie were both standing up and adjusting their clothes. "That'll be fifty dollars," Candy said, avoiding eye contact.

I slowly pulled out my wallet with a smile, keeping my voice as low as I could, given the blaring music. "Can you get into the system? Get a copy of the video?"

"Maybe." Candy's gaze flicked to her boyfriend, still over by the wall but barely restrained, like a leashed Pit-Bull eager to defend its territory. She sent him a sultry smile, but when she turned back to me her expression had hardened... and my heart sank because I'd seen that face before. "But I ain't risking what I got here." She grabbed the money I'd barely pulled from my wallet and stuffed a twenty and a five into her bra. "Not when Leroy's marrying another girl."

I glanced at Cheri-Pie, but she just shrugged and took another twenty five from my wallet before dipping her gaze and hurrying off.

Looking back at Candy, I felt myself get pissed off by the sudden change in attitude, even though I knew we had only precious seconds left. "I thought you said you loved him?" Yet another example of how so-called 'true love' was anything but selfless and generous.

Candy just glared at me again... but this time I saw tears shimmer in her eyes and knew I was getting to her. Even so, it wasn't exactly safe to be having this conversation here and now. I was betting there were rules about hanging around a client once she'd been paid, and frankly my reproductive organs weren't up to another round. As Candy's eyes flickered to my right and widened, I could almost feel someone - perhaps the famous Gun - approaching. We were out of time.

"Meet me for a coffee somewhere," I said quickly.

Candy shook her head, then pasted on a seductive smile. Taking her cue, I stood up as if I were leaving, and pulled another ten from my wallet like I was tipping her for a really good time. "We need to talk some more," I argued as I pushed the bill delicately through her thong's side, careful not to make more than passing contact with flesh but making sure to block any view of her mouth from whoever was coming up behind me.

"I can't," she mouthed, telling me they were now close enough to hear us speak, even over the club's loud music.

I let my eyes do the talking, milking the beseeching puppy-dog look for all it was worth and hoping I didn't just look constipated or horny.

I guess it worked, because after an anguished eye flick toward whoever was coming for us, Candy leaned in and murmured into my ear: "Nine thirty San Fernando, one hour." Then she pulled back, sucked in an offended breath - and *slapped* me.

I watched her speed away, bikini top held to her breasts, and wasn't surprised to feel someone's heavy hands on my arms a moment later. As I was swung around to face Candy's pissed off boyfriend, I braced for a beating.

Chapter Nine.

I limped out of the club ten minutes later, a couple of hundred bucks lighter - fines, they'd said - and wearing several new injuries. Fortunately, whatever erection I'd had in the booth had gone down before the beating commenced, or I'd have been in an even bigger world of trouble. As it was, I wouldn't be getting happy for the next few days without causing myself serious pain. I had to admit, other than the well-placed groin kick, Gun and his bouncer friend had actually held back, but I figured that was more out of fear of getting shut down than any sense of compassion.

In addition to being blackballed I'd also been blacklisted, which meant that my photo now sat on a wall of shame just inside the door. Fortunately, they'd caught my features in a rictus of pain that rendered me almost unrecognizable, but I still cringed at the idea of Len seeing me up there next time he stopped by for a visit. Maybe I should explain the circumstances to him ahead of time. Although I knew he'd been cutting back on such activities since Kaylee came to live with him, so I probably had a while.

Sliding slowly into my seat behind the wheel, I pulled out my phone and tried to distract myself by checking messages while I waited for the immediate agony to subside. There was an apologetic message from Kaylee's drama teacher, letting me know my van had been towed the evening of the musical and where it had been taken to.

Nice of the guy. I memorized the name of the impound lot and resigned myself to paying an arm and a leg to retrieve it, which would - *shit* - need to be this afternoon. Being without it on a job kinda felt like having a missing fifth limb... and if my lead at the Marriott worked out I'd *definitely* need it later on.

Wasn't Sunday meant to be a day of rest? This one was turning out to be a doozy.

But hey, at least I wouldn't hit any rush hour traffic as I criss-crossed LA.

The question was, did I try to fit in the hotel thing before I went to the address Candy had given me? My groin said *hell no*, but I bribed it with visions of hotel ice machines and it acquiesced, no matter how hard (no pun intended) it was gonna be to make that work without getting water stains all over my pants.

Some things were just worth it.

One successful hotel wedding reconnoiter and fifteen minutes hiding out in a restroom cubicle with an ice bucket later, I stared at a giant rat and tried to ignore the sounds of screaming echoing in my skull.

I'd double and triple checked all possible combinations of the address, but in the end I'd had to accept it: Nine thirty San Fernando Blvd. was the Burbank location for a Nutt E. Nibbler restaurant. Last time I'd been at one had been Kaylee's sixth birthday party. After three hours - which had felt more like three days - of fishing kids out of ball pits, breaking up fights over who got to play which arcade game, and brushing tomato-covered pizza and spaghetti out of my clothes and hair, I'd sworn to never darken their doors again short of a drug raid or the apocalypse. Fortunately for me, back then you'd needed to have a child in tow to get through the doors, so the likelihood had been a remote possibility.

But apparently the rules had changed since those days. At the door, no one had batted an eyelid at me walking in minus kids. In fact, unless my eyes deceived me, there was even beer and wine on the menu. I pictured bored drunks choosing their local Nutt-E's as a daytime watering hole, then realized they wouldn't; the place was far too bright and loud for any self-respecting wino. Although if they added marijuana to the menu, I bet junkies would get a kick out of the large animatronic squirrel that stood in the center of the floor, jerking periodically to a painfully G-rated rap song...

Yeah, my focus was for shit. An avoidance tactic that was dumb and dangerous in my line of work, but probably inevitable given my task today.

I turned my attention back to Candy as she gave her order, waiting until the waitress had departed before opening my mouth.

Candy beat me to it. "I know what you want, and the answer's no. I won't do it."

"Do what?" I asked cautiously.

"Whatever you want me to do to help Leroy. I already went to the fucking cops," she fumed, taking a deep gulp of her white wine that half emptied the glass.

I met the scandalized eyes of a woman ushering a red-slushie-covered child toward the bathroom, but couldn't tell if she'd heard the expletive or was offended by the day drinking. Or maybe it was both.

"It ain't my fault that dumbass detective didn't believe me!" Candy continued, aggrieved, and I decided not to mention I'd been one of those dumbasses not so long ago. "And now you want me to ruin a good thing I got going with Gun!"

I could see her point. Still, it sucked knowing that digital proof of Leroy's innocence existed, if only we could get ahold of it. "Look," I said, "I was wrong to ask you to get the tape for us. All I'm asking for now is a little information on how Gun has it all set up." I put on my best non-threatening expression, perfected by years of playing Good Cop in interrogations. "You said he can erase the security video remotely. So what if we go in when he's not there? Keep him in the dark until it's done?"

Candy snorted. "Gun's paranoid. If someone tries to access his system - hell, even unlocks the office door - he knows about it." She gestured to her left wrist, making a ring around it with her fingers. "Even if he's asleep, his watch vibrates and wakes him up." She grabbed her drink again and took another hefty gulp.

And here I'd thought Gun was just a glorified bouncer who thought an Apple watch looked cool.

I had to wonder why he was so cautious about their security footage, too. Was it possible the club was taping the action inside some of the private rooms and doing a little blackmail on the side? All of which would make him even readier to hit the 'delete all' button.

On the other hand, that could represent a lot of potential income. "You think he'll wipe everything just because an alarm goes off?"

I knew I sounded skeptical, and Candy scowled at me over the rim of her raised glass, no doubt pissed at my not believing her completely. "He has backups in the Cloud or whatever." She tossed back most of what remained of her Chardonnay. "He can wipe the servers at the club any time he wants." As she reclined back in her seat, glaring at me defiantly across the table, I caught a hint of satisfaction in her face.

Maybe she was just proud of Gun's abilities, but I didn't think so.

No, I thought she was gaining a kind of satisfaction from throwing obstacles in my way. For neatly blocking the path of her ex's ticket out of trouble. She might have gone to the cops initially, but now she'd had time to think about it, she was ready to let Leroy go to jail. *Happy* about it, even.

But why? She might be jealous of Tanya, but if he was

in jail no one would have him. Was she really that petty?

I tried another tack. "You realize Leroy could go away for years?"

Candy puffed up in her seat. "I'll wait for him." She took a final gulp of wine, muttering almost into the glass, "Not like that *skank* he's engaged to."

Ahhhh. I was beginning to see the light. Candy thought good-girl Tanya would drop Leroy like a hot potato if he went to prison... leaving him available for other people. So I just had to convince her that wouldn't work. To gain her cooperation, I needed to make her believe Tanya would never abandon Leroy.

But how could I do that?

Dammit. There was only one thing I could try.

I just didn't know if I could pull off the lie.

I'd lied a hundred times as a cop, first when I'd been undercover, then as a detective.

I'd lied to suspects in interrogations, telling them whatever I had to - within legal limits - to get their confessions.

I was *still* lying to my own family about the events of a year ago - to Reesa, too. And they might never understand or forgive me if they found out. But I'd had no time to think; no choice to make at the time. And once I'd made the decision, I'd had to lie to protect it.

So I guess the question was: if I could lie about something so huge, to the people I cared about most in my life, why couldn't I spin a story for Candy? The answer was, I *could* and I *would*. Even if the words stuck in my craw.

"I get it, you know?" I started off slow, going for the empathy approach. "Why should their happiness come at your expense? I just..." Breaking off, I leaned back in the booth and sighed. "I just know Tanya's heart is gonna break over this." I frowned across the table at Candy.

"You ever seen them together?"

"No."

Her answer was surly and unencouraging, but I took out my phone anyway. I was armed with visual aids, thanks to the power of Instagram and Facebook, and I pulled up the most nauseatingly cute of the photos I remembered seeing on there when I was drunkenly checking out Leroy's pages last night. The one I had in mind - and yes, it was even worse sober - showed Tanya and Leroy eating a bowl of pasta together, in a loving recreation of that scene from the 'Lady and the Tramp' movie.

Barf.

I put my phone down and spun it around so Candy could see it. "I've never been a big believer in true love." Understatement of the decade.

Candy - eyeing the phone only distantly - huffed her agreement and reached for her glass again; finding it empty, she held it high and waggled it about, the universal signal for wanting a refill. Although, as the only employee in our section was an over-subscribed Nutt E. Nibbler impersonator attempting to entertain a dozen screaming eight-year-olds, I figured it would take a while in coming.

"But I gotta say, these two... well, they've really changed my mind." I felt a cold shock travel down my spine as I said that, but at least I wasn't vomiting into the nearest trash can. Maybe I could fake it through this after all.

Reaching across the table, I scrolled until I found the photo of Tanya and Leroy in matching Star Trek uniforms at Halloween, then onto a selfie of them laughing and screaming as they reached the apex of a theme park ride. I'd only seen Tanya distraught or terrified in person, but I had to admit she glowed and looked almost beautiful when she was happy.

I glanced up to see Candy's eyes reluctantly drawn to the phone's screen and figured she was seeing the same thing. "They look happy together, don't they? Like they fit.

Like they were..." I cringed inwardly, "*meant to be*."

Not that I *believed* in crap like 'soulmates' or anything, I told myself firmly. Even if Leroy was cleared, I still gave them a year together - max.

Candy grunted, seeming unimpressed, but as I kept scrolling on through the photos she didn't take her eyes from the screen. I stopped on a blurry, badly lit photo showing Leroy down on one knee in a romantic restaurant. The proposal had obviously been snapped in a hurry by some entranced spectator. Even so, the angle was good and captured Tanya's reaction perfectly. If I wasn't mistaken, Candy's eyes misted up slightly.

She reached for the phone, clutching it tightly as she brought the screen closer to her face. She sniffed, and now I was certain her emotions were engaged. "So romantic," she croaked, then began scrolling through the images herself, seeing the smiles and happiness on Tanya and Leroy's faces. One perfectly manicured nail swept up to wipe a tear off her cheek. "No wonder he wouldn't cheat on her with me," she mumbled unhappily, then shot me a nervous look.

I guessed she hadn't meant me to hear that, but it wasn't like I hadn't already figured out what she'd been hoping for when she invited Leroy to the strip joint that night. It was as obvious as Cheri-Pie's bellybutton ring that Candy's job had never been in danger - hell, she was *dating* one of the strip club's owners. Which meant she'd simply been trying to pry him away from Tanya. Nothing like another woman wanting a guy to make him seem more appealing, right? I was guessing Candy had found out he was getting married and decided maybe he was her dream guy after all.

Unlike her, Leroy Baldwin had turned it around after high school. Stayed clean, gotten a good job. He probably looked like Prince Charming compared to the toad-like Gun, who might have some dough but wasn't exactly a guy you wanted to take to your reunion. Leroy hadn't mentioned her coming on to him, but we'd been cut short on time. Or was he just so fixated on Tanya he hadn't *noticed*?

I guess love made people blind in a whole slew of ways. Hell, I should know. I hadn't seen Jenny and Michael's affair until she was standing on my mom's porch with him, two months pregnant.

The only question was, why bring Leroy to a sleazy strip club to convince him he was better off with her? Unless she'd simply been trying to lead him astray. Maybe she'd figured the club - and her story - would provide the best chance for scantily-clad seduction without making him suspicious. Or maybe she'd just wanted to break up his engagement and hadn't cared how she did it, from playing on old affections to offering a ménage with the other strippers. I had to give Candy credit: she'd thrown every weapon into her assault.

I reached over and took her hand in mine. "Candy," I said seriously, "you are an incredibly sexy woman, and any guy in his right mind would *kill* to sleep with you."

I heard a loud 'tch!' of righteous indignation from the aisle and realized a gaggle of kids was just passing by. Fortunately, the only people who'd heard me seemed to be the leading parents, but from the stink eye they were shooting us I figured they'd be reporting in to the management. *Shit.*

I needed to pick up the pace if I wanted to convince Candy to help before we got tossed out on our ears. I wasn't expecting another beating, but I wasn't sure my self-respect could take being blacklisted again so soon - this time from a children's restaurant - and if word leaked out it wouldn't look good for my investigator's license either.

Returning my attention to Candy, I continued, "So I think that tells you how much he must truly love Tanya, right?"

Yeugh.

I worried I'd start believing this crap if I said it enough times.

Candy wiped another tear from her eye and scrolled on to the next photo... and let out a startled hiccup as she saw it. Yeah, I'd known that one was coming up at the end. No kidding, Leroy had actually given Tanya a Golden Labrador as a Christmas present, and the image showed the cute blonde puppy squirming in Tanya's arms as she kissed Leroy under mistletoe. That photo was so cheesily romantic, greetings card companies were probably in a bidding war over it already.

My eyes flicked from Candy to the restaurant manager, who I could see bracing himself to come throw us out. I needed to time this just right. It had been a risk, pushing the 'true love' and 'soulmates' angle so hard. Candy might've scoffed and argued Leroy would be happy with whoever floated his boat, or that she'd beat Tanya in a beauty contest any day of the week... but I'd hoped not.

Pretty sad that I was banking on an ex-con stripper with a shady, jealous boyfriend being less emotionally damaged than I was myself, right?

Still, it looked like it was gonna work. Candy was still staring at the 'Mistletoe Puppy' photo like it held the answers to all the mysteries of life. "Will you help them, Candy?"

She blinked up at me, teary-eyed.

I forced down my own nausea and said, "Will you help Leroy get his happy ending?" Belatedly I realized the phrase 'happy ending' might have another meaning to a stripper, but it was too late to change it now.

Candy's lip quivered, and I knew I was so close I could *feel* it. I tried not to let myself be distracted by the manager, now approaching slowly but doggedly over Candy's left shoulder, as I stared into her eyes. Just a few more seconds...

"Will you be the fairy godmother in their story?"

Candy's red-rimmed gaze held mine. "I will!" she cried

defiantly. Grabbing her coat and purse blindly, she surged up out of the booth, sending the nervous manager stumbling back into a cluster of two-person tables. "I'll do whatever I have to!"

&

An hour later, the memory of our conversation was still like nails on a chalk board inside my head. Fortunately, I had plenty of other things on my mind.

Unfortunately, this meant I found myself driving somewhere I didn't want to go... *again*. At least this time it wasn't because my internal auto-nav had gone batshit crazy. No, this time I was deliberately driving back home to meet up with Len... who had offered to drive me to the impound lot. Well, not so much offered as demanded. Which did not bode well for the time we'd be spending on the road together. I knew Len's eagerness to spend time with me wasn't out of the kindness of his heart, so I was braced for whatever he wanted to talk about in the car. Just me and him, with no chance of Kaylee overhearing or me walking out. Which was gonna be about as much fun as sticking my head down the toilet and flushing it.

I'd actually asked Joey to drive me over there, but it turned out he'd never gotten his license in the US, which explained why he was renting one of the most expensive suites in the city but relying on Lyfts to get around instead of some flashy rental car. I guessed I could understand why a busy child actor turned rock star hadn't had the time - or the need - to learn to drive himself around.

What I couldn't understand - or forgive - was him blabbing about my request to my father, even if the man was standing next to him and had ears like a highly trained celebrity gossip. Next time, I was dropping off the famous person in his hotel suite, instead of giving in to Kaylee's plea to 'hang out' with him because I was worried he'd drink himself stupid by the evening if we left him alone.

"You getting the kid back with his wife?" was Len's opening gambit as I pulled the old station wagon out onto the road.

I'd wondered why he'd insisted I drive, and now I had my answer: all the better to pump me for information, of course. I could feel him staring at me from the passenger seat, tracking my facial expressions for lies. I still considered lying, just on principle, but what was the point in winding him up when we'd be stuck in close proximity for up to an hour. "Yeah." Didn't mean I couldn't keep my answers short.

"Hmph." Len paused, then snorted disparagingly. "Guess some things never change."

I could've let it go... should have, probably. But I didn't. Maybe it was the snide note in his voice; more likely, it was the fact that I didn't have a clue what he meant, and that bugged me. "What do you mean?" There was no response, so I looked over to see him picking his teeth in the mirror. "Hey," I prompted, "what did you mean by that?"

He glanced over at me, his expression sour. "You were always trying to play 'matchmaker' for your mother and me."

What? I screwed up my face in disbelief. "No I wasn't."

"Yeah, you were." Len sounded pissed off. "I'd bring you home, and you'd drag me in to dinner, land every fucking guilt trip you could on me."

I guess I remembered a few of those times, right after they'd first separated. But I hadn't wanted him back with Mom, exactly. I mean, sure, that had been part of it, since I'd known she was miserable without him... for some reason. But really, I'd just wanted things to go back to normal. I'd wanted my father to come home in the evenings, like he used to once upon a time, and kiss my mother and sit down at the table with me and Michael, and be the protector of our family.

But no way was I telling him that, laying out all my childhood insecurities.

Instead, I forced myself not to react. "I don't remember."

"Well you were a pain in the ass, believe me." Len yawned loudly, leaning back more comfortably in his seat.

I fixed my gaze on the road ahead, trying not to give in to the urge to yell at the man. Because those years had been hell for my mother and me. Michael had been older, a teenager with his own interests and friends. But I'd been a nine-year-old kid who didn't know his father was a drunk who slept with any badge bunny who'd buy him a drink. And Mom had been a hard-working woman with two kids, desperately trying to cling onto her dignity even as she hoped for Len to come back to her.

I wondered suddenly if she'd even wanted him back for herself? Or had she only wanted him to come home for me and Michael? The latter actually made me feel better - even if it also made me feel guilty. I'd never understood why she'd accepted him back into our lives all those years later, right before her death, even with the whole AA / recovery spiel he'd given us. Had that been for us, not for her?

"You hear me?"

I glanced over at Len, who was looking peevishly at me. "Sorry?"

"I said you need to figure out your own love life before you start bossing other people around."

"I'm not bossing anyone around..." *you fucking asshole*, I thought.

"S'not what your brother told me."

My brain froze for a second. "Wh-what do you mean?"

Len sounded pissed off now. "You ever think if you hadn't been dicking around with his head, he mighta come to you when he needed help?"

Okay, what the hell? I noticed the car start to edge into the next lane and forced myself to focus on steering. "He was screwing around on his wife," I said, trying to keep the anger out of my own voice. And probably failing miserably, but that was always how it was when it came to Michael and Jenny. I'd met her first, *loved* her first... and then big brother had swept in with his swagger and bullet scar and dangerous assignments. Next thing I knew, Jenny was pregnant with Kaylee and I was having to suck it up and act happy to be best man at their fucking wedding, then play the friendly brother-in-law and uncle for life.

And then, just a few months before Michael died, I'd seen him leaving a bar with a woman hanging off his arm. They were clearly going somewhere to fuck, and I knew it probably wasn't the first time he'd cheated on Jenny, either.

"I told him to keep it in his pants or I'd tell her," I ground out.

"You threatened your own brother."

I heard the disgust in Len's voice and shot him a look, equal disgust in my own eyes. *You stick with blood* was the code my father lived by. Didn't matter if it was red or blue - your blood relatives or the cops around you. Everyone else fell by the wayside; didn't matter if you'd sworn to protect their rights or stay faithful for the rest of your life.

I'd never understood why my mother wasn't as important to him as those other ties. It was like he couldn't trust anyone he didn't share or spill blood with.

"You ever heard of HIV?" I shot back at him. "Gonorrhea? Jenny had a right to know."

Len scoffed. "Mikey was smart enough to use a fucking condom."

Dumb enough to get in bed with fucking drug dealers, though.

But I wouldn't say that out loud, because then Len would say something back... and I didn't want to hear my father defend him. I'd already had my illusions shattered enough when it came to the men in my family. Sure, I knew Len didn't always play by the book on the job, but if he ever tried to justify what Michael had been doing...

that'd be too much. It was the reason we never talked about it - on my side, at least. I'd always assumed Len didn't speak of it out of shame or anger at what his son had done... but if he still had Michael up on some kind of pedestal, after everything? I didn't think I could stay in the same house with the man.

Even now, the reminder of how badly he'd treated our mother was salt in the wound. "So that makes it okay to cheat?" I snarled at him. "Is that what you used to tell Mom? 'Hon, I'm dickin' around, but don't worry, I'm using protection'?"

"Leave your mother out of this!"

"I can't!" I spat out, pulling my eyes from the stopped traffic ahead to glare at him. "Why'd you think I hated Michael so much for cheating on his wife?"

I realized I'd just confessed to hating my own flesh and blood - a cardinal sin in my father's book. But to my surprise, he just smirked back at me angrily. "Oh, I know *exactly* why. And it had nothing to do with me and your mother."

"That so?"

He shook his head. "Reason you hated seeing Michael cheating on Jenny was you always wanted her for yourself. Even though she chose him over you!"

I said nothing, turning my gaze back to the road and the now-trickling stream of traffic. Inside, though, I was seething.

I'd always figured Len knew about my past with Jenny; he'd been out of our lives at the time, but he'd had fifteen years to hear about it since. He'd never mentioned it before, though - and now he was bringing it up, all this time later, and implying that I'd... what, made eyes at my sister-in-law? Tried to steal her back from my brother?

If anything, I'd *avoided* Jenny as much as I could. At first, because I was still bitter, and seeing her so deeply in love with Michael had hurt too badly. Later, when the pain had faded to a dull ache, I'd carried on keeping my distance. I still hadn't forgiven Michael, so family interactions were still strained... and while Jenny had seemed to want more from me at times, I hadn't wanted to get tempted into an affair that was driven by vengeance. Or do anything to make it hurt worse again.

But what really pissed me off was that Len was *still* taking my brother's side. I guessed even Michael's death and disgrace couldn't stop him being my father's pride and joy.

Which wouldn't have mattered, if it hadn't been made so clear to me that I was the disappointment.

We drove the rest of the way to the impound lot in mutually-agreed silence.

As I pulled the items I'd brought with us from the back seat of the station wagon, though, I could sense Len hovering more than usual. Most times he gave me a ride somewhere - we're talking since I was old enough to not need 'coddling' in his eyes - he'd sit behind the wheel ignoring me as I grabbed my stuff, then take off the instant the car door shut. One time he'd taken off so fast he didn't realize something had gotten caught in the back door until he heard it banging up and down on the freeway. Meanwhile, I'd been bawling my eyes out back at the summer camp, after screaming for him to stop while I watched my favorite backpack holding my Superman lunchbox get dragged along the road that led out of the park.

I'd consciously avoided baggy clothes for years after that, just in case the next time *I* was the one caught in the door.

I figured the lingering this time was because he regretted what he'd said, but as usual I was mistaken. "You gonna be home by nine?"

"Not sure. Why?"

"Harry booked the range, but I don't like leaving the kid alone at night." Len limped around to the driver's side and climbed in, slamming the door.

"I'll try," I called out, so he'd hear me through the glass.

He ignored me and started the engine, then drove off in a cloud of dust.

I stood there a moment, watching him leave, and wondering what he'd actually do if I wasn't home by nine. Would he still go out, or stay home? The crazy thing was, Kaylee was plenty old enough to be left alone in the house, but I remembered being less than half her age when Mom had worked evening shifts at a grocery store, and Len had left *me* home alone to go drinking with his cop buddies. For all I knew, he hadn't 'liked' it then either, but it sure as hell hadn't stopped him from having his fun.

Without further ado, I made my way over to the office and paid to get my van released. I could already see it was fine, as they'd left it sitting out front. It wouldn't fit into the regular spaces, I was guessing.

I checked the time - better hurry if I was gonna make it to Joey by six.

Not to mention the other stop we needed to make later on.

Joey had been fine with leaving off the makeup and piercings and wearing the outfit I'd told him to get into. He'd also been fine with me picking him up along Sunset, thus avoiding my nemesis who'd probably have called the cops if I'd driven the van into the Sunset Spire driveway. I pictured that dickwad valet squawking in rage, turning bright red in the face as I clipped the top of their dumbass awning. Huh. Maybe I should've gone with it. Joey had even been fine with waiting by the van as I hauled my 'secret weapon' out the back of the Burbank Marriott, then posing for selfies with the grinning waiters who'd helped me.

The only thing Joey wasn't fine with, apparently, was sitting around waiting for something to happen.

And we'd only been here fifteen minutes.

"What if they already went in?"

"They didn't," I said calmly, not lowering the binoculars from my eyes.

We sat a long, Beverly Hills block away from our target: a massive faux French Chateau, largely hidden behind high hedges and gates. It reminded me of the place where Michael Jackson spent his last weeks, and it had almost as much security, which I admit made me a little nervous about our method of entry. But hey: no guts, no glory. At least in the private sector, the worst they could do was basically tell us to go away, or - if we made it in there before we got caught - drag us back outside.

Which was a lot safer than wearing a wire to a cartel member's birthday party, not knowing they were strip-searching everyone at the door... or having your swastika temporary tattoo somehow *peel off* in the rain, in the middle of a neo-Nazi fundraiser. Both of which had happened to undercover cops I knew.

Worst case scenario here, Bethany flew to Europe without talking to us, and -

Pain struck at my temples then settled to a dull throb, reminding me the stakes were higher than on my usual jobs. I hissed and winced, trying to rub the residual ache away with my fingers even as I kept my eyes glued to where cars were arriving and partygoers getting out. It was still on the early side, so I'd spent more time watching bored valets and security than guests up until now. On the other hand, Gerry was practically hosting this event, so you had to figure he wouldn't show up last.

Right?

I felt Joey fidget in the seat next to me. Was he about to cut and run? Charge up there on his own and yell 'I'm a rock star, let me in!'? That might've worked at any other party, but I had a feeling Joey Russo was banned from any of Gerry's events at this point in time. I looked out of the corner of my eye to see Joey watching me with an intensity that made me nervous

It's never a good sign when clients get all thoughtful like this. The last one decided to crash the stakeout I was running on her ex, and I ended up with a *lot* more video of her committing property damage on a Motel 6 than of her cheating spouse.

"Joey, I can feel you boring holes into my skull."

I glanced over to see him looking worried. He gestured to my head - which I realized I was still rubbing like I was polishing the best silver - and asked, "Another migraine?"

"Uh... yeah."

I'd mumbled something about migraines earlier to explain all the sudden pain attacks I'd had. It just sounded better than hallucinations, psychotic episodes, or supernatural curses.

I went back to staring down the block, but Joey wasn't done yet.

"You don't have, like, a brain tumor or something, do you?"

"No," I replied firmly.

Strictly speaking, I guessed some medical explanation was still on the table. But depending on how things went in the next few hours, I was hoping I'd have an answer, one way or another... I just wasn't exactly sure what I hoped it was. I knew at least some brain tumors could be treated, whereas I still had little idea what Mara had done to me and even less idea of how she might fix it.

"That you know of," Joey muttered depressively.

I'd like to think this was all a touching degree of concern for me, but it was mostly the mood he'd been in from the time I'd picked him up. He'd convinced himself Bethany wasn't coming or that she'd already gone, so he was seeing the world through mud-colored glasses right now.

"Any updates?" I asked, hoping to distract him so I

could focus on watching the house in peace for once.

In my peripheral vision I saw him pick up the tablet in his lap and take a look. I'd set it up to show all the social media feeds for Gerry's agency and The Birdies, plus all the ones Gerry had himself. I was hoping the dumb schmuck would tweet their arrival, just like he tweeted everything else, including which type of breakfast waffles he was eating and when he took a really great dump... okay, so he hadn't tweeted that last one *yet*, but I was sure he had a big enough ego that he thought the world would be interested.

The first pumping music and loud shrieks echoed away from the party, and I saw colored lights switch on somewhere in the huge rear garden. Freaking *searchlights* also soared upward into the sky, just one Bat-Signal short of being useful.

"Pretty big party for an unknown group," I murmured.

Joey snorted in contempt. "It's all about marketing, not talent, these days. Celebrity feuds and getting on TMZ."

I decided not to comment on the fact that his *own* music career had been built on his cute former TV personality. Plus honestly, how many people got famous due to pure talent anyway? I bet even Helen of Troy was nothing special, she just had a load of bragging cousins.

"The Birdies," Joey scoffed, still enjoying his mini rant. "What a dumb name. Had to be Gerry's idea."

"I guess they picked it to sound retro."

The stony silence that followed told me either that Joey disliked me defending Gerry's latest discovery, or that 'retro' wasn't a word I should be using this decade... probably both, actually.

Fortunately, I was saved by the loud *bleep* let out by the tablet Joey still held. I heard his sharp intake of breath before he said excitedly, "Gerry just tweeted they're en route to the party!"

I grinned and shook my head. "Gotta love social media."

Truly, a stalker's best friend.

Ten minutes later, we watched as a massive gold Mercedes pulled up to the curb outside the mansion. Through my high-powered binoculars I could see Gerry and Bethany emerge - heck, I could see the ankle bracelet Bethany wore - but at my side Joey was still anxious.

"Is it them? Is it them?"

"Yeah."

I lowered the binoculars and went to hand them to Joey, but he was busy reaching for the door instead, eyes fixed on the distant Mercedes.

I could tell where he'd be headed once he set foot outside the van, so I grabbed him before he could get out. "Hey! We have a plan, remember?"

Joey shot a conflicted look toward the rear of the van, from which a faint *drip-drip-drip* had been sounding for the past fifteen minutes. "If it doesn't work -"

"It will!"

I hoped.

I tapped a warning on the divider as we pulled up to the mansion's gated entrance, then leaned casually out the window and gave the three security guys my best idiot grin. "Hey. Beverly Hills Events." I'd seen the name of the catering company from my vantage point earlier. Of course, that didn't mean the van *I* was driving magically had the right name on its side.

A guy holding a sturdy tablet computer checked the screen then stepped forward, eyeing me suspiciously. Both he and his machine looked like they were built for the Navy SEALs, which seemed like overkill for a Birdies fanfest. I wondered if the heavy protection was for The Birdies or to stop Joey getting to Gerry's precious daughter before they left town. "Your van says 'Epic Events'."

I glanced out my window, like I'd forgotten this. "Oh, yeah - we just expanded, took over those guys. Haven't had a chance to repaint everything yet." I saw the fractional doubt on the big guy's face and continued merrily, "Just call up to my supervisor - they'll tell you it's legit."

I rapped on the divider twice as I finished speaking, the signal for Joey.

The first security guy glanced back at the others, and one lifted a radio to his lips. "Gate to house, come in."

Shit.

I rapped the divider twice again, harder this time, forcing myself to keep a good-natured but bored expression on my face even as the guard's radio crackled to life. But whatever response came from it was masked by the loud *crack* that came from the back of the van.

Instantly all three security guys went on alert, one reaching for what looked like a Taser on his belt. *Great.*

"What was that?" Popeye demanded, but before I needed to answer, Joey's agonized wail rose from the rear.

"Billy! It's coming *apart!*"

"Holy crap!" I pushed my door open and jumped out, but before my feet had completely touched down I was shoved back against the van's side, one meaty forearm held across my throat. I froze, playing the nervous van driver, which wasn't a hard sell since I was outnumbered, outmuscled, and outgunned here.

"What's going on?" The words were growled right into my face, bringing with them some of the worst bad breath I'd smelled in a while. Bizarrely, it reminded me of the old days, interrogating a suspect after letting them stew in a room or a holding cell for hours; except this time, I was on the other side of the equation.

Another loud 'crack' came from behind my back, inside the van, and I hoped things hadn't progressed to the point of uselessness. "You hear that?"

"Yeah, what it is!?"

"Let me go and I'll show you!"

Reluctantly, the behemoth loosened his grip, and I

hurried to the van's rear - followed by the scowling threesome - then wrenched the doors open before they could stop me.

Inside, Joey stood in a pool of water, the front of his white waiter's uniform soaking wet as he clung desperately to a large, misshapen block of ice. Closer inspection revealed it to be more like *two* large bodies of ice, apparently newly calved with a jagged break between them.

Ignoring the various squawks from the goon squad behind me, I scrambled up into the van and spoke urgently to Joey. "You think it'll hold until we get up there?"

Joey's convincingly wild-eyed look of panic told me he hadn't lost those juvenile acting abilities. Toss in a photogenic mutt and two improbably tolerant parents, and it would've been just like an episode of his TV show. "I don't know! I think we lost a whole face already!"

"What the fuck is that thing?"

I turned around to see the three guards staring at us in confusion.

"It's the fucking Birdies! Can't you *see* that!?" Hoping to hell they had truly vivid imaginations, I shot the mess in Joey's embrace a glare. "Frickin' ice sculpture. I *told* them we should've used the refrigerated truck!" I turned my glare on the three men behind me. "'Course, if we'd been able to drive straight up there, we might've been okay! They've got a whole setup waiting for us - gonna feature the thing in a new music video or something!"

The men exchanged nervous looks, and I knew our entire plan rested on which way they jumped next.

Lucky for us, Joey had a great sense of timing. "Billy, I can't hold it much longer!" he cried out, artistically bracing his legs as if holding the pieces together took a Herculean effort.

"Okay, okay!" Popeye broke first, waving me toward him. As I climbed out, he slammed the rear doors shut then practically dragged me back to the driver's seat, issuing instructions the whole way. "Go up there, save

215

the... save the freaking sculpture or whatever..." he thrust me back behind the wheel, "and get your damn supervisor to call me - okay?"

"Okay! I swear, I will!" I threw the van in gear and hit the gas the second the gates opened ahead of me. As we accelerated up the slight incline, no doubt leaving a trail of water droplets in our wake, I lowered the window and yelled back, "Just as soon as it's safe!"

Three minutes later the van was parked in a deserted spot at the side of the mansion, and Joey and I were being pounded by music and the screams of over-entertained celebs and beautiful people from the garden beyond. We were also huffing and puffing as we heaved our rapidly melting ice sculpture out onto the nearest piece of grass, where the two halves cleaved fully apart with satisfying finality.

As we stood back, trying to recover our breaths, Joey was the first to speak. "How'd you get it made so fast?"

I shot him a puzzled look. "Made?"

"Yeah - you know someone in the business?"

I frowned at the decaying edifice on the lawn, trying to see how anyone could mistake it for a genuine attempt to reproduce the three 'Birdies' brothers. Sure, when I'd shown it to Joey I may have used the words, "It's an ice sculpture of The Birdies and it's melting, okay?" But I'd figured he knew I was just giving him direction, like in his acting days. "You think that looks like The Birdies?"

Joey frowned, twisting up his mouth as he regarded the object in front of us, clearly trying to pick out facial features. "Well... I mean... it's not *perfect* -"

I concluded that the power of suggestion was truly alive and well in LA. "You did notice we picked it up from a *hotel*, right?" I'd left Joey in the van, blocking the loading bay, while I paid two waiters to help me wrangle it out of the ball room without attracting too much attention.

He scrunched up his face. "Well, yeah..."

I pointed to the tiny sliver of orange-pink flesh stuck to the ice. "It's left over from a wedding banquet. Some kind of fresh fish display." The three 'heads' were actually three mostly melted-down sea-shells, and when I'd got there it'd had pieces of shrimp, salmon, and lobster still strewn all over it, which I'd had to pick off before I could cart it away. Even so, it had been pretty much perfect. The fact that it'd survived until now in any kind of state was also pretty fortunate, but we'd lucked out with the temperatures cooling off the past day or so.

Joey jumped as a fluffy white cat surged out of the bushes by his side then proceeded to jump up onto the ice and start licking at it happily. Come to think of it, there *was* a definite fishy odor. I sniffed and wrinkled my nose. "You don't smell that?"

Joey was still staring at the sculpture with the eyes of the newly awakened, like he couldn't believe we'd gotten away with it. But there was no time to bask in our minor glory; we needed to maximize our advantage before the three stooges down at the gate started calling up here for an update and discovered they had intruders on the premises.

"Okay, so we probably don't have long before the security guys figure out we're fakes." I glanced around, seeing no sign of anyone other than the fish-enthusiast feline. "You stay here and wait for me."

Joey opened his mouth to protest, but I cut him off.

"Stay out of sight and I'll get what we need! Okay?"

I could tell he was just itching to crash the party and drag Bethany off to one side, but no *way* was that happening under my watch. Nope - to avoid drama and potential bloodshed, I was going to corner Gerry and show him the proof we had, then *he* could ease the way with Bethany.

I thought it was a pretty decent plan myself.

Back to that saying about plans and enemies...

I'd figured on the 'enemy' being Gerry's goons, so I'd just been hoping my waiter's uniform and fake mustache would throw them off long enough for me to get close to him.

Of course, I hadn't reckoned on the small army of young, entitled celebrities and hangers-on who also stood in my way. I'd been outside for nearly twenty minutes already, trying to reach Gerry's location. Attracted by the weird cacophony of a sound check going on beyond the amplified pop, I'd finally spotted him near the back fence, alternating between yelling stuff at the guys up on a temporary stage and ranting into his phone at someone else. And for the past ten minutes I'd been attempting to work my over to him.

But every time I got close, my tray was decimated - zombie-piranha-style - by the hordes of young men strutting around in swim trunks, or by the masses of size-zero women in tiny bikinis, who'd probably be vomiting it all back up before the end of the night anyway. Just looking at their visible rib cages and skinny thighs made me worry about raising a teenage girl in this country.

But back to my current predicament...

I peered toward Gerry again. I guessed I could head over there with an empty tray... but nah, someone like Gerry and his boys would see that coming. With his level of fame and career-making ability, he'd probably had everyone from waiters to mail delivery guys hitting him up to listen to their singing or their demo album over the years, and I was betting his security team was well-versed in keeping such people away from him. Which meant a waiter approaching with an empty tray was a big no-no.

On the other hand, I wasn't sure how much longer Joey would wait for me back at the house. As I'd discovered during our short stakeout, 'Joey' and 'patient' didn't belong in the same dictionary, and if he blundered in before I was ready he could screw up everything.

Gritting my teeth, I picked up my *fourth* tray of hors

d'oeuvres from under the anxious eye of the party planner and headed back into the fray. As I strode across the huge garden, taking the poolside route as the fastest way to the stage, I decided that this time I would keep going even if the gannets ate everything. Or heck, maybe I should tell people I was taking it *to* Gerry, so they wouldn't try to eat it first. He was the boss, after all. Who in their right mind would get in my way?

"Waiter!"

I kept walking, dodging the bodies splayed out across the grass next to the pool.

"Hey, *moron*! You leave your hearing aid at home?!"

I glanced over to the group of a dozen or so scantily-clad male and female bodies lounging in the shallow end of the pool. "Sorry, sir, this is for Mr. Warnock!"

"Dude..." another white-clad waiter grabbed my arm, cutting off my escape, "that's Nick Birdie's entourage, you better get over there!"

Blowing out an irritated breath, I somehow forced a neutral expression onto my face and carried my loaded tray over to the group in the pool.

It wasn't hard to pick out the one who'd been yelling at me, since he was now smirking up a storm at my expense. The guy was a skinny, nighttime-sunglasses-wearing moron, wedged improbably between a couple of D-cup beauty queens running their red-tipped nails all over his hairless chest. No doubt he was busy coming up with more snarky comments, but I was more worried about whether I could keep my own snark reined in. Usually I figured as long as I didn't punch anyone I was good, but the last thing Joey needed was me getting tossed out of here.

As I reached them I figured I'd give it one last attempt. "I'm sorry, sir, but I was told to take this over to Mr. Warnock and The Birdies."

The skinny kid tugged off his shades and glared up at me, even as the twin babes either side of him pouted in malicious enjoyment. "Good thing I caught you, then!"

My heart sank as I recognized Nick Birdie from the posters spread across Gerry's Instagram and Twitter feeds. I'd assumed the band was over in the back with Gerry, dealing with the sound check... but apparently they had people to stand in for them on the boring stuff. *Great.*

Forcing myself not to scowl, I grudgingly moved over to him and knelt by the pool, offering my tray. Hands clashed as the guests around him fought over sushi rolls and miniature dumplings; at least they'd empty the thing in seconds and I could get back to stalking Gerry again.

But Nick Birdie wasn't done with his entertainment yet. Clicking his fingers rudely in my face to get my attention, he then waved to his own features like he was George Clooney or something. "You didn't recognize all this?"

I stared back at the pimply, pock-marked skin, partly concealed by a thick glaze of cover-up that looked like it'd been laid on with a spackle; long, stringy hair that reminded me of a Walking Dead zombie; and the red-tinged nostrils and dilated pupils that told me he'd snorted something illegal very recently.

I fought the urge to reply 'All *what?*' and instead mumbled a barely audible, "Sorry, sir."

Nick chortled, shoving his shades back on and leaning back against one of the buxom beauties, basically using her biggest assets as a throw pillow. "It's okay, man. You can't help your advanced age. Guess they don't get many of the 'new tunes' in the old folks' home, eh?"

Half the pool cracked up. The rest were still too busy stuffing their faces.

Staring down at my now-empty tray, I sucked in my annoyance and started to move away... until a happy notion occurred to me. "Uh, Mr. Birdie -?"

"No autographs," he bit out, more interested in plumbing the depths of the redhead next to him, or at least the depths of her cleavage.

"Oh, no, sir," I said quickly, aiming for humble. "I just

wondered if you knew about the ice sculpture, up at the house?"

That got his attention back. "Huh?"

"Of you and your brothers. I believe it's a gift from, uh..." I frowned, trying to look as doddering and ill-informed as humanly possible.

"Who?"

"A... a Miss... Smiley Ficus?" I frowned harder. "Or was it... Mikey Silas?"

There was a second's pause as Nick's brain put it together. Then he was surging up in the water. "Miley freaking Cyrus sent us an *ice sculpture*! Woo hoo! Yeah! You hear that, baby?" High fives resounded through the air as he tried to hand-slap everyone within range. Shoving tanned legs and oiled bosoms aside, he slipped and slid across the shallow end as he made for the steps out of the pool, attention returning to me as he climbed out. "Where is it?"

"Just to the left of the house. But, uh..."

Nick paused in the middle of pulling on his robe. "What?"

"You might want to hurry, sir." I tried hard to look sorry. "Before it melts."

I was still smirking at the memory of Nick Birdie hurrying across the grass as I closed in on Gerry.

At last.

Although getting any closer was gonna be a pain. His bodyguards hovered just a few feet away as their boss continued to rail at the team setting up the stage, and I already recognized one as the guy I'd accidentally nudged into the pool the other day. I doubted my disguise was good enough to fool him for more than a second or two.

Just as I was debating what angle to tilt my tray so it wasn't as obvious it was empty, a phone went off, punching out what was most likely the latest hit on Gerry's label. Casting the sound check team a final glare, he put the phone to his ear and stomped away from the noise... heading straight in my direction.

This was it, now or never.

"Warnock," Gerry snapped into the phone, then scowled at whatever he heard. "Then try another goddamn airline! My Bethany travels first class!" He glared at me as I failed to move out of his way... then his mouth dropped open as realization dawned. I gotta say, I was kind of impressed he recognized me at all, seeing as he never seemed to actually look in my face when we met before.

"You!" he fumed, anger rising as he turned to his flanking bodyguards. "Toss him out!"

Before they could grab me I ditched the tray and backed up quickly, holding up my phone and hitting 'play.'

Over the speaker, my recorded voice rang out: *"You're the Sophia Wilde Gerry Warnock hired to lie about sleeping with his son-in-law?"*

Sophia's nervous *"Yes!"* was followed by *"I-it wasn't my fault! He said he'd kill my career if I didn't help!"* before I hit 'stop' again.

I'd done a little editing and the end product really worked, if I did say so myself.

It sure seemed to work for Gerry, whose face had turned a lovely shade of puce, even as he gestured for his swiftly encroaching bodyguards to cease and desist.

And with that one act, I knew we had him. "In case you're wondering, I also have it on video... oh, and I can prove the photos are fake, too." I grinned at Gerry, starting to enjoy myself.

He growled. "What do you want - money? How much?"

"Nah." I rubbed my head absently. "Wouldn't be good for my health."

If Gerry's face had been capable of it, his eyebrows would've shot up past his retreating hairline - as it was, they merely wiggled a little. "Well you must want *something*. What is it - a job? You wanna cut a demo?"

"I want you to give the kid a chance."

"What kid?" Gerry scowled, then gaped at me as he finally got it. "*Joey Russo?*" Fury and satisfaction warred in his eyes. "I knew he only married Bethany to get to me!"

Now *I* was the one confused... until I realized how he'd taken my words. "You're an idiot, you know that?" Gerry stiffened, probably in shock at being talked to that way by anyone. "He doesn't give a shit about your label, he just wants a chance with Bethany."

Gerry eyed me in disbelief. "If you believe that, then you're the idiot."

"You ever stop to consider they're actually in love? Maybe I'm just not as cynical as you," I retorted, then caught myself.

What the hell?

Had those words really just come out of *my* mouth?

Fortunately, before Gerry could seize on my momentary pause as evidence of doubt, the sound of violently shattering glass had us both swiveling around to look back at the mansion.

Or maybe 'fortunate' wasn't the right word, I thought, as I watched a chair sail majestically through the air before splintering apart on the patio beneath, sending revelers and catering staff alike scrambling for cover.

"What the *fuck*?" Gerry breathed out next to me.

A second later another item of furniture - probably a footstool - soared out of a third floor window after the chair. It, too, plunged to the patio beneath, but this time it found a more impressive target in the form of the entertainment station into which an iPod was plugged. The loud music abruptly cut off, replaced by a loud scream of fury emanating from the windowless bedroom.

Dammit - I'd told Joey to stay out of sight of anyone. *Especially* his wife. Hell hath no fury, right?

"Bethany!" I had to give Gerry credit. If that anguished squawk and the speed at which he took off across the grass were any indication, the man really did love his kid.

I sped into action, too, because I didn't want Gerry ripping Joey apart before I arrived.

Or Bethany killing Joey herself, for that matter.

Chapter Ten.

I reached the bedroom via the back stairs, which gave me about ten seconds of lead time on Gerry and his muscle. Before I could enter, another loud crash resounded from inside the room.

"Bethany, baby -"

"Don't call me *baby*!"

I peered inside in time to see Bethany pick up a small side table like it weighed nothing at all. Okay, so it probably didn't weigh much - the thing looked like it'd struggle to support a small wine glass, which probably meant it was worth a fortune... I winced as she flung it toward Joey on the far side of the room and it shattered against the wall.

"Baby, you'll hurt yourself!"

I shook my head at Joey's words. If I were him, I'd be more worried about her hurting *me* right now.

Bethany grabbed a matching side table and lofted it high into the air. "Oh, I've been working out! I hit the punching bag all day... I pretended it was *you*!"

Her aim was improving; Joey only just managed to twirl out of the way as the second table impacted the wall. I cringed as I pictured the bill. Gerry was definitely losing his deposit if he'd rented this place.

"Baby, please, I never cheated on you!"

As I heard the grunts of approaching Neanderthals behind me, I decided that was my cue and stepped into the room. "And we can prove it."

Bethany paused in the act of picking up a truly humongous perfume bottle - she appeared to be running out of objects, in fact - and for a second I thought we had her. But even as Gerry and his men entered at my back, the former puffing and blowing, Joey had to go and put his foot in it.

"I never even *liked* Sophia, baby!"

With a howl of fury, Bethany hurled the bottle straight at him. Not expecting it... because clearly, the kid was a jackass... Joey failed to duck, dodge, or dive this time around, and it caught him right on the temple. He went down with a cry.

"Joey?" Bethany seemed stunned, like she hadn't really expected to hit him either. "*Joey*?!"

"Bethany -"

Evading her panting father's outstretched hands, Bethany raced across the carpet to collapse at Joey's side. "Joey! Joey, wake up!" Tears dripped from her eyes as she clutched at him, terrified, then started smoothing his hair back from the reddening mark on his face.

More than a little concerned myself, I took a step forward... then noticed Joey's fingers twitching as he fought to remain still under her tender ministrations. I hoped Bethany didn't notice, because even in her current mood she could still turn on him, and at close range she could do some *serious* damage with those super high stilettos she favored.

"M-maybe we can g-get past this..." Bethany's face twisted up as she cried even harder, "m-make a fresh start..."

Regardless of how I felt about love myself, the genuine pain in her voice made me want to punch Gerry in the face. I shot him an evil look and made sure my voice carried across the room. "You tell her, Mr. Warnock, or I show her the proof."

Bethany looked around at us, and the heartbreak was right there in her eyes as I realized she'd misunderstood my words. She probably thought I had photos of Joey banging his entire backing group.

"He never cheated on you, Bethany," I said firmly - and felt a sense of shock that I was arguing *for* a spouse's fidelity. Possibly for the first time.

Cynicism entered her face as she started to shake her head. "I saw the photos, and -"

"The photos were fake, honey."

Everyone in the room - me included - looked around in surprise as Gerry stepped forward. Even Joey raised his head and blinked uncertainly.

"Wh-what?" Bethany stared at her father in confusion. "What do you mean?"

Gerry shot me a glare that would've killed my singing dreams, if I'd had any, then forced an apologetic smile onto his face as he approached his daughter. "I, uh..." The smile slipped, his voice turning whiny. "I meant it for the best, baby girl..."

Bethany's face set into an outraged mask. "Daddy!" Something told me she knew daddy dearest well enough to guess where this was going.

From his position down on the carpet, hand still clutched in Bethany's, Joey beamed in delight.

Ten minutes later I stood on the patio far below the missing bedroom window, only half-listening to the blazing argument still going on upstairs. Although maybe 'argument' was the wrong word, since the loudest phrases ("always interfere!" "serve you right!" and my personal favorite "have you arrested!") had all been yelled by Bethany, while Gerry's replies had mostly consisted of gruffly inaudible pleadings with a touch of a whine; kind of like the family dog apologizing for peeing on the furniture and promising to go outside next time.

I hadn't heard much out of Joey, but if he had any sense he was keeping out of it and milking the situation for all it was worth. Wasn't like he had any reason to defend

Gerry. On the other hand, I had to admit that at least Bethany's father cared about her welfare... even if the way he showed it made him a borderline sociopath. I couldn't imagine Len caring who I married; although with Kaylee, I knew he would. Of course, she was just a kid, and parents tended to be more protective of girls, but still...

Shaking off the errant thoughts, I checked the time - nine fifty five - and wondered if Len had stayed home after all. Either way, I wanted to head there myself as soon as possible.

I mean, I'd done my job, right? The lovebirds were back together, and surely that meant no more crazy balls of light flying around; no more vicious headaches, cross-LA drives, or compulsions to keep them together.

Although to be honest, after what I'd seen before, I'd expected a *bit* more fanfare at the end. I banged experimentally on my sternum. Nope - nothing.

Maybe I really had hallucinated everything.

Deciding I might as well just leave, I wandered over to the side of the house, where my van was still parked next to the now heavily melted block of ice. To my surprise, Nick Birdie stood over the latter, staring down at it despondently. No... there was no way -

He looked up and saw me, zero recognition in his eyes as he asked, "Did you see it before it melted?"

Amused by the fact that he was treating me like a fellow human being - probably because I'd shed my white waiter's jacket - I decided to play along. "Absolutely. Very realistic."

The young pop sensation looked even more crestfallen at that, barely wincing as the growing pool of icy meltwater nudged his bare foot. "Really?"

I couldn't resist. "Oh yeah. I mean - look..." Bending down, I picked up a stray bit of ice that was curved into a kind of hook and held it up for him to view. "They captured your nose perfectly."

Nick Birdie's bloodshot eyes went wide. He clutched at his own nose, eyes darting wildly about him, before speeding off into the house - presumably in search of a mirror.

Grinning now, I headed for the van, only to pause again as I heard my name being called. A moment later, Bethany and Joey came around the side of the house, looking relieved not to have missed me.

"Lyle!"

I flinched as Joey pulled me into a tight hug, but the sight of Bethany's happy face over his shoulder made me resist rolling my eyes.

Joey stepped back and grabbed Bethany's hand, linking their fingers tightly together in a grip they both seemed to need. "We can't thank you enough. Talk about going above and beyond the call of duty!"

I flicked my gaze heavenward and thought Joey didn't know how right he was. There'd certainly been something 'above and beyond' about the past few days, and I was looking forward to putting it all behind me. Hopefully once Leroy's alibi was firmly established he'd be out of trouble, and then Mara would undo everything and I'd never see her again.

Or I'd never see her again period*, in which case I'd finally 'fess up to the doctors and get that MRI I needed.*

Bethany sighed. "I can't believe I fell for Dad's stupid lies."

Joey hugged her shoulders comfortingly. "It's okay now. We're done with it."

She turned her head to look up at him - I hadn't noticed the height difference before; yep, she was wearing flats, so I guessed she'd thrown her shoes at him too - and stared into Joey's eyes. "I promise I'll never doubt you again."

"I love you, Bethany."

"I love you too."

As their lips met in a sweet kiss, I felt a mild burning

sensation in my chest. Looking down, I saw a stream of bright white spheres drifting out from where the tattoo lay over my heart. A few inches from me, it split in two, half of the spheres moving almost lazily for Bethany, the other half for Joey -

- and as the first spheres entered their chests, the stream increased to a flood that made me stumble back just at the sight, even though I couldn't feel the force of it this time.

"Look out!" I heard Bethany cry, as my legs went out from under me - slipping on the meltwater, I realized, as my arms pinwheeled in the air. Then my head slammed into something cold and sharp, and the world disappeared from sight.

I opened my eyes to the cool white walls of a critical care hospital room. Shit - had I impaled my skull on a shard of ice? For a moment, all I could think about was it being some kind of karmic retribution for mocking Nick Birdie - which would've been grossly unfair, I felt.

But then I caught sight of my old patrol uniform, carefully folded on a chair. A twinge of déjà vu hit me as I realized this was another memory. Then all I felt was dread, as I remembered the one and only time I'd been hospitalized during that period of my life...

As if on cue, the door to my room opened and Jenny walked in. Just as I remembered it, her pretty eyes went wide, filling with tears as she took in my battered form lying in the bed. I'd been first on scene at a domestic assault, the guy about to start in on his teenage son when I got there. He hadn't been armed or especially big, so I'd tackled him, taking him down to the ground as he cursed at me drunkenly... only to be knocked over the head with a glass mixing bowl by his equally drunk wife. She'd spent the next thirty seconds kicking me as I lay there semi-conscious, praying for my backup to arrive and scared of what the father was doing to the boy. I'd been lucky the bowl was poor quality or I might have lost my life that night; as it was, I'd had a concussion and enough bruises that the hospital had called my next of kin.

Jenny hurried to my bedside, gorgeous as ever to my bleary eyes, although I never admitted that to myself usually. But my defenses were low tonight - and she seemed different too, as she clutched my hand in hers and brought it to her cheek. I felt liquid skate along it, and realized she was crying over me.

"Don't cry," I said, my voice sounding odd due to my swollen, split lip.

"I thought you'd been shot," she murmured. Then she bent forward, and I felt her hair sweep over my face before her lips found mine in a kiss.

Despite the pain I was in, for a moment I reciprocated eagerly. Jenny was the first and only woman I'd fallen in love with; the woman I'd lost my virginity to; the only woman I'd ever bought a damn engagement *ring for. Except before I could propose, I found out she was sleeping with my brother -*

And with that thought it all came back to me. Jerking my head back, I pulled away from her, looking toward the open door in a mixture of guilt and anger. What if Michael had come in - or my father? What if it had been Kaylee? My niece was only six years old, but that was old enough to know her uncle shouldn't be making out with her mother.

Jenny's expression was pained, as if I'd been the one to dump her. "I-I'm sorry -"

I felt all my old anger surge up inside me. "What the fuck, *Jenny?" I'd finally gotten to the point that I could go over to their house for 'family dinners' without needing to get drunk that night just to fall asleep; I'd even considered asking out another cop - a woman in the Computer Crimes Unit - instead of just screwing random women I met in bars, most of them self-confessed cop groupies. And now Jenny was screwing with me again?*

Her gaze shot to the doorway, suddenly anxious, her hands retreating away from me as she backed up a few feet.

"You chose Michael," I hissed through puffy lips, though I really wanted to scream it at her the way I was screaming inwardly. "You don't get a second chance with me!"

"I'm sorry!" She blinked back tears, eyelashes fluttering wildly. She'd always been one of those rare women who cried beautifully. "I

just..." she waved a hand helplessly, "Michael, he's..." more tears, "I think he might be cheating on me."

I felt myself slowly grow cold as I realized: it wasn't about me.

Jenny's sparkling sapphire eyes fixed on my face, her expression pleading. "He's not the man I thought he was, Lyle. He's -"

She cut off abruptly as voices came from the corridor. A moment later, they became recognizable as Len and my brother. I saw panic come into Jenny's eyes, a kind of desperation as she jerked away from me.

"Jenny?"

Avoiding my eyes, Jenny moved away from the bed - and away from me...

"Jenny!"

I jerked upright - and found myself looking into Bethany and Joey's worried faces, Gerry's substantially less-concerned visage looming behind theirs. I was lying on a lounger on the patio, maybe twenty feet from where I'd slipped.

Joey exhaled in relief. "Thank fuck!"

Bethany's response was more nuanced. "Who's Jenny?"

I avoided giving an answer by swinging my legs off the white fabric cover - now dirt-streaked, I saw, thanks to my wet shoes and clothes - and immediately clutched my hands to my head in agony. For a second I thought it was the curse, and was almost scared to open my eyes in case I saw glowing spheres shooting between all three of us again. But a gentle probe of the back of my skull told me the source of my current affliction was nothing more than an old-fashioned goose-egg.

"You want some ice for that?" Joey offered.

Given how I'd injured myself, I cracked my eyes open enough to glare at him, and he had the grace to look embarrassed. "I just want to go home. I think." I slowly stood up, wincing as the action sent shards of pain through me. Okay, maybe I should rethink the ice. But seriously, how unfair was it that I beat my curse only to get a head injury the same damn evening?

"We'll drive you home," Bethany offered.

"*Whatever* you need," Joey added. "Any time, anywhere."

I heard a grunt followed by a less than enthusiastic "Sure" from Gerry, and figured Bethany was behind it. Knowing her, she'd probably kicked him.

I wasn't sure how much I could bank on his goodwill in future, but having an IOU from someone with his influence could definitely come in handy...

Which was when the crazy thought occurred to me. "If you really mean that -"

"Of course!" Bethany insisted.

Was I really gonna do this? Exhausted, soaked through, and nursing a headache that might be a concussion?

Then I thought of how I hadn't acted, back when Jenny had tried to tell me something about Michael all those years ago. Angry that she'd only wanted to use me, I'd told myself I needed to focus on recovering from my injuries, and after that... well, life had moved on, and by the next time I saw her she didn't seem unhappy. But maybe if I'd spoken to her about what she said, she wouldn't have been sucked into that life along with my brother. Maybe I could've changed her fate.

Just like I could change Leroy Baldwin's if I acted now.

I took a deep breath, trying to summon enough energy. "In that case, I could *really* use a favor."

The term 'media frenzy' didn't do justice to the scene outside 'Boobies' at midnight. And all it had taken was literally ten seconds of social media activity, times three:

@GerryWarnockProducer: Proud to announce my beloved daughter Bethany is engaged to Warnock Prod. hit artist Joey Russo!

@JoeyRusso91: Hey fans, want you all to be first to know I'm in love with the beautiful @RealBethanyWarnock #MyFutureWife

Bethany had simply posted a selfie of herself and Joey, grinning into the camera over her engagement ring, with the caption 'Looking forward to being Mrs. Bethany Russo' on her Instagram feed. It had already blown up with more than fifteen thousand likes, despite most of the east coast being asleep.

Okay, so they were already husband and wife. But the still-subdued Gerry had grumbled about missing their wedding, and Bethany had talked excitedly about 'rebooting' their marriage. Hey, at least she hadn't said 'consciously re-coupling.'

Then we'd all just sat back and waited for the paparazzi to arrive. Alerted to their whereabouts by Gerry's earlier tweets about the launch party, the first news trucks and motorbikes had appeared in under ten minutes, and there'd been enough of a swarm to bring traffic cops within twenty. Even I had to feel for the Birdies, who'd had to go on stage after being abandoned by first Gerry then most of their audience. Half the party guests had clustered around the terrace, seeking autographs and selfies with the Couple of the Night, while the other half gave interviews and were photographed by the waiting reporters outside.

It seemed that the combined impact of Gerry, Bethany and Joey was greater than the sum of their parts, especially after someone spread the rumor that Gerry had resisted their relationship at first... Yeah, I might have had something to do with that one. It helped that some devoted Joey Russo fans had taken screenshots of the great producer's angry (and recently deleted) tweets about his former client over the past month, and were now posting them all over the internet, much to Gerry's ire.

We had let things simmer for another five minutes, then given the waiting press a tantalizing - but deliberately unsatisfying - glimpse of the lovebirds and Gerry, as we'd rushed out to his chauffeur-driven car. Even Gerry had looked kind of energized by all the attention as we'd driven away, and I figured pretty soon the fact that he'd insulted his new son-in-law on Twitter would just become 'great PR' in his scheming little mind.

I just hoped he bore that in mind when we reached our destination.

Concerned they might give up on us during the half hour journey to Glendale, I'd had Bethany and Joey send out cryptic social media updates at first... until I pictured a paparazzo checking Twitter from the back of his speeding motorbike. But even without the extra inducements, the paparazzi train had stuck to us like glue the whole way; it probably helped that we took surface streets rather than risk losing them on the freeway.

We were followed just as closely as we hurried from the car to the front door of the club, the newshounds spilling off the backs of bikes or out of news trucks then flanking us scarily fast.

"Gerry! Gerry!"

"Bethany! Why are you at a strip joint?"

"Joey! Is she gonna strip for you?!"

I saw Gerry's head swing up, eyes bulging as he took in the bright neon 'Boobies' signage looming above him. At that moment a flash bulb went off, immortalizing his look of horror. Before he could balk, however, I pushed a hundred dollar bill into the hands of the startled bouncers and shoved the others inside ahead of me.

Behind us, I heard the bouncers calling for backup as they prevented the growing number of paparazzi seeking entry. I smirked as we passed the huge sign that read 'No photos or video!'... then lost my smugness as we came to the wall of blacklisted customers. I was still on there of course, my 'mug shot' front and center, although I hoped the fake mustache and slicked-back hair would hide my identity for long enough.

The four of us entered the club to the beat of loud hip-hop, overlaid by Gerry's hissed protests. "Taking my own daughter into a *strip club*?!" he ranted. "Do you know what this is going to do to my reputation?"

Bethany patted her father placatingly on the chest, the same way I'd seen parents soothe their screaming toddlers. "Relax, Daddy. Story is, we're just checking out a location for Big-Z's next music video."

Gerry glared impatiently at her. "What?"

"Don't you think? It'd be perfect for *Sleazy*." Bethany added in an aside to me and Joey, "Big-Z's new single, it's gonna be huge."

To me, 'Big Z's were something you needed after a forty eight hour stakeout, but from the interest I saw on Joey's face I figured I was the only one confused.

Or maybe not. Next to us, Gerry had ground to a halt, looking puzzled. "How do you know about that?"

"I'm not just a pretty face and Instagram Influencer, Daddy." Rolling her eyes, Bethany hooked her arm around Gerry's and pulled him out onto the main club floor... where we were greeted by the sight of five sets of thong-divided butt cheeks, set atop legs made longer by fearsome stripper heels, gyrating in rapid circles to the appreciative whoops of a small but enthusiastic crowd who'd gathered up by the stage. The booths were mostly empty, maybe for that reason, but a couple of guys were each getting a lap dance: one loud and raucous in his approval, the other watching in silence, seemingly mesmerized by the pneumatic Cheri-Pie undulating above him.

Joey blanched at the sight of all the exposed female flesh and shot his wife a nervous glance - hey, who could blame him, given recent events - but Bethany ignored it all in favor of continuing to school Gerry on her value to his company. "Half your artists play their new tracks for me first, just to make sure they're ready."

Gerry was clearly stunned by that one. "Wh-what? When did you start -?"

"I've been going into the studio since I was *twelve*."

Bethany looked offended. "Didn't you always *want* me to get involved?"

"Yes!" Gerry was starting to recover now. "But I thought you were bored when I made you an intern."

"That's because you wanted me to," she made air quotes, "'start at the bottom and work my way up.' I could've Ivanka'd the *shit* out of it, but you had me answering phones and *filing* the whole month!"

Joey looked a little stunned by his wife's shameless demand for greater nepotism, while I kinda wanted to applaud Gerry for actually trying to do the right thing for once. But we needed to change the conversation from Bethany's career ladder to the matter at hand... especially as I saw movement over by the manager's office next to the stage.

As I'd hoped, it was Gun - real name Roberto Hernandez - who'd emerged and was even now skirting the two booths with the energetic lap dancers, his suspicious eyes fixed firmly on the four of us near the entrance. I wondered if he'd checked the camera feed for the parking lot, and if so whether he'd recognized Gerry or just freaked out at the number of cameras and news trucks.

I also wondered just how well my fake mustache was hanging on.

Gun paused right before reaching us to address a nearby bouncer. "What the *hell's* going on out there?"

The other man gave a bewildered shrug. "Don't know, boss. But we got a dozen guys with cameras wanting to get in and take pictures of some celebrity couple.

Now Gun's eyes swung back to us and unerringly fixed on Bethany and Joey. They were the only ones holding hands, after all; not so much of the PDA between me and Gerry. He frowned, as if trying to puzzle out who they were, but I doubted Candy's tough-guy boyfriend was an avid fan of TMZ and Perez Hilton or boy bands from the noughties.

Fortunately, my plan didn't rely on him recognizing any

of us by sight.

"Mr. Hernandez?" Bethany swung her hand out toward Gun with a smile, exuding the dazzling charm and panache of an experienced corporate shark. I wasn't the only one starting to look at Bethany with new eyes, I saw, as Gerry and Joey both wore slightly dazed expressions too. "Apologies for bringing all of this media attention to your door," she continued smoothly, "but we had no idea the entertainment press would follow us when we left our album launch."

I was seriously impressed. Bethany had just managed to drop in two references to press coverage of the club *and* a strong hint that we were Important with a capital I, all before Gun could utter a word in protest. In fact, I could see our target was impressed too, his face scrunching up as he shook her hand and clearly tried to figure out who she was.

Bethany spotted that too, and went on without a pause, "I'm Bethany Warnock, and this is my father, Gerry. Also my h-," she caught herself, "*fiancé*, Joey Russo, and our - uh - assistant." Her gaze flicked to me briefly. "Eric."

I tried to look as bland as possible in case Gun looked my way, but there was no need. He might not have recognized their faces, but he'd recognized the other men's names the moment Bethany said them.

Excitement showed in Gun's own face as he leaped forward and shook Gerry's hand like it was going out of fashion. "Wow, man! You're - you're, like, a *legend*. What are you doing here in Glendale?" He turned his attention on Joey next, pumping his hand just as eagerly. "And Joey Russo, in my club!" He glanced around hastily, like a fifties hostess wanting to make sure the living room was ready for visitors. I wondered what he was looking for: discarded thongs on the tables; dubious stains on the booths? Or vice versa? Apparently satisfied with whatever he saw, Gun urged us forward and called for champagne and glasses as he led us to a large VIP booth with the best view in the house.

As we sat down, the music changed to a thumping industrial beat, and with it three leather-clad, dominatrix-like strippers strode on stage, sexily snapping whips and canes. I shot a wary glance at Bethany, but she only smirked back at me, though I thought she looked just a little red in the face. One of the strippers was Candy, I noticed, and hoped everything was ready. I'd texted her from the mansion before we left, but we hadn't had much time to arrange it all.

"So..." Gun sat on a low stool opposite us, forcing us all to look toward him - and at the stage - as we spoke, "what can I help you with?" His gaze ran professionally over Bethany. "You wanna try out... learn some moves for the bedroom, maybe..." he winked at Joey, "my girls'd *love* to help with it."

Bethany wisely distracted Gun's attention from the thunderous expressions of her menfolk by leaning across the table and beaming at him. "I'm flattered, but we're actually scouting for a location."

"For a music video?" Gun's eyes flashed interest. "And what would 'Boobies' be getting out of this?"

Bethany further proved her professionalism - and acting abilities - by not even cringing at the corny name of the place. "Obviously we'd pay to hire the club for however long it took."

Gun pursed his lips, looking thoughtful. "We don't generally hire the place out. We'd need to work out a rate, compensate the wait staff and the girls for lost tips. Plus, I mean, we could lose our regulars if we're closed for the day."

I saw Gerry open his mouth to scoff at that claim, and I wanted to slap him across his Botoxed face. Sure, we all knew the publicity they'd get from being featured in one of Gerry's music videos would bring in a load of new customers, more than enough to offset any existing 'clients' who got pissed off and walked away. But we were trying to make Gun happy here, not rain on his parade.

Fortunately, Bethany spoke before her father could voice his thoughts. "Completely understandable," she soothed, then let herself look pained. "Of course, while we do love the authenticity, we have the backup option of a sound stage."

To my relief, Gun played along instead of getting angry. "How about you hire our people as extras and dancers? Like you said, authenticity matters, and my girls are *very* good at what they do." His eyes slid to me and hardened. "I'm sure 'Eric' here can confirm that, since he was checking us out earlier today."

Well, I guess that answered my question about whether the fake mustache held up to inspection; he'd clearly ID'd me as the guy who'd taken liberties with Candy and gotten slapped then beaten up for my trouble.

I let myself look nervous, and finally Gun looked away. His voice was hard, though, as he addressed Bethany directly. "Don't bring him back again." I had to give the man credit; it didn't seem like he was a forgive-and-forget type, even when money was in play, which boded well for the women who worked here.

I also had to give him credit for his intelligence. His style was in your face and a little coarse, but his negotiating had been smart and he'd seen through my disguise in under a minute. All of which was... unfortunate. Much like a con artist, any cop or PI preferred tangling with morons. Worse, if Gun had set up the monitoring system as Candy described, he was both smart *and* paranoid.

On which note...

I looked away from the negotiation, making it seem like I was leering over the stage action when really I was checking the activity around the office door. Hard to tell if anyone was in there or not, but I hadn't seen anyone else go in since Gun came out, and every spare body seemed to be busy helping with the craziness in the parking lot.

Which meant it was a *fairly* safe bet the office was

empty right now.

I caught Bethany's eye and gave a slight nod.

"Oh my *God*!" Bethany reached over and grabbed at Gun's watch. "I can't believe you have this model!" Seemingly oblivious to the fact that it was still attached to his arm, she dragged Gun's wrist over to show it to Joey up close. "Look, baby - doesn't it look comfortable?"

Joey had stayed remarkably quiet so far, and for an instant I was worried. But as his face fired with what looked to me like genuine excitement, I remembered his past. If he could carry a show that was basically 'Timmy's stuck in the well' for five ponderous years, he could easily pull this off. "Yeah - it *is* the same one," he murmured, grasping Gun's wrist in his left hand and running his fingers over the watch face.

From Gun's expression, I could tell he was torn between a dislike of being fondled and treated like a piece of meat - which was ironic - and having a fan boy moment here.

"Can he try it on?"

Gun looked up at Bethany's plea, his expression resistant.

"Please?" She made a face that would melt a thousand hearts. "I want to get him one for our engagement, but he's afraid it won't sit right on his wrist."

"I, uh -"

"Not much to ask, is it?" Gerry had stayed silent since we'd come in here, but this line was delivered with the innocent expectancy of a powerful man who was primed to take offense if denied.

Gun glanced once toward the management office, as if confirming the watch alarm wouldn't be needed, then reluctantly began to unstrap it.

As he passed it over to Joey, Bethany smoothed her hand up his arm. "You are just a *wonderful* man."

"Woo *hoo*!!"

The five of us all looked up instinctively as a rotund

figure came charging straight at our table. It was the enthusiastic lap dance recipient we'd passed earlier, clutching a handful of paper money. But just as I was sure he was going to collide with us, he dodged sideways, making a desperate plunge for the stage area.

"Hey buddy, slow down!" Gun yelled angrily, gesturing for the other bouncers to come over and deal with him. But before they could respond, the guy had dragged a chair over to the stage and was attempting to hoist himself up onto it.

"Shit!" Gun jumped up from the table, shoving chairs aside as he hurried to join his bouncers in securing their runaway patron.

Meanwhile, up on stage and deep into her routine, Candy turned around and snapped her whip down viciously -

Joint howls emanated from the spot as Candy and the customer both screeched, one in shock, the other in pain. The fat guy clutched at his hand, cradling it to his chest and rolling about in agony, even as Gun leaped up onto the stage with two bouncers behind him.

I snuck a quick look at the management office. No one was near or appeared to be watching the door. *Great.*

"Oh God... oh God!"

"It's all right, babe!" Up on stage, Gun cuddled Candy to his chest, glaring violently at the still-moaning customer as the man was carefully hoisted to his feet by the bouncers.

I stood up, backed into the shadows, then began making my way quickly along the wall -

"Hey, you! Stop!"

I looked up to find Gun's gaze fixed on me, and froze. Huh. I'd really expected him to be distracted for longer.

With a quick hug of Candy and a glare to his boys, Gun jumped off the stage and approached our table. "Where are you sneaking off to, huh?"

I tried to look baffled. "I-I was going to find the

restroom -"

"No, you were trying to get backstage." Gun turned his furious gaze on Bethany et al. "Do you know the disgusting things he said to my girlfriend up there?"

I shot a nervous glance toward Candy. How much had she embellished the story since I'd left? I could swear I caught a glint of amusement in her eyes as our gazes met. Then she covered her face with her hands and dramatically burst into tears.

Oh, shit.

I resisted the urge to run for it as Gun stalked closer. Yeah, I'd told Candy to make a scene, but I hadn't quite envisioned this. I made a quick calculation: five bouncers working the club, with three still up on stage, meant only two potentially between me and the exit. And I could take two guys, I was pretty sure.

Unless they'd called in backup, of course...

"Hang on a second." To my eternal gratitude, Joey stepped forward, putting himself between me and the all-but charging Gun.

"Get out of my way!" Gun bit out. From the stage came a sobbing wail, and I wished Candy would just shut up for now. Talk about immersing herself in the role...

"Look." Joey stood firm, and I noticed Bethany looking impressed. "Let's get rid of this guy and get back to talking business, okay?" He shot me a disconcertingly authentic glare. "We had no idea *Eric* was such a douche bag."

"He'll never work in this town again," Gerry pronounced with relish, looking at me like his fondest wish would be to arrange it personally.

I gave an involuntary shudder and realized something: if you were powerful enough, that line didn't actually sound cheesy *at all*. But he was only acting, of course.

I hoped.

As I was escorted to the club door, I cast a stealthy glance back at the management office - and Leroy's best chance to prove his innocence - out of the corner of my eye. But it was almost midnight and I was exhausted... and potentially still mildly concussed.

I sighed under my breath. Well, I'd done what I could tonight. Everything else would have to wait until tomorrow.

Chapter Eleven.

The loud banging on my door reminded me of the mercifully brief period when my father had been put in charge of getting me and Michael off to school in the mornings.

"You got another guest," Len growled, not sounding happy about it.

Blearily, I fumbled for my phone and lifted it up to check the time.

8:05 a.m.

I groaned. Not super early, but I hadn't exactly slept well last night.

By the time I'd gotten home and debriefed an over-excited Kaylee on the conclusion to the Joey-Bethany love story, it had already been after two. In telling the story, I'd made the mistake of including the bit about hitting my head and passing out, and a grouchy Len (who'd come down to complain we were keeping him awake, even though he acts deaf as a post whenever it suits him) had then insisted on waking me up every hour for the rest of the night. Just to be safe, he claimed.

Between the late bedtime and moody wakeup calls, I'd probably slept all of three hours total.

"Who is it?" I called out, hoping Len could still hear me.

My door opened and after a moment he came in, frowning his bushy, gray-streaked eyebrows at me in unconcealed disgust. "Well, you look like crap again."

Normally I'd have come back with some snarky line about how he should look in the mirror, or at least told him it was his fault for constantly waking me up. But for whatever reason - maybe the sleep dep, or everything else going on right now - his words hurt too much.

It didn't help to be lying in bed with him towering over me, either. It was times like these that made it hard to remember I was a grown adult and not still a kid getting reprimanded by my father for doing something wrong. Of course, for most of my childhood, Len had only been the absent threat used by my mother, not the one actually doling out the discipline. Even when he lived with us, Mom had never ratted us out when he'd been drunk, which had been most times he'd been home after I hit seven. But there'd still been plenty of times I'd fallen foul of him directly and he'd walloped me until I cried.

Annoyed, I threw back the sheets and pushed to my feet, stupidly satisfied when I bested him by a few inches. We'd been pretty much the same height for years, but finally age and arthritis had begun shrinking him... and great, now I felt like a jerk for being proud of it, no matter our history.

I turned away from him and headed for the closet, dragging the last clean shirt off its hanger then wincing as I remembered it had turned pink after I'd washed it with some of Kaylee's underwear. She'd laughed and called it metrosexual chic, then complained that I was taking revenge when I said she could wash her own clothes in future. In reality, I'd realized I couldn't keep washing her bras and panties in with my stuff if I refused to actually *look* at them.

Wordlessly, I pulled on the shirt and reached for my pants, waiting for Len to make some dumb joke about the color...

"What the *fuck*?"

Right on cue. Leonard Gregory Thatcher, everyone. What a dad.

I turned to face him as I pulled on my pants. "It was an accident. Let it go, okay?" I started to do up the shirt's buttons. "I'm too tired for your shit this morning."

To my surprise, Len stepped forward and tugged my shirt wide open above where I was buttoning it. "An *accident*?" For a second I thought he was going to rip the shirt off me altogether - then I realized he wasn't looking at the material. He was staring, aghast, at the new tattoo on my chest. "What, you fall onto a tattoo gun or something?!" He licked his thumb then poked it into me, rubbing his saliva forcefully across one of the circles of color. *Yuck.* Even though I'd done pretty much the same thing in the Urgent Care cubicle, that had been my *own* skin I'd been assaulting with my *own* bodily fluids.

Yanking away from his touch, I shoved past Len and continued doing up the shirt as I headed for the door, snagging my shoes and socks from the floor en route.

"Don't tell me it's *permanent*?" he called after me, horror evident in his voice. I wasn't sure if he was upset about tattoos in general, or that mine was of the 'hippy-dippy' variety, as I knew he'd describe it. Not that I'd had any choice, but I wondered if he'd have complained as much if I'd gotten a bald eagle clutching a Beretta in its claws.

Deciding not to wait for Len to say more, I jogged down the stairs barefoot and strolled into the living room.

No one there. Huh. Maybe he'd left my visitor outside the front door?

I opened it and checked, but the street seemed devoid of anyone there to see me, only a few dog walkers in sight across the road. Even though this morning's visitor had been given plenty of time to walk or drive away, it reminded me of the time my elderly nemesis had vanished into thin air, and that left me unsettled. I'd been hoping for Reesa, but what if Mara had finally been ready to talk, and I'd lost my shot at finding out what the hell was going on in my life?

I hastily pulled on my socks and shoes, then hurried

back toward the stairs, intending to get an answer from Len this time... but the unexpected sound of female voices from the kitchen had me changing direction.

"So what happened?" Kaylee was asking as I burst in through the door. Her head swiveled toward me in surprise, but her companion answered as if she hadn't noticed my hasty entrance.

"Well, obviously I couldn't let the marriage go ahead..." Mara nonchalantly picked up her coffee, "so I started a small stampede." She was wearing a neon pink velour tracksuit that was already burning my retinas after only two seconds.

Kaylee sounded way too impressed. "A *stampede?*"

Mara looked please. "Well, only a little one, but it did prevent the ceremony very nicely."

There was a lot I could have said to Mara right about then: not least, a demand that she stay away from my family. Instead, the words that came out of my mouth were, "So *you're* allowed to stop a wedding, but when *I* do it it's a felony?"

Her gaze finally shifted to me, eyes unblinking behind her usual Day-Glo orange glasses. "Your situation was completely different. *I* prevented a disastrous match between two people who would have made each other miserable; *you* prevented two soulmates joining forever."

Kaylee regarded me with concern from her seat. "Did you really do that, Uncle Lyle?"

I felt like dragging Mara into another room - or gagging her - but instead I answered my niece. "I had to take the groom to jail, Kaylee."

"But your uncle's about to prove he's innocent so that the happy couple can reunite." Mara smiled warmly at Kaylee, but I could see the smirk on her face when she turned to me. "Isn't that right, Lyle?"

I ignored her and turned to Kaylee. "What's she been telling you?"

"Just that she's a Matchmaker, and that you're gonna

be working for her on some cases." Kaylee frowned. "I don't see why it was such a big secret, though - I mean, we already knew you were helping Joey..." Her eyes went wide with excitement. "Oh, oh - did you see the news yet? Isn't it *awesome?*"

Her tone of voice suggested that world peace had been declared, but when she held out her smartphone to face me I wasn't surprised to see the TMZ website. The bold headline read: 'Pop king Joey Russo back with hit rock ballad dedicated to shock fiancée, Bethany Warnock.'

"I *totally* said he should do ballads!"

"*Hit* rock ballad?" I muttered skeptically, but Kaylee just nodded enthusiastically.

"They released it on iTunes at like 3 a.m. Pacific, so it hit the east coast airwaves right before commuter traffic. One point two *million* downloads in six hours." She sounded so knowledgeable about this stuff; maybe Bethany could set her up with an internship. Nepotism, right?

It was all beyond what I wanted to deal with, anyway. I still remembered when music came out on CDs, and had been freaked out when my fancy new setup at the office didn't come with a CD/DVD drive as standard. Of course, my setup was now nine months old, which I guessed made it pretty much ready for the landfill in most people's eyes; the newest version probably didn't even come with a keyboard.

Jesus. If the world started moving any faster it would come off its axis, and pretty soon we'd need a time machine just to keep up with all the latest 'necessities.' Fortunately, we'd probably blow ourselves up at some point and reset everything. An evolved cockroach would probably be standing right here, going through the same shit all over again, in fifty million years.

The doorbell saved me from expounding out loud on my profound thoughts. And also, to be fair, from accusations of being a Luddite.

"I'll get it!" I yelled out to forestall another of Len's moans about how he should get paid as our butler, and hurried into the front hallway.

I opened the door to the welcome sight of Reesa, grinning at me on my doorstep.

Grinning.

"Really?" I breathed, almost afraid to ask.

She held up a small USB drive. "Yep."

I grinned back at her and ushered her inside, sending up a silent prayer of thanks to the gods of private investigation.

The plan had worked.

Re-entering the kitchen, I was relieved to see that Mara hadn't fled the second my back was turned. I took the USB drive with a flourish, then plugged it into my waiting laptop.

"Hi, Reesa," Kaylee greeted her cheerfully. "You want some coffee?"

Reesa smirked and took a seat at the breakfast bar. "I never say no." I saw her send a cautious smile to Mara, who smiled back pleasantly in her 'resident grandmother' pose. But I wasn't stopping for introductions until I'd shown Mara exactly what we had.

I found what I was looking for, clearly marked in the drive's files, then swiveled the laptop around to face the group and hit 'play' before joining them myself.

On screen, time- and date-stamped footage played, showing Leroy Baldwin locking his car and moving nervously toward the back door of the club.

The playback switched to another view at that point - now from a camera positioned over that door - and showed a tear-streaked Candy peering out nervously, then ushering him inside.

"He doesn't come out again until eleven oh five. I checked both doors, and there's no one who could possibly be him, not even in disguise." Reesa sounded pleased with herself, and she had every right. Although I took some credit for figuring things out.

You see, I'd known that no amount of distraction would get Gun's eyes off me as part of Bethany's group, especially if he recognized me from before. So instead I used that to our advantage... along with a couple of other tricks.

Specifically, a couple of lap dance customers.

The raucous fat guy had been Gary in a padded suit. And while he'd charged the stage, drawing Gun and the bouncers' attention, the silent customer had snuck into the manager's office, using a keycard supplied by Candy via Cheri-Pie.

The silent customer being Reesa, of course.

I'm pretty sure most women would react badly to being called up out of the blue after eleven at night and asked to wear drag to a strip club so she could hack their security files. But not my best friend.

Nope... despite having less than an hour's notice, she'd gotten a fake beard and mustache from somewhere, and she'd been at Boobies getting the Cheri-Pie treatment by the time we arrived.

Once into the manager's office, Reesa had needed time to access and copy the right files. Despite Gary's commitment to his role, I'd worried that he'd be subdued too soon. Hence Candy's artfully wielded whip, followed by my fake bid to get backstage. All drawing the attention onto the stage and me, and away from the watch and office.

Fortunately, all of that had given Reesa enough time to get in, copy what we needed, and get back out. After which she and Joey had rendezvoused in the restroom, so she could wipe all traces of the system alerts before Joey handed Gun back his smart watch.

The only real roll of the dice had been whether the

manager's office would be empty or not, which was why the chaos outside the club had needed to be so huge, to pull everyone off their regular jobs.

Not too shabby, if I did say so myself, for a plan I'd come up with after getting knocked unconscious at the end of a *very* long day.

I pressed pause on the video and turned triumphantly to face Mara.

To my frustration, she looked pensive rather than pleased.

"Together with Candy and Cheri-Pie's statements, that should be enough to exonerate Leroy," I said, wondering if maybe her eyesight was so bad behind those orange disasters that she couldn't figure this out.

She pressed a finger to her lips in thought. "I should think so, yes."

"And...?" I prompted.

Her only response was to blink at me as if waiting for me to explain my question. Which, of course, I couldn't do in front of Kaylee and Reesa without them thinking I was insane.

Fighting to keep my cool, I moved toward the doorway. "Mara, would you join me in the living room for a minute?"

Her only response was a mild smile before she stood up and elegantly walked out past me.

I turned back to give some bullshit excuse for the private conversation, only to find Reesa getting up from the stool where she'd been sitting. "I guess my job here is done," she said, swinging her purse up onto her shoulder. "Nice to see you again, Kaylee." But I knew that blank expression she was wearing, and it always hid pain or anger. She thought I was blowing her off - again - even after all she'd done for me.

And I couldn't let her leave that way. "Don't go!"

Both women gaped at me, and I realized that had come

out like an order.

"Please stay," I said more calmly, taking a step closer to try to convince Reesa just how much it meant to me. "Please, Rees, I... I really want to talk to you." I sensed Kaylee's interest and added, "To thank you properly, I mean."

With a puzzled frown, Reesa eased back onto the high stool she'd just vacated. I could just see the faintly reddened skin around her lips where the fake mustache and beard had been glued, and I had the sudden crazy urge to lean in and kiss it all better...

My panicked eyes shot to Reesa's - but instead of frowning at what must have been a wild-eyed look on my face, our gazes connected and held.

"I'll wait," she said softly.

I really wished we were going out... I mean, *hanging* out... today. And hell, why couldn't we? I only had to get the evidence to Leroy's lawyer. That would only take - what, an hour? We both had flexible jobs, after all, and Reesa didn't seem in any hurry to leave, now that she knew I wasn't blowing her off.

I just wished I didn't have Mara to deal with first. But this was my chance to *finally* corner her for info, now that I'd ticked off every task she'd set me.

"I'll be back in a few minutes," I promised, then hurried out of the room.

I practically ran into the living room and saw - to my relief - that Mara hadn't evaporated into thin air. The realization that she'd disappeared before and could again had me cutting to the chase before I lost my chance this time. "So am I free of this now?"

Mara ignored my question, instead tilting her head like a bird and regarding me. "Oh my, you do look tired."

I persisted, "I got Joey and Bethany back together, and Leroy's getting out of prison, so -"

"Well, yes," Mara interrupted. "I suppose it's very likely

they'll let him out now."

"Then I'm done, right?" I found myself bouncing slightly on my feet, nervous energy meaning I couldn't keep still, despite how exhausted I felt. "No more crazy headaches? Or having my decisions taken away from me? No more being forced into taking nutcase clients when I'm too busy for their crap?"

Mara gave a little smirk. "You weren't *that* busy -"

I pulled my hands into fists to avoid stomping across the four feet of carpet that separated us and putting my hands around her wrinkled neck. "Dammit, Mara: *answer me*!"

"You want answers?" Her expression was suddenly quite serious.

"Yes!"

"You want the truth?"

"What did I just say?"

Her mouth opened again... and for a split second I was convinced she was going to *A Few Good Men* me.

Instead, she seemed to shrink in on herself, and sighed softly. "I'm sorry."

"*Sorry*?" I'd seen Mara play ditzy, dim-witted, and dotty; full of quips, excuses, and more lies than a politician's press release. But for a reason I couldn't name, this version of her was the one that unnerved me most.

She flopped down onto the sofa as if genuinely relieved to be off her feet, then sighed again and stared up at me. Seconds ago, I'd wanted to wipe the amused expression off her face. But now that she'd dropped whatever defenses she usually kept raised, I saw the tiredness behind those wrinkles; a strain I thought might have always been present, now that I really looked.

I looked into her eyes and asked quietly, "Just tell me: am I done with this or not?"

Mara closed her eyes. "I'm afraid," she said slowly, "that isn't up to me."

"What the fu-?" I cut myself off; took a deep, calming

breath, and tried again. "What do you mean?"

But deep down, I think I knew already. Or at least, I'd suspected it wouldn't be that easy. What had been done to me... it was...

Okay, I could admit it.

It was Otherworldly.

Oh sure, I'd pondered whether Mara was a witch, someone who'd done something woo-woo to me. But really, I hadn't believed it. Not when she was the only person I'd seen pulling my strings. And the whole time, I guess my rational side had been stockpiling ideas and theories. Like her being some deranged former con woman, trying to atone for her crimes by helping people, and bringing me - and maybe others - in as a reluctant partner, by hypnotizing and/or roofieing me.

But that didn't explain the visions. Or the tattoo, which at least two others had now seen, meaning I couldn't be hallucinating it. Not unless Mara had tampered with the entire water supply, or performed some kind of mass hypnosis on half of LA County.

And there was a point at which even... okay, I could think it... at which even *magic* became more believable than elaborate conspiracy theories.

Besides...

I pressed my fingers between the buttons of my shirt, running them gently over part of the tattoo and feeling a weird warmth coming from underneath my skin.

Yeah. I hadn't wanted to acknowledge that either. But it was like the tattoo was *alive*. And I knew what I'd felt when those crazy balls of light were whizzing in and out of me. Or even when I'd felt pain whenever I turned away from helping Joey or Bethany. It was like I'd been feeling the pieces of their souls, trying to get out.

I sank into the armchair opposite Mara and stared over at her.

She smiled sadly back at me. "I chose you for a very good reason. But I'm still sorry."

I swiped a hand over my hair, which should be standing up on end with all the shocks I'd had over the past few days. Instead it only felt unkempt and overly curly; a remnant of the crappy night's sleep I'd had, thanks to Len. "You chose me to be a..." I couldn't say it, "um..."

"A Matchmaker. Yes."

"But I don't believe in this crap!"

"But you *are* very good at it," she returned, then scoffed gently. "My first... ooh, dozen outings... I was never as efficient as you. Two sets of soulmates mended in under three days, and one of them not even yours?" She smiled happily. "A natural, oh yes."

I processed what she'd just said. "You... *you* were supposed to connect Leroy and Tanya?"

"Yes." Mara shot me a peeved glare. "And do you know how *long* I'd worked on them? At first he wouldn't even go *into* the library, let alone speak to her at the circulation desk. Months of effort and I was finally ready to bask in my success, when you ruined things at the last possible minute!" Losing her ire, she folded her hands primly in her lap. "I thought it only fair that you fix what you broke." She rubbed at her chest as if it pained her. "I'll be quite glad when everything's put to rest."

I stared at her, aghast by what she was implying. "You... you had those... those things in you for *months*?"

"Part of their souls," she said, confirming what I'd somehow already known, then gave me a piercing stare. "And once you embrace your role, you'll find it won't hurt; simply guide you to what you're meant to do next."

Embrace my role? Talk about rubbing it in that I wasn't done yet. "And what if I refuse?"

Mara waved away my concerns, seeming to forget her apologies from earlier. "*Pshaw.* Like I said, you're a natural at it." She gave a smug little smile, like one of those proud parents crowing over their child's success. "Give it a few months, and I bet you'll be shooting up the rankings!"

Rankings? How many 'Matchmakers' were there?

But before I could ask, Mara lost the smile and cast a guilty look upward, like she'd just farted in church. "Not that we keep track of such things, of course," she added quickly.

Her reaction derailed my train of thought, making me wonder something I'd pushed firmly aside before. "Do you... uh... work for... umm...?" Giving up on voicing my question, I slowly uncurled my right forefinger until it pointed up at the ceiling.

Mara didn't nod, but she didn't laugh at me either. Instead, she licked her lower lip thoughtfully with her tongue. "You know, I'm not really sure." Suddenly her head twitched to one side, as if she'd just heard the doorbell, and she sent me a warm smile then stood up.

I stood too, wondering why I was even considering letting her go. Aside from convincing me I was in a world more trouble than I'd even realized, she hadn't exactly told me much. Or really anything at all, now that I thought of it. Well, except for the small fact that it wasn't over - oh, and that I may or may not be working for some kind of a higher power.

And why would that worry me at all?

"But this doesn't make sense." I stepped forward, making a last-ditch argument. "You're telling me some higher power is worried about who people are *dating*? What about violent civil wars? Famines? Cruel dictators committing human rights abuses every day?"

Mara regarded me for a long moment, a glimmer of pain in her eyes, and I suddenly wondered where she was from originally. But then she smiled - and it was the fond smile of a teacher educating a student who'd fallen behind. "We don't change governments, we change people, Lyle. Think of it as a grassroots effort. Change from within. 'Make love, not war' - hmm?" Her smile widened. "And we *are* planet wide. Have been for... oh, a *long* time."

I felt a shiver go down my spine. I had a feeling she was talking about far longer than I'd been alive. Like maybe a few thousand times.

"Well," she said brightly, "time for me to go now. Goodbye, Lyle."

I wanted to protest that she still hadn't really told me anything, but instead I found myself pulled into those big, owlish eyes. As I lost myself, I realized dully that she must have removed her glasses at some point -

- then suddenly it was dark outside, and I was standing by the window in my old one-bedroom apartment, phone squeezed tightly to my ear.

"You have to help us!"

Caller ID had shown 'number unknown' and the woman was whispering and sobbing over the bad line, but I'd instantly recognized the distraught, frantic voice. I'd always know it anywhere, any time. "Jenny? Where are you?"

"We're on the boat! Please, Lyle!" Her voice was more of a hiss now, quietly terrified.

"Are you in danger? Who's with you?" I'd been watching TV seconds earlier, some post-apocalyptic sci-fi show that stretched the limits of plausibility, but now my mind was racing through crazy scenarios of what the hell could be going on in real life. Everything from someone trying to steal their boat with only Jenny and Kaylee onboard, to Michael having collapsed with a heart attack or worse.

"Michael! Michael's here too!"

"Is Kaylee there?"

"No! She's at home."

I grabbed my holstered service weapon and keys off the table in my living room and headed for the door. "What's going on?"

"They're coming for us!"

"Are you at the marina? Which berth -"

"They have guns!"

Now I swung back around, heading for my landline phone. "Stay on the line, I'll call 911 -"

"No!"

She sounded so vehement - so loud - that I was scared she'd just attracted the bad guys to her, whatever was going on. "Keep your voice down!"

"You can't tell anyone!" Her voice was hardly any quieter, veering into panic.

"Why?" All I heard for several seconds were her sharp, rapid breaths. "Jenny -"

"Michael stole something, all right? You can't tell anyone!"

What was she talking about?

"Promise me you won't!"

"Jenny -"

"Swear it!"

I reached for the handset, knowing I had to do what was right. It didn't matter what Michael had or hadn't done, 911 could get someone there first. Better to be in jail than dead, no matter the charge. "Jenny, please, you have to tell me where you are!"

"Swear you won't tell on Kaylee's life!"

The promise I finally gave her would come to haunt me. It certainly kept my foot pressed down hard on the accelerator the whole way to San Pedro. It was 3 a.m., so the 110 freeway was empty, and I knew where the traffic cops hung out.

Even so, their boat was ablaze by the time I arrived - no one aboard left alive.

"Uncle Lyle?"

&

I jerked awake, loopy as hell with the remnants of my nightmare still echoing inside my skull, yet at the same time feeling weirdly rested.

Kaylee stood next to me where I lay on the recliner, my second favorite coffee mug quivering in her hands. By that, and the drips I could see trailing down its sides to the mercifully beige carpet, I could tell my sudden motion had startled her. She looked pleased, though; relieved, actually. "I *told* Grandpa the smell might wake you up."

I frowned as I sat up, kicking the footrest back into place as I remembered everything that had just happened, from my conversation with Mara to the unpleasant dreams of what had happened almost a year ago now.

That *bitch*. She'd done it again. And... *fuck*! What time was it?

My gaze shot to the wall clock, surprised to see it was only seven oh five.

Wait... it had been gone *nine* when I woke up. Which meant -

"You've been asleep all day." Kaylee pressed the coffee mug into my numb fingers, and the warmth and familiar aroma felt good. "I was getting worried," she went on, perching on the sofa arm opposite, "and so was Grandpa. Even if he wouldn't admit it."

I said nothing, gulping the coffee greedily instead. I could just imagine Len's response to me occupying his favorite chair all day, and concern over my health wouldn't have come into it. But if Kaylee wanted to believe he cared, who was I to correct her. "I'm surprised neither of you tried to wake me."

"Grandpa wanted to," no shock there, after last night, "but Mara said it wasn't the concussion, you'd just lost too much sleep over the past few days."

I frowned, wondering how the hell she'd persuaded my bullheaded father without a medical degree and copious X-rays. Then again, she had tools at her disposal that weren't exactly available to ordinary mortals. Kinda like Reesa's 'Batman' basement, but -

I struggled up out of the chair, almost tripping on the arm. "Is Reesa still here?"

Kaylee looked puzzled. "Did she wait around all day for you to finish sleeping? Uh, no." Then she must have seen something in my face, because her mouth fell open with a soft little "*Ohhh*."

Shit. The last thing I *or* Reesa needed was to make Kaylee think we were an item. I put on as nonchalant a face as I could, forcing my voice to sound unworried. "I wanted to make sure I paid her, that's all."

My niece regarded me dubiously, not being a complete

fool. "I guess she won't mind waiting until you go for that drink. She said she'd call you."

I tried not to let my relief show. Then another worry bubbled up in my brain. "*Shit!* I wanted to get the security tape to -"

"Leroy Baldwin's attorney? Yeah, we know. Don't worry, Grandpa took care of it."

Which could mean anything. "How?" I asked warily.

Kaylee rolled her eyes as only a teenager can do. "*Relax*, will you? Some assistant came and picked it up this morning." I sagged against the side of the sofa, and she regarded me with an ancient expression. "You really don't trust Grandpa, do you?"

I thought about it for a second. Did I trust him with Kaylee's safety? No question. With her hopes and dreams? Maybe.

With *my* hopes and dreams?

Never.

I realized I'd taken too long to answer, but when I looked at Kaylee she was already onto the next question. "So... is Leroy Baldwin the guy you arrested at his wedding?"

I hesitated, wondering if I should go back and address the non-stampeding elephant in the room; namely, my relationship with my father. But in the end I chickened out on it. "Yeah. He skipped bail."

She scrunched up her face in question. "But couldn't you have just waited until after the ceremony?"

I did it so I wouldn't be even later *to your musical, dammit!* But I wouldn't put that on Kaylee. I was the one who took on too much that day; the buck stopped with me. I went for a half truth instead. "You kinda have to arrest criminals when you see them."

She still looked troubled. "I guess. But it must've really sucked for the bride-to-be."

I hadn't thought about Tanya in a while.

"Did she know he was supposed to be in jail?"

"She knew." I pictured Tanya's impassioned pleas to her father. "She didn't believe he was guilty, though."

"Did she try to stop you taking him?"

Yeah, by inciting her heavyweight father to beat me up, but I didn't feel the need to say that. The less Kaylee thought my job involved physical harm, the better. "She, uh, verbally defended him," I said carefully. "Very intensely."

"Must've been high-key embarrassing," I didn't really know what that meant, but Kaylee sounded impressed, "like, happening at her own *wedding*. But she still stood up and defended him? That's crazy romantic."

Unable to reply, I managed one of those rictus-like half nods, half smiles that could pass for agreement if she didn't look too deeply, then headed for the kitchen and more coffee. I was also aware that my stomach was grumbling noisily. Mara might've let me get some damn *breakfast* before she hypnotized me again.

Kaylee followed, still chatting away happily. "Anyway, you'll be on the other side from now on, right?"

"Hm?" I asked absently, heading for Len's coffee maker when I saw it was already on. Even if the 'real' stuff was too bitter for my taste.

"Now that you're a Matchmaker and all."

I was too busy pouring out lifesaving java to take that in for a moment, but when I did I huffed out an irritated breath. "It's only a *part time* gig." At least it had better be, or I'd lose what little remained of my sanity.

"I guess." Kaylee sounded momentarily disappointed, then perked up. "Cool business cards, though - don't you think?"

I looked around, mildly surprised that Kaylee even knew what a business card was in these days of bluetoothing contact info between smartphones, and even more surprised that she sounded impressed. My niece was holding up what seemed like a pretty ordinary white card rectangle; the background didn't even seem to be cream or ecru or any of those off-white colors designers use when they want to look like they're earning their pay. Atop this, in bold, black letters, the card read:

MARA K THETCHEM

and was in all respects pretty similar to the one I'd seen before, except the word "Matchmaker" was missing.

So what? was my immediate response. Okay, so it was minimalist and elegant, I guessed, but I couldn't see why my artistic young niece thought it was so amazing.

But then... it was the weirdest thing. The longer I looked at the letters, the more they started to shift and weave, coming apart and re-forming, then sliding up, down, and sideways, until finally they were in a straight line again. Only this time, they spelled out:

THE MATCHMAKER

I took a moment to shiver at the sheer freakiness of it.

Then - as the creep factor began to wear off - I realized something: The one thing I'd known about Mara was her name... and now it turned out it wasn't even real.

Dammit.

"I guess you'll need different ones, though." Kaylee sounded disappointed. "Unless we can figure out a cool anagram for 'Lyle Thatcher'...?" She wrinkled her forehead. "Cat Hell..."

"No." I stomped that idea flat. Even if I'd wanted to - or found an anagram that actually worked - I sure as hell didn't have Mara's supernatural ability to animate my business cards the same way.

"Mara must have changed her name - you know, legally - to make it work, right?" Kaylee asked innocently.

I didn't trust myself to answer, since I suspected 'Mara' changed her name whenever it suited her; probably twice a day and three times on Sundays. I forced a smile that was more of a grimace, then tucked the card into my pocket and went back to doctoring my coffee the way I liked it.

As I worked, Kaylee slid onto a seat and played around with her iPad. "Did you ever think about changing your name, Uncle Lyle?"

"Not really." Except for that first year out of the academy when everything I did seemed to be compared and contrasted - usually unfavorably - with the reputations of my older brother and father. But I'd gotten over it... eventually.

I'd figured Kaylee was just making conversation, but when I turned around from putting the milk away I found her staring into the distance, a troubled expression on her face. I'd seen that look before, but not in months. Honestly, I'd been hoping never to see it again - ever - and it made me realize Kaylee wasn't asking these questions just for the hell of it. Which in turn made me realize I owed her a more complete answer.

I started with a question of my own. "Why - you thinking of swapping 'Thatcher' for something else?"

Kaylee looked up at me and winced. So much pain in her face, I wanted to go over there and hug her. Except maybe there was a better way.

I forced myself to sound casual. "Might do the same myself," I said. "Maybe I'll change my first name too while I'm at it. I've always felt like more of a James than a Lyle..."

Kaylee gave me a long, dubious look, then seemed to accept that I wasn't teasing her. "I wouldn't really do it," she said finally. "At first, maybe. When Mom and Dad were all over the news. But it got better once I stopped being teased at school." She squinted at me then, like she knew what I'd done about that.

So sue me: the second Kaylee had come home in tears, I'd stomped on her teachers until they'd dealt with the troublemakers. It had only been a week after the funeral when she started school again, Len and I having decided it would be worse to keep her home and ruin her academic chances too. Maybe we should've waited until things had died down more, but the story had been like a zombie: we'd think it was dead, but every few weeks some new revelation would come out. About how Michael had facilitated drug and weapons deals, or how Jenny had helped - knowingly or not - to launder the money he made via shady real estate sales. And then the columnists and talking heads would start in on it again.

One guy at the Los Angeles Post in particular had made it his career, for a while, to dig into where the dirty money went and whether the rest of us in the family were involved. The bastard must have even conned his way into their funeral service, because right after it another article came out, talking crap about how we showed no remorse and were "teaching Thatcher's young daughter that crime is okay if it means Mommy and Daddy can spoil you all the time." Yeah, well, I'd had to give a speech about my lying, cheating, thief of a brother in front of my innocent niece, who'd been bawling her eyes out since we left the house. So sure, I'd played up how devoted Michael and Jenny were to their only child.

The reporter had also gone on about how my new business was rumored to have 'underworld ties,' and how Len owned a house in an 'up and coming' part of town. This being the house my parents had moved into when Silver Lake was a total dump, and had paid a thirty year mortgage on since.

Bottom line, the guy was a real prick.

I'd love to meet C. H. Bannerman some day when *he* was down and out.

My father chose that moment to re-enter the kitchen, pausing on the threshold when he saw my scowl. "Thought everything was hunky-dory? What is it now?"

"Nothing," Kaylee and I said in unison. But that was a lie. She was still fragile, even if she only showed it about one percent of the time.

And me?

I'd spent most of my adult life believing my brother was a bastard because he'd stolen the love of my life. The worst thing hadn't been everyone else thinking he was perfect; it had been me not being able to disprove it, even in my own mind... his theft of Jenny aside. I hadn't even blamed Jenny after a little while, not after she had cried on me and apologized so sweetly, and had been so clearly and desperately in love with him - not to mention so very pregnant. So I'd just shoved all of my frustration and anguish down and away from her, sending most of it over to the easier target of Michael.

That anger had festered over time, and part of me had rejoiced when objective proof was provided that Michael was, indeed, a bad guy. Of course, that proof had only come with his murder and Kaylee losing both parents, which meant I'd taken on the guilt for being a selfish prick too. But hey, at least now I had plenty of other things to occupy my mind.

Always good to find a silver lining.

"Wanna help me cook?"

"Sure, Grandpa."

Trying not to dwell on the fact that my mother would've fainted in delight if Len had even once offered to get the ingredients out, I got out of the way of Martha Stewart hour. The fact that my father wasn't a half bad cook made it even worse, of course... but I wasn't dwelling, was I? I'd offered to help once, but he and I had nearly killed each other - and knives were within too easy reach in a kitchen - so we'd come to an agreement that we provided food on different nights. I say 'provided' because I typically ordered in from a local restaurant; it was healthier and cheaper than me cooking and either poisoning us or burning the house down.

Pushing away from the counter, I carried my coffee mug into the living room and set it down, lying back against the sofa and taking my phone out. I'd been ignoring it all day - not by choice - and I felt out of the loop and behind.

Opening up my work email - my personal email contained little that wasn't either a begging letter from some organization or an offer of discount coupons from CVS or RiteAid - I scrolled down the list and worked my way back up again chronologically.

Bethany had certainly lived up to her promise to help me, referring me to three friends and two celebrity-endorsed charitable organizations already. Perusing the messages, which - reading between the lines - ranged from theft of jewelry to some minor blackmail, I supposed the rich and famous were just naturally more drawn to trouble than the rest of us... or rather, troublemakers were drawn to them, maybe. Either way, it was enough to keep me going for a few weeks in terms of work, and I figured these were all people who could afford my rates. Add to that the amount Joey had already transferred into my account - and I had the email notification to tell me he'd been more than generous - and I was looking set for a while.

I still didn't like the whole Matchmaker thing. Having no choice about something always drove me crazy, and I hated being used as some higher power's pawn with no idea if there was even an end date to it. But I guessed the rewards from grateful rich couples might come in useful sometimes.

I had a sudden vision of Mara, clad in a sari at a gigantic Indian wedding and receiving a gigantic ruby from the father of the bride. I shook my head, wondering if I'd conjured that up myself, or if she was somehow dabbling in my thoughts from afar.

What could couples like Leroy and Tanya offer, though? Bodyguard duties and fine forgiveness down at the library? Hell, even Joey and Bethany could backfire when the inevitable split happened down the line. No, I couldn't think of any grounds they could use to sue me, but that's what pricey lawyers are for, and I figured I'd be the first person they blamed given all the gratitude they were heaping on me now.

Yeah, yeah... call me cynical, I know...

Moving forward to this afternoon's messages, Leroy Baldwin's attorney had emailed me - and, I discovered, called and texted me, mostly asking me to call him back - a collective total of thirteen times. I was worried the Boobies evidence had been bounced as inadmissible, but when I finally listened to his voicemails the guy sounded like he was high on something.

Turned out it was success.

It had been too soon for the courts to act, naturally, since justice moved at a speed that was ponderous at best. However, tangible proof of Leroy's alibi had already convinced the lead investigator on the case to go after the other suspect they'd identified but dismissed due to lack of evidence. They'd shown up at his door, and the man had broken down and confessed. In a twist of fate, it turned out he'd actually been a *guest* at Leroy and Tanya's wedding, and had been guilt-stricken ever since I nabbed the groom on the way to the altar. Leroy should be out of jail in no more than a couple of days.

"I don't know what possessed you to take this case on for nothing," the lawyer finished; cannily not offering to pay me, I noticed, "but you've impressed me and my firm. We'll be coming to you again. Ed White was also extremely grateful and asked me for your contact details, so I'd expect to hear from him too."

Given how my last encounter with Ed had ended, I kinda wished the lawyer hadn't shared my work address. Still, it wasn't like he couldn't have looked it up for himself at any point. I hoped if he hadn't shown up to my office for revenge before now, he'd be coming with warmer feelings this time. A check would be nice, but honestly after what I done to his daughter - however legitimate my actions had been - I figured we were about even now.

Pretty content with my life at this moment, all things considered, I finished checking through everything, then checked my spam folder out of habit.

Four seconds later and I was tensed up again, ready to punch through a wall.

The email from two days ago was innocuous - at least, as far spam emails went; the kind of dumb con job a preschooler could have seen through. 'Hoping for yur asistence,' read the subject line. The email itself began, 'Greetings, I am Mr. Joseph K. Smith, former bank to His Highness Prince Namdewin of Namibia,' before it moved swiftly on to the fact that there was $100,000 sitting in an account somewhere, and would I like ten percent of it to assist in retrieving the money? It was riddled with poor grammar, spelling mistakes, and dubious claims concerning the largess I would be receiving.

But that wasn't why I reacted so badly to it.

Not at all.

➷

I let myself into my office right before eleven that night. Despite the sleep I'd recouped today I felt like crap again, and only my need to retrieve a certain item from my safe could have dragged me away from the lure of a nice, comfortable bed - and the chance to feel one hundred percent before I tackled my promising new client roster in the morning.

Telling myself not to delay things any further, I locked the door behind me, then headed into the back room and went straight to the safe. Opening it, I stared in at the thing I always hated to use. But sometimes you just don't have a choice.

Taking a deep breath, I took out the burner phone I'd owned for almost a year now and turned it on.

Carrying it into the front office, I put it down on my

desk and stared at it. I was too scared to keep it in the house; too horrified at what could happen if Len or - god forbid - Kaylee found it. Even though I kept it password protected and deleted the call and text logs religiously - just like I did the messages in my spam folder, then overwrote them with a nice piece of software - I couldn't take the risk that they might find it and get into it somehow. Len had enough connections it'd probably be easy if he decided to try, and Kaylee went to a large enough school that there had to be at least one hacker she knew...

Okay, yes, I was paranoid. But even with no call logs, no numbers stored, I couldn't get out of my mind what would happen if it rang and one of them answered instead of me... what would happen if *Kaylee* was holding the phone the next time she called -

Drrrrr. Drrrrr.

The phone vibrated on the desk. And as always happened, I felt my legs turn to Jell-O and my heart to a mound of ice. But if I didn't answer now, she'd only call again. And again. Until maybe eventually she'd get reckless and do something stupid. Like call the house, or even show up in person.

Taking a deep breath, I unlocked the phone and held it to my ear.

"Hello, Jenny," I said.

THE END

ABOUT THE AUTHOR

Claire Elaine Newman has a doctorate in atmospheric physics from the University of Oxford and spends her days working on the Curiosity Rover or predicting the climates of Mars and Titan.

When she isn't exploring real worlds using a numerical weather prediction model, Claire loves to create fantasy worlds in her novels, typically kept company by plenty of decaf Tetley tea, milk chocolate, and her beloved cat Sparky.

For a **FREE** short story set in the world of The Matchmaker, and for news about upcoming books, please visit Claire's website at:
https://thematchmakernovels.wordpress.com/

26886228R00164

Printed in Poland
by Amazon Fulfillment
Poland Sp. z o.o., Wrocław